Arion Rising

by

Jackie Anders

Edited by: Amanda Hardebeck & Jackie Anders

© 2019 by Jackie Anders and Static Pen Publishing.

TED Talk quote used with permission.

Printed in the United States of America

First Printing, September 2019

ISBN-13: 978-1-7336817-5-9

DEDICATION

Arion Rising is dedicated to my grandmother who I miss every single day. My grandmother was the one that saw the talent and abilities in me long before I did. I would simply brush the compliments off as her just being biased. She was the one who introduced me to books and painting as a child and to the piano before I could even write a single sentence. I still remember the nights we stayed up way past two in the morning reading books or watching QVC. She was, is, and will always be my biggest fan, even in Heaven.

CHAPTER 1

Houston, Texas
2017

Rapture

Never lose hope, never give up because good days really are to come. That's my motto. Or at least that's the motivational quote off a church flyer covered in bird crap and street grime on the corner of Willis and Park Avenue. Most days, I had trouble believing it. But not today. Sitting at the city park and clutching my crowning achievement, I repeated the words over and over again.

"Tea Lane, a homeless reject, somehow managed to snag the title of Best in Show from all the other affluent teens in Houston's Regional Science Fair."

I … I really did it.

I clutched the small, round medallion hanging over my still jittery stomach. Everything went so fast earlier. It was a whirlwind morning that started with getting my name tag, doing the presentation, then receiving the medal. After a long and agonizing road of research and interviews to get me to today, my head was spinning. Sitting tall with this huge achievement, I finally believed something good could happen to me.

The only problem, I had no family to share it with.

I mean, I did have my friends on the corner of Milam and Beech Street who I called family ever since I became homeless. I guess they counted, but it wasn't enough.

Dang it if the thought of my lost brother didn't cross my mind again. I brushed it away and the warm tears before they managed to flood my vision.

"Not today, Téa. Not today."

Even with the win, the person I really saw myself as, came back to mind too. I wasn't anything special. If the judges really knew how I really saw myself, they would have given the win to someone else. Not a girl who used to blow up in elementary school by kicking and screaming uncontrollably. Who would spend more time in the principal's office in trouble than in a classroom.

I wiped a tear that threatened to fall and decided to shove those torturous and useless memories away with the ones of my lost brother. This day was my happy day. I needed to let myself be happy for a change and take this stepping stone as momentum on my way to being the first Latino woman astronaut to spacewalk. Yes, that was my goal, and I was going to achieve it. One day.

The sweet scent of spritzed honeysuckle all through the city park had me entranced as I unwrapped my sandwich and eyed the rich mayo that seeped out. Nothing was better on a picnic sandwich than extra mayo. This was the best celebratory lunch ever, even though I was eating alone. Ugh, enough of that! I took a sip of my sweet tea while noticing the new landscape. I hadn't been to the park since before Hurricane Harvey hit and flooded most of Houston.

Now, sand was piled up high on both sides of the creek's banks where the flood waters rose and then fell away leaving behind this wavy, outré topography. What a shocker. We really didn't see that hurricane coming. At least not one *that* bad. I could still hear the cries for help. The helicopters and boat motors polluting the air with reminders that there were more families trapped.

I still saw the deluge of the Stygian-like water rising farther and farther until it engulfed the city to its rooftops. But we weren't the lost city of Atlantis like I read in my school books. No, surprisingly we stayed above sea level. However, we're still rebuilding with the bodies of the fallen being found in alleyways and newly drained basements as recently as last week.

Shaking off the mournful thoughts, I ran my palm over the virgin grass in front of me and followed the rays of the sun down the hill.

"What is that?" I thought.

I scooted in closer and saw a strange looking acorn. It looked to be an albino one. Do oaks even shake off white acorns? I had never seen one like that and one that was unusually divot free and shiny. The odd object was just sitting there, barely surfaced above a rift in the sand. What was more surprising is that it was encased in a material similar to resin. My curious fingers couldn't help it any longer. I grabbed it. Despite the temperature outside being in the seventies, it was surprisingly warm.

Feeling around it with my curious fingers, I found a small hole below a patch of gold? "Huh?" I searched through my pocket and pulled out a spare string that was supposed to be used for my science project. I put the thin string through the hole, creating a nice necklace. It was an even better purpose for the excess string. Then I tied it around my neck just enough that the object dangled a few inches below my collar bone. I smiled at my two new achievements and went back to my celebratory lunch.

As I finished my sandwich, I noticed I was starting to get one of my migraines. The annoying pain in the rear headache always came after stressful events. I reached into my backpack and pulled out some pills to rid myself of it. After swallowing two, I laid back on the cool grass and watched the sun dance among the clouds. I was asleep before I knew it.

It was all a blur. None of the sounds could be made out. It was chaos.

Nothing made sense until …

"No!!" a little boy cried out among all the rising eerie screams. He was surrounded by blankets of suffocating smoke. His eyes … They weren't right. They were brown. At least, they had looked brown. Now, they were iridescent gold. The swirling smoke pulled away like in a vacuum to reveal gruesome silhouette figures approaching him and the young girl he held. He screamed again, but this time a strong rumbling sound followed sending intense shock waves through the ground. Layer upon layer of dirt slipped away under his feet.

"Rosa, please, no!"

Suddenly, a huge ocean wave appeared out of nowhere and crashed all around. Drowning out everything.

I woke instantly. Pulling myself back to reality, I felt for the charm. It was hot against my chest, probably because of the sun. I felt my jeans and jacket. They were dry. I took a breath and noticed my migraine had receded to only just a small aching pain in my left temple.

"Thank God."

I picked up my lunch scraps and left the park, but with that odd dream still on my mind.

CHAPTER 2

Superficial World

Later that afternoon, I reported to work at Tacky Tacos. I could tell my friend and coworker, Kiki, had missed me. She met me at the counter with a fizzing fountain drink in one hand and my apron in the other.

"It must be nice to be able to take off when you want. But good thing you came in early today. Boss man is already on a roll."

Kiki took off work a bunch, too. Leroy, our boss, frowned at her reasons more than mine. I guess I earned that having worked there for two years. Kiki had only been at this joint or even had a job for three months.

"Back away Kiki, senior staff member coming through," I said and grabbed my apron. I was in a picking mood today.

"Funny." She rolled her eyes at me.

I walked passed my fiery brunette friend and noticed a new guy in the back. A tall and rugged looking guy. He was leaning over washing dishes and seemed to pay us no mind. I looked to Kiki.

"New victim?"

Her eyes lit up. "Oh yes, just started yesterday. His name is Ben."

She emphasized the *n* sound in his name alerting me to her interest in him. I set down my small backpack and greeted him.

"Hello, Ben."

Ben turned his head slightly to glance my way and gave me just a small nod. He had a nice tan, angular face, and a strong horizontal jaw line. With all that, his dark hair laying just above his strikingly sexy dark eyes, made me easily see why he had Kiki's attention.

Kiki leaned over to me. "If he wasn't so bashful and strange acting, I'd jump on that," she whispered and continued to ogle her new conquest.

Ben lifted his head again as if to inquire. That was when I noticed how incredibly uniquely colored his brown eyes were. I assumed he was Hispanic because of his dark features, but those eyes. They were chocolate brown but with a silver outline around the irises. I'd never seen eyes like that before.

I stepped passed Kiki. "Ben, pay no mind to her. She's not house trained."

"Hey!" Kiki said and slapped me on the arm. I was the only one of us three that laughed at my joke.

Leroy walked in the front door making his presence known by loudly barking into his cell at some innocent soul on the other end of the line. He hung up and addressed me when he got closer.

"Glad you're back, Téa. I heard you did very well Saturday."

I tied my Tacky Taco's bright orange apron around my waist. "Yes sir, and thank you for the morning off."

Leroy smiled. "No problem at all. Listen, we won the bid for the Hero Luncheon in a few weeks. We're going to be busy, Téa. You know how crazy banquets always are. But this one in particular is for the men and women who helped our fellow Houstonians during Hurricane Harvey. It is important that we make the best showing."

"Yes, sir."

Leroy was obviously excited. "You know, the profits from this would help with the debt I ran up to fix this restaurant after that blasted storm put ten feet of water in it."

He gestured to our new dish washer, "That's why I didn't mind taking on an extra hand when he showed up looking for work. Have you met Ben?"

"Yes, I did."

"Great!" Leroy turned on his heels to head to his office. His freshly shaved head glistened under the room's bright fluorescent lights.

I addressed Kiki as she walked back up. "Busy, busy we'll be."

She snorted. "I guess. So, you won?"

I was not one to boast. "Yes, I did."

"That is awesome! So what did you win?" She had a little bounce in her step as she skirted around me to grab another tray.

I frowned. I didn't want to say too much. The new dish washer had now come up to the counter to grab Kiki's first tray of empty Coke glasses. He impatiently removed her tray of dirty dishes off the counter. He had a tall, strong build and a tight expression planted on his face. I wasn't sure if I was going to like having someone so strange and intimidating around.

I grabbed my order pad and finally replied to Kiki, "Some money."

I wouldn't say aloud how much in case this new guy was a thief. I knew I shouldn't judge a person so quickly, but being cautious was an important part of surviving on the streets.

"Really? So what are you going to do with it? I know, let's go out and celebrate! Oh, let's start with a Snapchat selfie!"

She popped out her pink, glittery iPhone case from her pocket and leaned into me with a big cheesy smile.

I broke away. "Sorry, Kiki. I've already started spending it."

"On what?" Her heavily glossed bottom lip protruded slightly.

"I bought two dozen warm blankets and new tents for the homeless on the south side of town before coming into work."

"The homeless?" She dropped her small chin down to her chest, and her usual perky facade fell away to one of concern.

"Do you think that was wise? You have to think about getting a car for college, Téa. And what if you don't get that other scholarship? Foster care doesn't cover everything."

I wiped up the counter and noticed Ben now staring at me from the other side of the counter. When he held the stare longer than customary, I nervously retreated to the dining area to take table five's order. Boy, did this Ben guy have an intense stare. I couldn't decide if I should be flattered or worried.

"Two Snappers and two Cokes," said one of the frat boys at table five.

I smiled. "Coming right up."

As I headed back towards the kitchen, the mom with the rambunctious child at the booth next to the frat guys asked, "Ma'am, I'm confused. What is a Snapper? It says on the menu that it consists of fried egg, brisket, hash browns, and taco sauce. It doesn't have fish in it at all."

I about died. I got that question a lot but never from a mom with a kid by her side. I had to control myself as usual. Think happy thoughts. Be patient with people.

"It's a different special taco every week, but we always use that word for its name. We aren't called Tacky Tacos for nothing."

Her heavy foundation gave her a very obvious makeup line below the chin and by her ears. She looked at me unamused. "And?"

I looked around at the other families in the diner and leaned in to whisper in clarification. I pulled back and she cleared her throat.

"Very well then." She slapped her toddler's hand for spinning their menu. I tried not to notice her venting her frustration on her child.

"Yes, ma'am," I said taking that as my chance to get away so she could process that info. I walked briskly back to put in the new order.

Kiki met me at the counter while I was typing it in. "What's wrong?"

I noticed then that Kiki's dark shoulder length hair had been curled at the ends with a flat iron, almost as if she knew we'd have a hot new guy working with us.

"Nothing. Just a shocked customer."

She laughed. "Oh, another one of those."

I laughed back. Then, she stared at me with one eyebrow lifted. "What is that around your neck?"

"Do what?"

She pointed her long, slender finger at my chest. "That."

Oh, my new charm. "It's nothing. I found it at the park." I tried to brush her off.

"Really? It's neat looking."

"I think it's really old. The floods from the hurricane must have unearthed it."

She kept her eyes glued to it. "As devastating as that storm was, a lot of great things did come out of it."

Kiki's shoulders curled over her chest as she slowly dug for a washrag in the lower cabinet. She had lost a family member who drowned in the flood waters off of I-10. He was the police officer everyone talked about that saved a young child. When he went back for another, he drowned. The media still ran hero footage on him.

"Téa, you ever hear of *Antiques Roadshow*?" she asked when she stood back up.

"*Antiques Roadshow*?"

"It comes on PBS. It's a bunch of people selling old crap."

"Hmm." I tapped *enter* on the keyboard to send off my order and noticed a group of college students come in wearing their University of Houston t-shirts.

Kiki continued, "They are coming to Houston next weekend at the George R. Brown Convention Center. You should bring it for them to check out. They have experts from all around the world that look at the antiques and assess their value. It could be worth some money! And the top looks like real gold."

I just nodded and walked towards my new customers thinking about what she told me. Money? This old thing could really be worth something? I could use the money for a down payment on a car! Handing the menus to the young girls at my table by the door, my eyes noticed movement coming from the back to the front of the diner.

Ben's thick dark hair was now covered by a Houston Astros cap, and he wore a grey and white jacket over his faded blue jeans that fit him well. Too well. He stopped at the door to zip up his jacket. Then, those strange-colored brown eyes looked up and caught mine. He nodded slightly. I looked down at my new guests. Their attention was now on Ben, too. I pulled my pen out of my jeans' pocket and cleared my throat.

"Welcome to Tacky Tacos. What can I get you girls?"

That was when the female customer with auburn hair and angelic features finally acknowledged me. "Three servings of him!" she said pointing at the front door where Ben still stood. All the girls at the table laughed. I couldn't help but smile.

Ben didn't do what I expected a good looking guy to do. He didn't smile or take that as his opportunity to approach the model perfect girl in front of me. Instead, he acted nervous and walked out of the diner quickly.

Mind blown! I turned and winked at the flirty girl. "Good one."

She replied, "Well, he is hot! But not very sure of himself, huh?" She frowned. "I don't know if I like low self-esteem guys."

I pondered her words for a sec. Him, low self-esteem? How?

"No, he probably just has a girlfriend."

She straightened up in her seat. "Nope. Even the taken ones come running when I flirt."

Then, one of her brunette friends tapped her shoulder. "Stop, Emma! I'm hungry."

Emma shrugged. "Okie dokie. We would like three chicken cilantro tacos, two Cokes, and one water."

"Coming right up!"

I picked up the small paper menus and pivoted back towards the kitchen. After about thirty minutes, Ben came back into the kitchen. Without a word, he put on his apron and got back to washing dishes. I didn't know why I stared longer than usual at him while he washed. But something about this mystery guy had my attention. Arms sculpted worked perfectly in tandem grabbing dish after dish and scrubbing effortlessly. Ben lifted one shoulder to wipe sudsy water off his subtle cleft chin, and I did nothing but stand there watching. He could have easily caught me staring, but he never looked up.

I turned to fill a few glasses with Coke, and turned back to continue to admire how he kept working without hardly stopping. As if he were on a mission. I touched my lips involuntarily as I watched his serious work ethic. Ben stopped mid rinse and with narrowing eyes, finally looked over at me. He lifted one side of his mouth. He knew he busted me. I fidgeted with the glasses on the tray and turned to head back to my tables. The rest of the night, I avoided my wandering thoughts and kept it focused on my job. My mind kept thinking about Kiki's insight into my charm anyway. Could I really get some money for it?

CHAPTER 3

Trials

Monday morning, I was sitting in class listening to Ms. Harrison go on and on about Texas history as my eyelids started to droop. Squeezing my wrist or changing positions in my desk seat wasn't helping like it usually did. I was still really worn out from my weekend. I heard the words Sam Houston this, Sam Houston that, and then the weight of my head was too much for my neck. Stretching out, I tried to make it look like I was just adjusting into a more comfortable position. But before I knew it, the lights went out.

"Téa Lane!"

Oh no, it was Ms. Harrison's nasally, shrill voice. She woke me instantly. Crud. Several amused eyes stared at me from all different angles around the classroom. I cringed while realizing I did in fact fall asleep in class again. My hands were shaking like leaves. I shoved them into the pockets of my hoodie.

A vexatious yet subdued laugh tickled my left ear. Another reminder that my attempts to stay awake had failed. On top of that, I knew exactly who that was laughing. It was that Lexi Sampson girl. She loved to see me fail. I fought the urge of wanting to stand up and punch her pathetic

18

Stepford Wives' face. A few years back, that would have happened. But counselors and behavior specialists had taught me ways to counteract that anger.

However, I am a work in progress.

Maybe just this once, I could slip up. No, not going there. Not worth it.

I took a slow breath in and a slow breath out and focused hard on my teacher instead. I was better than that now. Heck, I was closer to my dreams than ever before after my big win Saturday. I had to stay focused.

"I'm sorry Ms. Harrison. I didn't realize," I said, embarrassment still swallowing my voice. I wiped my mouth with the back of my hand while slowly sitting up straight in my seat.

"Maybe a little detention will spur on some effort," Ms. Harrison said with one hand on her wide hips and the other irritatingly waving all around in front of her.

I started seeing red again. I coaxed myself back calm by whispering to myself, "In and out, Téa. In and out."

However, that didn't stop what I thought to myself, "Shut up, Ms. overly short and annoying queen bee."

But "Yes ma'am," was what I finally said. I shrugged my sore shoulders. I wasn't going to let my attitude ruin my chance at graduation. However, I hated history. I had a huge disdain for this class and this teacher. I just had to survive it. My charm under my shirt reminded me that I had something to look forward to in the short term, as well. This weekend, I may be getting me some quick cash!

Ms. Harrison interrupted my thoughts again. "Class, do your research with the citations of which website you used.

I'll take anything that is not Wikipedia. Now, Téa, you need
…"

Ring, ring.

Thank you, Jesus. I was saved by the bell. Another
student jetted out the door removing all attention away
from me. Ms. Harrison turned her head to unsuccessfully
holler at him. Then, her short self reached up as best she
could to grab her whistle above the white board. I was
thankful that I was at least a little taller than *her*.

The boy that had her distraught was Freddy Wells, the
most hyper student in our entire grade. Freddy was
notorious for his lack of patience and not pushing in his
chair before exiting. I was always thankful when the ADHD
students gave me a buffer from overzealous teachers every
now and then. Go Freddy! Now, I was no longer in Ms.
Harrison's sights.

Standing up onto my own petite gait, I frowned at Lexi
Sampson as she just snickered back at me. Then, she tossed
that perfect hair over her left shoulder to begin her daily
flirting with one of the other massive football players.

Rushing into the hall with my boulder-weighted
backpack, I averted my eyes to try to steer clear of everyone.
I let my long hair fall over most of my face, as a shield in a
way. A foreign sensation in my temples that felt like a needle
stabbing me in the head left me wanting to vomit. In
response, I closed my eyes to try and counteract the pain
from possibly another migraine. Thankfully, it passed as
soon as it came. I didn't have time to be ill again.

"Téa!"

Tommy, who used to be my friend, came up confidently through the herd of teens that retreated in his wake. He was the only one that didn't date cheerleaders or spend his weekends with his fellow football players. No, he liked to hang out with indigent loners like me and try to humiliate us. At least that was how he saw me, and what he did to me. Ha! No matter how long we had known each other, there still was a lot he didn't *really* know about me.

"Go away, Tommy!" I made the final steps to the school's exterior door, hoping he wouldn't follow. I hadn't forgiven him yet.

"Just let me give you a ride," he said shrugging his broad shoulders. As usual, his pale green polo shirt was flat ironed, his hair combed over to one side with not too much gel, and his skin perfectly shaven.

"No, I've got my bike."

"Téa, it's raining. You can put your bike in the back of my truck."

His pleading eyes looked down at me and then off to the sheeting rain. The school's entryway awning was currently shielding the peril he wanted to protect me from. It was easy to fight off the offer at that moment until I actually had to step out into that mess.

I pulled out my handy rain coat from my backpack and slipped it on. "No, Tommy."

I waved and dashed away to my bike leaving him behind. I was still mad at him. We had been friends for a long time, even though we were so completely different. But we did have a good friendship until he screwed it all up.

It didn't take long to unlock the bike chain and leave campus. I had hoped to avoid the heavier rain. However, the ride on the soaked streets slowed my plight. When I got to the first intersection, the rain finally stopped and the ache in my stomach and head eased up. I wasn't over what Tommy did, and he knew it. I mean, just because I had never had a boyfriend didn't give him the right to meddle in my life.

After a few blocks, I pulled in at my favorite Jason's Deli on the corner of Washington and Bentley Street. I needed a warm place to have dinner and prep some more for the presentation I was going to be giving at the science fair. Mrs. Nguyen was smiling at me with squinty dark eyes from behind the counter when I walked in.

"Téa, you such a good girl and work hard. Why no car?" she asked in her cute ESL way.

I narrowed my eyes at her. "Saving my money."

She shook her head at me and asked, "The usual?"

"Yes, ma'am."

She scooped out the shredded chicken for my Southwest Chicken Pita. "Studying hard?"

I lifted my head up. "Oh yeah."

"You do fine. You a smart girl," she said and sipped on her hot tea after serving me.

My mouth fell open. "Yea, thanks."

I retreated to a corner booth with my tray of coffee and dinner. No more compliments, please. The space around the booth was so empty that my footsteps were the loudest sound. I had maybe two hours before dinner traffic came through and made this place too loud. I used a napkin to dry off my face and pulled out my binder. It was going to be a long afternoon. I was behind in Calculus because of the time I put in for my science project instead of doing my classwork. I sipped on the stout coffee and indulged in my two pitas with extra mayo, courtesy of Ms. Nguyen.

CHAPTER 4

Home Sweet Home

Two or so hours later, I waved goodbye to my deli friend and headed towards home by way of Louisiana Avenue. When I rode in, I saw a new crew of beggars lining the street with their *help me* signs written in Sharpie black ink on old produce boxes. Ever since the devastation from Hurricane Harvey last August, new faces were becoming more and more apparent. The last few months, it made me nervous if I had to ride down this street. However, it was the quickest way to get home. I just made it a point to be extra cautious.

A few more turns, and then I was rounding the corner to Lyon Street. Packed with bars, eateries, and shops decorated in the bright primary colors of red, yellow, and orange, it showed Houston's true colors. Almost all these establishments included signs adorned with huge tamales and loud Tejano music that escaped into the street. I caught a whiff of the pungent tar scent that barely masked the sour sewer stench that always radiated through the street's cracks and crevices. It was especially bad after hard rains like the one today.

I parked my bike by the fire hydrant on the corner and sighed. It had been a long day. I was beat. The chain I always used to secure my bike clanked as I locked it up to the metal post under the porch of the Mi Casa Diner. That bike was all I had. I pulled my black binky out of my rain coat's pocket and quickly pulled my hair up into the hat. The goal was to never stand out. I should have cut off all my hair in the fall when the lice were running rampant, but my hair and Latino heritage were the only good attributes I got from my mom. Looking at my wavy light blonde hair in bathroom mirrors was the only way I could remember what she looked like.

Just as I finished and rounded the corner, I spotted Robert Carr. At least that was what he told me his formal name was when I first met him. I had never called him by that name, though.

"Uncle Bob!"

"Hey, Téa. It's going to be a colder night than usual tonight."

He was bundled up by the makeshift fire pit we made out of a barrel laid on its side. He grinned at me with his pearly whites that stood out like bright headlights against his dark skin. I shrugged and dropped onto the flattened box next to him to take in some of the warmth.

"Good thing the rain stopped."

"You like your new and dry box? I flattened it out for you." He winked at me before continuing, "Now young lady, even without the rain, I wish you had taken that old lady up on her offer for that room and board. At least for a few nights."

I got his concern, but I knew I could survive now that we were approaching spring. What I was really worried about was another ridiculously hot summer out here. I usually tried to work more shifts at Tacky Tacos during the day in the summertime to beat the simmering heat. I truly believed that if it wasn't for Willis Carrier inventing air conditioning in 1902, the Gulf Coast would not be as inhabited as it was today. It was just way too hot here in the summer.

I replied with a hint of petulance in my voice that I regretted instantly, "Don't start. You know how I feel about people."

"Téa, when you first came out here last year, the spring was in full swing. You have no clue how horrible it gets out in the elements during wintertime and early spring."

"If you can survive it, I can."

"I was trained to survive things like this." His tone was laced with regret.

He never brought up his military past. Just little snippets here and there and the random nightmares that he tried to hide from us. One thing I figured out, is that he lost his mind somewhere between Iraq and the States.

I held up my finger at him. "I know, but I've been through a lot too." I said it in a joking way. No one, not even my colorful friends out here, knew about what really happened to me. I kept it that way.

He pulled up his coat and shivered. I really enjoyed my evenings with this vet. He had a cold exterior, but deep down I could tell he cared about me. He turned to me again.

"I wish you weren't so hard headed. As smart as you are, you would think you had more sense."

Then his left eye twitched, and it was my unpleasant reminder that he wasn't one hundred percent all together. My other friends out here were already asleep on the curb a few feet from us. It was a good thing. I worried about them sometimes, too. They would do some really strange things that would draw the wrong attention to them. I had learned to tune them out. They were harmless. But they did like to put on a show similar to a jester for a king when innocents walked by with their snobby noses lifted higher than this street's Chase building.

I leaned back onto my elbows and looked over at everyone. Here we all were stacked in one on top of the other, pretty much. That's okay because it allowed me to smell the smoke floating through my sinuses signaling Pam's last cigarette for the night. I relaxed knowing that she was safe after another long trek across the park. Her tripod legged dog, named Unlucky, limped by me. He stopped to see what I brought home from the school's cafeteria.

"Now, Unlucky, you know if I keep feeding you chips, you're gonna get fat."

He barked and almost woke up the neighbors. "Ssh … next time," I told him.

A ritzy couple walked by headed for the downtown theatre in a fancy suit and sleek black dress. I couldn't help but admire their perfect physiques. They were all put together nicely like they came from somewhere special and had an amazing life to go back to. Unlucky barked a squeaky high pitched tone at them, so I pulled my damp blanket up to hide my face. I guess I was the only one on this block that still held out hope for *normal* one day.

Suddenly the neighborhood instigator, Sam, cursed at a cop by the curb. Then, he sashayed oddly towards me with his big toothless grin. The cop scowled at him but decided to pay no mind to what he deemed as trash at his feet. Sam flicked the mythical hair, that he didn't have, at the cop as he got closer to us. He had been bald for as long as I have known him but told us he would love some long girlie hair like Dolly Parton. As if on cue, Pam yelled something vulgar to Sam to throw off the cop. She followed it up with more mindless rambling while Unlucky nipped at Sam's feet.

"Unlucky, get back over here. I'm going to sleep," she told her dog and laid back in her tent. Me, them, all of us here, we were no different than everyone else. We looked out for each other too.

Once we were all settled in for the night, the mix of body heat broke the chill in the air. A band of misfits, we were. But in some ridiculous world, we were family. Currently, this was my only home. I didn't know it any other way anymore. I laid back and aimed to finally get some real rest. It didn't take long, and I was out.

"Rosa, hurry!"

I heard the young boy yell out again in Spanish. He swung open a heavy door of what looked like a monjeria and ran in to huddle down on the sandy floor inside. The lone candle lighting the room dimmed a bit almost extinguishing us into complete darkness. I studied his young face and the setting for a second before realizing that I was having that odd dream again.

I pulled my hand away from his noticing my hand was as tiny as his.

"My name is not Rosa," I told him.

He ignored me. He wore his long black hair tied behind his head. His dark skin, long nose, and other strong facial features reminded me of a Native American Indian.

As I started to hear a shuffling of feet outside the door, in came a man dressed in a white floor length robe that was tied at the waist with a thin horse hair rope. When my eye caught his collar, it made me think that he could be a priest. He had a balding, mottled scalp and his back was slightly hunched. I went to stand thinking I would be more of his same height but he still towered above me.

"Who are you? What is going on?" I asked and this time noticed that my voice was childlike. I was in the dream this time.

He turned back towards us. I could see now that his robe shown stains of splattered mud and viscous manure.

"Child, sit and stay calm. Peta will look out for you. It will all be fine," he replied.

The boy, Peta, was now standing beside me pulling my arm trying to get me to sit back down.

"Sit, Rosa!" Peta told me and managed to pull me down this time. "Father Hernandez, I will protect her."

Then, a brush of cool sticky air danced over my sweaty face as the priest swung open the shutters on the adobe room's window from the inside. The blurred rays from the fires outside aided my view until suffocating smoke began to roll into the room.

Father Hernandez turned towards Peta and me. "Children, stay hidden in here and do not come out unless I tell you to," he told us in Spanish.

His menacing tone and lack of eye contact with us, now scared me. The worried man's dark brown eyes darted all around the small room like a nervous finch preparing to take flight. He wiped his shaky hands on the last clean part of his white cotton robe while he moved back towards the door.

"We're safe, Rosa," Peta said.

I looked down at my tan floral dress that was crunched under my tiny fisted hands. The white apron overlay was even torn at the hem. Peta kneeled down in front of me and spoke again, "I promise. I won't let anything happen to you." He picked up a pestle that was lying nearby. I guessed that it was in case he needed it. But how would a young child fight off what was going on outside?

I nodded as a few strands of fine blonde hair escaped from the donut bun behind my head. "Peta, my name is not Rosa," I told him again.

He looked me squarely in the eyes. "Don't talk. We need to stay quiet."

I went to speak again and then heard more screaming outside. I was hyper-sensitive to the noises and movement. And judging from the high-pitched weaponry sounds slamming walls and people in the courtyard, escape wouldn't be possible if I waited too long. Just then I felt heat penetrate the wall behind me. The room next door was on fire! I didn't know what was going on, but I did know that I didn't want to burn to death in this room.

The swinging door behind Peta signaled the priest's departure. Just as Peta was looking back at me, I jumped up to rush passed him and out the door.

"Rosa, no!" Peta yelled while jumping to his feet to follow me.

I managed to snake right passed the old priest and ran right in front of a ravaging horse. It slammed me hard sending me to the ground. All I felt was pressure all over my chest as I gazed at the dark sky above and heard the footfalls of the retreating horses.

Peta fell down next to me.

"No!!" he cried out as he laid over me amidst all the chaos. "Rosa, please, no!"

The now distraught boy grasped my face. I tried to mentally fight back against the devastation all around me and the fact that I was actually going to die. Peta rubbed his own face until his cheeks were red. Then, his eyes morphed from a dark brown to a golden hue. I stared into them shocked.

He reached to his right ear and pulled off his earring. I couldn't make out what it looked like in the dark.

"It is going to be alright, Rosa."

Without pause, he opened my mouth with one hand and forced his earring inside my mouth with his other hand. I couldn't move or fight him, I was suffocating from both the object in my mouth and the pressure on my chest from the horse.

Suddenly, we were surrounded by blankets of suffocating smoke and a few of the combatant men descending upon us. Peta screamed again, but this time with his scream came a rumbling sound of intense shockwaves through the ground.

Layer upon layer of dirt slipped away under us as he finally yelled, "Rosa, you must believe in us!"

Suddenly, a huge ocean wave appeared out of nowhere and crashed all around, drowning out the dream and everything all over again.

CHAPTER 5

Found Me

I woke up with the little boy still screaming in my ear. But it wasn't him making that noise. It was more modern. Police cars? Oh, thank God. I'm still alive. I was shaking and touched my chest and neck enjoying the ability to breathe again. Uncle Bob rolled over as I asked, "Uncle Bob, what's going on?" Then, sure enough, three Houston Police Department cars sped by splashing road residue all over us.

Uncle Bob readjusted his blanket and turned over like it was no big deal. "Nothing, just the usual. You've only been asleep one or two hours. Why are you so on edge lately?"

That's when I noticed everyone around me was still asleep undisturbed. "I don't know. Don't you think that's more than the typical amount of cars called out?"

"Na, seen more. Go back to sleep."

I laid there listening and watched the HPD's car lights fizzle out into the labyrinth of streets ahead. Something had me feeling uneasy, but I couldn't figure out what it was. Was it that dream I just had? The dream seemed so real, like I really was there. I could feel the fear, smell the smoke, and sense the danger.

Then an ambulance passed by making me almost jump up. I looked ahead. Had there been another gang shooting, a car wreck, or domestic dispute? So many things happened out here in this part of Houston. Violence was a given on any typical night.

I settled back down watching the street lights flicker. I started thinking about the time I had come close to death myself. It was still all too clear, the memories unfaded. I remember the looks on the people's faces that hovered around me, the sounds, and the smells. And I still questioned if I would welcome it again the way my mom had. But what comes with death? Do I just close my eyes and escape into darkness? Would the darkness be void of memories, emotions, and struggles? It had been tempting to find out back then.

I imagined death as all-consuming yet with the power to wash away fears and torture. Wash it all away like the high tide does the man-made dunes on Crystal Beach. It pulls them back recessively into the vast ocean. Pieces of that sand that were once connected for a purpose would then dissolve into nothingness. Floating around with no direction or goal. Would I be taken away for good into this world's depths and no one would care? If only someone cared. I went back to sleep thinking about my brother and how much I missed him. He would care about me as I cared about him. If only I could find him.

The next morning, I was running quickly through the halls to keep from being late for Mr. Edgar's class. I was just a few steps from the door when Mr. Henderson, the school principal, grabbed my arm.

"Ms. Lane, late for class again?"

He glared down at me with crude brown eyes and thick brows. His sharp bird-like features added to his stern look. Everyone knew not to cross him.

"I'm sorry, Mr. Henderson. My alarm clock didn't go off this morning."

He actually smiled at me and let go of my arm. "You know how many times I hear that excuse?" His black suit and frigid demeanor was in line with most governmental men that it made me wanna gag.

However, I gave him a pleading half smile. "Never?"

The principal dropped his own grin and shook his head. "You have so much potential Ms. Lane. If only you would make the effort."

But I do make the effort. More than most. If only he really knew.

"Maybe I need to make a call to your foster mom."

I quickly interrupted, "No, sir. She's been sick, and I wouldn't want to upset her. It won't happen again." In that moment, I was so mad at myself. I couldn't keep making these mistakes. If I did he'd find out the truth and then Foster Care would know.

"I swear. I'll get it together."

Mr. Henderson paused and looked down at me with a hard expression. "I hear your science project is top notch.

You'll represent us well at State, right?" He gave me another bitter smile. It stunned me.

"Yes, sir."

I wanted to melt into the grey and red striped floor beneath me.

"Good. KPBC will be reporting on it."

Typical, it was all about how they looked compared to other schools. "I know."

"You see, you are only able to attend this school because of your STEM scores. We turned a blind eye for you."

Then, he peered hard at me. "And you know what I mean."

"I know, sir. Thank you."

His physiognomy always had a perpetual frown. However, he surprisingly just smiled twice during this conversation. Almost like he wanted me to fail so his son could move up above me in class rank.

"Have a good day, Ms. Lane," he said and turned to walk off.

I pressed my palm against my constricted chest. It had been a tough morning. When my street neighbor, Pam, woke me up this morning to go make her rounds all over the city park, I knew something was wrong. I couldn't believe that I had forgotten to charge my cell phone the day before during dinner back at Jason's Deli.

Maybe it was all Mrs. Nguyen's congratulatory speeches that distracted me. I wasn't used to praise. Anyway, it threw off my regular routine. When I woke up this morning, my blank screen told me my cell was dead. That cell acted as my only alarm clock. I cursed the whole time I was rolling up my sleeping bag. Needless to say, my bed making efforts were messy because I didn't have time. Thankfully, no one on the streets ever cared anyway.

Then, I had to make a mad dash to the school, so I could sneak into the gym dressing rooms before Coach Levi came in. She always did her morning rounds just ten minutes before the morning bell. I lucked out and just missed her on my way in. I pulled my hygiene stash out of my locker and took the quickest hot shower I could before I got caught.

I'd been taking these showers for months and no one had noticed. They all believed my lie that I had wet hair in the mornings because I didn't believe in frying my hair with a blow dryer. The things people will believe because the truth was too outlandish for them to comprehend. Thank God, because I had come up with some pretty crazy excuses this last year.

The whole day in class after that encounter, I went over the changes I needed to make to my project before I took it to State. I was panicked. There was a lot riding on my performance at the next fair. That sad truth was made perfectly clear to me earlier. But, I still didn't feel confident. Confidence was not my strong suit.

However, the warning from the principal and my lack of funds for college meant I had to nail this. Unlike all the pimple popping rich kids surrounding me, I needed to win. I wondered what it would feel like to have a backup plan like my fellow classmates did. Parents, grandparents, uncles, and aunts to help me out like all the students around me had. I had no one. In order to survive, it was always up to me.

Tommy approached me in the library later that day with a smile like everything was all good. Typical. "Hey Tea! I forgot to tell you congrats on the win at Regions."

I glared. "Go away, Tommy." I walked over to the science fiction section and picked up *Bumble Bee*, a book about alien life on distant planets. My favorite kind of stories.

He followed me and shook his head. "Tea, we've been friends for forever. When will you accept my apology?"

I walked over to biology to find another book over reproductive cycles for my class. "Never."

As usual, I noticed Tommy carried not a single book. He never had to study. It was like he knew everything and school was just for fun. He laughed now and a few girls in the stacks smiled over at him. He stopped laughing and ran his hand through his light hair.

"I'm always going to be here. I miss you. I miss our people watching, we used to do at the park every Friday night."

His bright green eyes darkened a bit. "I really do miss you, my friend."

I looked at the huge red clock on the wall above the horror books. "I gotta go, Tommy."

He straightened up and took a breath. "I'll be waiting."

I waved without looking back. "You do that."

CHAPTER 6

Discoveries Found in Mysteries

The rest of the week was a little easier. No more encounters from Tommy or the principal. My charm was on my mind as much as the State competition, though. On Saturday morning, I locked up my bike outside the convention center. The building was huge. It took up two square blocks of downtown Houston. As it turned out, the *Antiques Roadshow* occupied every square foot of that building.

I didn't know which door to enter through or where to begin. Women passed by me drinking their Venti-sized Starbucks drinks with their deflated husbands tailing right behind them carrying a variety of different things. I decided to follow behind the husbands carrying huge paintings wrapped in blankets. I had nothing of value compared to all that. I couldn't believe Kiki talked me into this. However, I needed the money.

I paid for my ticket and registered at the jewelry booth. For item info, I just put old charm in the shape of an acorn and further described it the best I could. A tall man wearing a construction-like orange vest, similar to other workers there, ushered me over to an area marked 'Old World Items'. I sat there for what seemed like hours and scanned through Twitter, Instagram, YouTube videos, and played Words with Friends before finally I heard, "Ms. Téa Lane! A Téa Lane, please!"

I jumped up and grabbed my little backpack while heading towards the lady in red with long black hair. She wore a poncho-looking cover-up over leggings and black boots. Black rimmed glasses covered her dark eyes and sat on top of a long, prominent nose. She smiled politely at me as I got closer.

"Ms. Téa?" She spoke with an accent I didn't recognize, and her raspy voice was soft and low.

"Yes, ma'am."

"I am Alexandra Marks, but you can call me Alex."

She motioned towards a booth not far from where we stood. I took a seat on one side, and she sat across from me. The raven-haired woman crossed her legs and said, "I hear you have something interesting that you found at the city park."

I pulled my necklace off and handed it to her. She took it between her painted fingernails and frowned showing several deep wrinkles between her brows. It was the first time I was able to ascertain that she was an older lady, maybe in her fifties. Nothing in her face or figure had revealed that.

She held my charm up and made no expression at all now. My heart sank.

"I guess it's not worth anything?"

I shrugged and looked down at my pale hands clasped on my lap. I knew I shouldn't have gotten my hopes up. She hung the necklace on a small jewelry mannequin and pointed at the gold on top with a long thin stick.

"This is definitely gold. The gold acts as a case for the actual object. It is all surprisingly in good condition too, even though it's been outside in the elements for a long time. It's old. Probably three hundred years old, maybe older. The markings on the gold tell me it is Indian in nature. Native American Indian, in fact."

I perked up. "Really? How much do you think it is worth?"

She removed the stick and set it in her lap. "The timing couldn't have been better for us to make our rounds to Houston. People have been bringing in many Spanish and Native American Indian artifacts that were found after Harvey. But I'm sorry, this piece is not worth much. Really just the value of the carved gold. Maybe one to two hundred dollars."

I bit my lip. "That's it?"

"But it is a neat find. You should just keep it. Since you found it in the aftermath of this city's horrible tragedy, you should view it as a keepsake item. It won't be special to anybody but you."

When she stopped adding to her evaluation, I took that as a sign that it was time to go. I stood, thanked her, and slipped the string back around my neck. I guessed she was right. It was a uniquely different item. I should treasure and keep it. I resolved to let the issue go and headed towards my bike outside.

Traffic had gotten heavy, so I decided to sit on a park bench outside the George Brown Center and watch families head to Discovery Green Park for some family fun. I pushed back my emotions from the sight of kids with their loving parents to the disappointing news from a few minutes ago. Before I knew it, the park was filled with even more kids running around crazy and parents following behind in a frenzy.

Then, a black mini coup stopped on the road in front of me blocking my view. The tinted window rolled down halfway. Long black hair and black rim surrounded eyes met mine.

"Ms. Téa!"

I blinked for a second. "Alex?"

She looked around wide eyed with her brows pushed together. "You must come with me now! Can you trust me?"

"Ah, no. I don't know you."

"What if I told you I lied about your charm? That it is worth more than you would ever believe."

She had my attention, and I couldn't deny that she looked serious. Not only that, but she had to be reputable since she worked for the show, right? Either way, it didn't matter. My natural instincts were screaming at me. I'm wasn't one to trust people, but something warm ran up my body. It was like a tingling sensation from my toes to my neck. Then, without hearing, comforting words filled my mind: *safe, trust her.* On autopilot, I jumped up and made my way to her car. When I opened the passenger door, she had books and manuals spread out all over the back seat.

Her brown eyes were wide. "Great! Now, hurry. Put your bike on the rack."

I walked with my bike to the back of her car and fastened it to the rack. When I walked back around, she was still looking around nervously. I got in anyway. Did I actually get into a car with a stranger? For the first time in years, I trusted someone other than myself. We rode for a few blocks to the Marriott, and she didn't say a word. I followed her after she valeted her car and headed to her room on the tenth floor. When we walked into the plush suite, I immediately noticed three suitcases, two laptops, and several expensive black shoes lining the closet floor. She was there for the long haul. The whole show.

"Why did you leave the show early? Doesn't it not end today for a few hours?"

"Téa, sit down."

I sat down on a yellow and blue striped, wingback chair. Alex opened the mini bar and pulled out a small bottle of wine. Then, she opened the laptop that was sitting on the cherry wood table by the window overlooking the convention center. She began typing with amazing speed.

"I have something to tell you that may take you off guard. There is more to that charm than what I told you. Much more."

She stopped typing. "Will you please hear me out before you comment?"

"I came here with you, didn't I?"

She nodded and the toe of her black heeled boot tapped the side of the table. Alex shut her laptop revealing a cover with a picture of racing horses across it. Turning to face me more directly, she started, "They call it a Kabar."

I took in the way she pronounced it with a long *a* first and then a short *a* sound. I tried pronouncing it myself, "Kabar?"

"Yes. In Native American Indian cultures, the Kabar represents a seed from a very special tree."

"But it's not a real seed," I added.

She smiled. "What faith do you practice?"

I frowned and crossed my arms. "I don't."

"Your parents?"

"They're dead. But when they were alive, they were Methodist."

"I'm sorry for your loss." Her eyes dimmed. "Did you ever take Communion as a Methodist?"

"I wasn't old enough, but I knew the bread represented Jesus' body and the wine was symbolic of his blood."

"Exactly. And you said bread meaning that the bread turned into his body upon digestion?"

I shrugged. "I guess. At least that's what they believed, sort of a ridiculous notion."

She continued, "The same thing occurs with this seed. Right now it seems like just an acorn. But when it's ingested, it becomes something more."

I studied her long face without blinking. She had a stern disposition and a steady gaze. She didn't shrug, break eye contact, or stutter.

"You believe this," I said slowly. This wasn't my chance to hear that it was worth a lot of money. I was starting to feel aggravated instantly.

"Not only do I believe in the tales of my ancestors. I also believe in its purpose, which is why I brought you here to

talk in private." She leaned forward and took her glasses off
to clean them with her blouse. "Téa, only special people can
be in possession or ingest the Kabar."

I stood and shook my head. "I'm not special. There is a
mistake. Look, why don't you take it and pay me more for it
then. Say five hundred?"

I figured this was a good time to negotiate. In her eyes,
this thing had intrinsic value. "What do you think? Want it?"

"No. It is only meant for the one it chose."

"An object cannot choose a person. You're mistaken."
But then, I remembered. Something like this was shoved in
my mouth in my dream. I wondered how much I should tell
her. No, this is crazy.

She waved her hand. "No mistake. I will tell you one
more thing. Don't give it to anyone else either no matter
who tries to take it. And there will be ones who do."

I swallowed and my left hand instantly went to the
charm. "Like who?" There are others that may pay more?
My hopes rose.

Alex erratically lowered her head to look at the floor
around us. "I can't tell you that," she said and looked back at
the charm with childish eyes. "It is odd, though. They all
should have been ingested by now unless …"

She stood and walked within a breath of me to inquire,
"Who are you?" She looked towards her hotel room door.
There was a buzzing sound outside the room. It sounded
like a hive of bees. Alex's skin turned from copper to ghost
white instantly.

"I'm just Téa. Hey, are you okay? That's just a vacuum
cleaner." I said with a glum sounding voice.

She frowned and shook her head facing the door. "I only believed parts of the tales before. Now, I think I believe all of it."

With her face vulnerable from whatever scared her, she turned without expression to grab her laptop. She shoved it into its case and retreated towards her suitcases.

"Do you not hear them?"

"What's wrong? Hear who?"

Okay, so she is mentally ill and hearing voices just like my crazy mom.

"Nothing. I must check out now." Her eyes were now icy and distant.

I stood up and asked, "All of the sudden you're leaving?"

Alex smiled awkwardly at me without making eye contact. "I just remembered I have to get home for my brother's surgery in the morning."

I jetted towards her and cut her off at the door. "You're lying. What is going on? Is it that sound? That's just a vacuum cleaner or something. Are you loco? I know a lot of crazy people, I didn't take you as one of them, though."

She pushed me out of the way and opened the door looking both ways before stepping into the hall. She then turned back to look at me. Finally her eyes were acknowledging that I was still there.

"Good luck, Téa. When the time comes you'll know what to do, when you are ready. Just don't let that thing go."

The heels of her boots stomped down the marble floor of the hall as she ambled with luggage and laptops to the elevator. When the elevator opened, she disappeared. That was the last time I saw her. I walked back into the room and shut the door, deflated again. I figured the room was still paid up for the night since check out time had already passed, so I stayed to watch the television for a little while and stew over what just happened.

A few hours later, I went down stairs and was thankful that my bike was there. At least Alex had been in the right mind to take it off of her car. I took my bike and loaded myself and it onto the city bus from the hotel. The bus would bring me closer to my section of town. I guess something just didn't sit right. Whatever began making me nervous a few days ago, began building back up when Alex left. After I exited at the bus stop, I noticed the sun had set.

When I got on Main St., there was something out of the ordinary two blocks down that reinforced my fear. Workers had a manhole cover surrounded with ribbon and were standing around it in a protective fashion. I jumped on my bike and took a quick turn onto Sheppard instead. Sadly, my wheels lost traction causing me to fall off my bike. I hit the cement hard, and I couldn't ascertain what had happened.

I slowly stood up on uncertain legs and noticed my bike was just scratched up a little. However, I had huge scrapes on my knee and arms. The stinging pain caused me to have to walk and pull my bike back home. I moved slowly down the lane until it veered off of the city street into a small, grassy area away from the street lights.

A few steps into the darkness and the hair on my bloodied arms started to stand on end. Almost like they did when my foster father from a few years back, Rick, came home from work. I always knew something bad was coming when I felt that. I became acutely aware of trouble from an early age. A warm frontal breeze picked up and rolled down the street. I paused and pulled my small taser out of my coat pocket. No movement insight, but I could sense a presence. My heart started to race, and I thought I heard a voice in the wind. The rest of the easement was empty, though.

"Who's there?" I said into nothingness but got no reply.

The sounds of the wind turned into more of a buzzing sound. It was menacing and sounded like the sound at Alex's hotel. However, I blamed my mind.

"Come on Téa, nothing's here," I said to myself but peered hard into the darkness to make sure.

With my taser at the ready in my left hand, I grasped my bike with my dominant right hand and began to move again. Then, I heard another sound that I couldn't deny. Light padded steps approached me from the direction I was heading. I stopped and started to turn in preparation for flight back the way I'd come. But I now saw movement from the direction I'd come.

I stood frozen for a few short seconds. Seconds that felt more like five minutes, while I debated my options. Sweat beaded over my brow and fear gripped my spine. I worked hard to survive my past. Three years ago, I would have welcomed death. After my time with Ms. Adele, I was made to believe that life was worth it. I was prepared to fight for it now.

Suddenly, a dog popped out and pranced towards me from my original direction. Realizing that that way was now safe, I took off running with my bike as fast as I could towards the labrador. I didn't look back but noticed that the dog didn't seem bothered by whatever the movement was behind me. The lab passed by me and kept on going toward that direction while I kept on running towards mine.

CHAPTER 7

… And That's How it Goes

"One more second and the bell would have gotten you," said Mr. Edgar as I entered science class Monday morning. The medium sized teacher was dressed down in jeans and cowboy boots reminding me that it was rodeo week. Let me barf now.

"Good morning, Mr. Edgar," I said, keeping my eyes down low and briskly headed to my seat. I hated coming into class after everyone else, but my morning shower in the locker room felt so good after a night of scrapes and running. I lingered longer than I should have in the relaxing pipe-based waterfall.

I saw an empty seat and sat next to Ana. Ana Bromley was the sweetest girl of the whole senior class. She smiled warmly at me and handed me her staple Ticonderoga pencil she always had sharpened and ready for me in the mornings.

I nodded a thank you and relaxed into the maroon plastic seat. Mr. Edgar began science class the same way he did every day.

"Class, what would you like to know about your world today?"

He was a great teacher and never followed the required curriculum. I swear he never wrote a single lesson plan. However, I had never learned as much as I learned in his class. He was the best. As Mr. Edgar began explaining the theory of relativity and how it relates to our teenage lives, my mind drifted off. I was still freaked about Saturday night. To steady myself, I glanced around and noticed Ms. Lexi Sampson sitting in a new seat close to Tommy. He seemed fine with it. He even smiled at her several times. For some reason, it didn't sit well with me.

Ana leaned over to me to whisper, "Kyle broke it off with her."

I gasped. "What? They've been going strong for years."

Ana lifted a brow. "I know, but word is he's dumping her so he can be single when he goes off to college. He wants to spread the *love*."

She said it with a purr sound that made me want to laugh.

I responded back, "Typical for a jock."

"Don't knock them all. Tommy isn't half bad."

She peered back at him with her the eraser of her pencil between her lips. "Well, he *wasn't* half bad. He seems to be liking the slut flirting with him."

I couldn't comment. Or maybe I didn't want to comment. To reply to that would make it seem like I cared, but I didn't like him like that. He had always just been my friend, not that spoiled brat's.

Ana was turning her ruby ring over and over on her index finger. "You shouldn't be so mad at him."

"I ... hey deserve each other anyway."

I wanted to drop it. I knew exactly why Lexi was moving on Tommy. She knew we had had a falling out and there was no way she was going to pass that up. *There is always a girl like her in every school, job, and organization*'. That was what Ms. Adele used to tell me not long before she had her stroke.

She'd been the only foster parent who'd really cared for me and didn't abuse me. She was also the one that taught me how to speak and carry myself correctly. And the one that would hug me all night after through and after my violent breakdowns. Too bad I knew the State of Texas foster care system wouldn't let me stay with her after her stroke.

My redheaded friend nervously peered her big brown eyes back behind us again. "Yeah, I guess you're right."

Ana seemed to pout like it hurt her too.

"It's fine, Ana. She's easy and Lord only knows guys like easy, especially him."

Ana made a sour grape face. "Téa, stop that. He's a good guy. He's already apologized about that picture and removed it from Instagram."

Was it my damp, freshly showered hair soaking the back of my shirt or the embarrassment of seeing that pic again that gave me a chill?

"Stay out of it, Ana."

"But you do have a hot body. You should show it off."

"Ana!!" I seethed.

"Ms. Lane!" I heard Mr. Edgar announce. "Please read us the quote by Elon Musk that we just saw on our TED Talk video and explain to us what you think it means," he said impatiently. Dang, if my outburst didn't get me the wrong kind of attention just like that swimsuit picture Tommy posted without permission.

Ana reached over and circled on my notebook paper the quote that I thankfully jotted down during the video.

"Um ..." I was so embarrassed as my eyes tried to adjust to read my own shorthand messy handwriting.

"You know, from their CEO?" Mr. Edgar said helping me out. Whispers from behind my back shot daggers into my pride.

SpaceX was one of my favorite corporations. I should've known every single one of Elon's published quotes by heart.

"From the video?"

"Yes, Téa, and it was also referenced by *Silicon Valley Business Journal* in the article I just assigned."

I swallowed nervously and read it.

"'There have to be reasons that you get up in the morning and you want to live. Why do you want to live? What's the point? What inspires you? What do you love about the future? If the future does not include being out there among the stars and being a multi-planet species, I find that incredibly depressing.'" (TED 2017)

I sat back in my chair wondering what answer Mr. Edgar was looking for besides the obvious. Thinking about the context of where the quote was also published, the *Silicon Valley Business Journal*, I decided to go with what that quote meant to me.

"To me, the quote says we all need a goal or a dream that will keep us going. For Musk, it's space exploration. Truth be told, I guess it's the same for me."

"Yes, Téa, I figured it was. Therefore, I would like you to take the lead on your group's presentation over SpaceX's current space exploration program."

Then, he turned to Michael at the front of the room. "Michael, you will take the lead for your group and report over oil exploration in the Gulf of Mexico. They just made a new discovery. Go to NOLA.com for news on this."

I sat there relieved as my teacher moved from team to team assigning topics for our exploration presentations.

Ana leaned in again. "Mr. Edgar likes you. However, I'm not complaining. Since I'm in your group, we always get the coolest assignments."

❈ ❈ ❈ ❈

When first period was over, I jumped out of my seat but was immediately detained by my teacher. "Téa, stay for a sec. I'll write you a pass for next period."

"Yes, sir."

I slid back into my seat not knowing what it could be about. The science fair? I sat watching hormonal teen boys trying to inconspicuously check out the girls as they all walked out of the classroom.

Mr. Edgar sat on the desk in front of me. "Congrats again your advancement to State."

"Thank you."

"I just heard that Shell Corp. is handing out a $10,000 scholarship to the winner at State *and* promised an intern spot for next year."

I drummed the heel of my Reebok's against the floor. "Really? That's great! I wasn't expecting any more than maybe one thousand dollars more than what I was awarded at Regions."

"Yep. So are you still good with working after school on it with my help? There are some things we need to perfect."

"Definitely. I already took off work for a few days after spring break too."

"Good."

He smiled genuinely at me. If I had a father, I imagined that would be what a dad's pride looked like. He slid off the desk and checked his cell. Girls always talked about how good looking Mr. Edgar was. He did have some redeeming qualities. In fact, those Wrangler jeans he was in were probably stopping a lot of hearts today. To me, someone in their late thirties was more like a father-figure than eye candy.

With that I stood up with a little more pep in my step. I was extremely excited with the scholarship and intern news.

"Thanks, Mr. Edgar!"

Things were looking up! At least until I got to second period and received a note that I was wanted in the assistant principal's office. Fear traveled up my chest and to my neck wanting to choke me where I stood. What if it was the foster care people? Did they find out?

All during class group work, I ignored my fellow students' bickering over failed plans on spring break. How I wish I had trivial things to worry about like they did. I was so jealous. Second period was another class that drug on and on. When my group finished our research, I went back to watching Mrs. Shaw's rustic clock tick by slowly from 9:05 till 10:15. It was agonizing.

I got to the principal's office down the hall by 10:16 and walked right into the reception area. No one was at the front desk, but the television was on. It was reporting about a woman's body being found this morning in one of the city's manholes. The reporters said she was in town on business. I tilted my head and for a second and wondered . . .

Then I heard Ms. Jolly, the school secretary. "Téa! Come in!"

I walked into her small office and watched her smile at me. Ms. Jolly was a chubby lady with a thick middle and spiked hair. She neither held her tongue nor acted professionally. Students gossiped that the powers that be have been trying to get rid of her for years. She didn't care, not Ms. Jolly. I imagined that she had something on them that she had been holding over those big dogs' heads for a long time.

"Hi, I got a note to come in." My eyes were darting around her office looking for stuffy governmental workers with cheap suits and store-bought hair colors. If I was found out, I didn't know what I'd do. I wasn't going back into a bad foster home.

Ms. Jolly leaned over the L-shaped counter showing every bit of her round, huge cleavage above her low cut blue blouse. Like I said, she didn't care. That woman did whatever she liked.

"I'll tell you a secret."

"Yes?"

"Just say you know nothing."

She leaned back and took a sip of her coffee. Per the other rumors, it was probably laced with vodka. She giggled at me before picking up her phone to call the assistant principal in the next office.

"Mr. Powers, Téa Lane is here to see you! No … no … not this one. I think it's a mistake, too. Oh, okay, so she's free to go?" Ms. Jolly winked at me then.

"Sounds good, I will let her know."

She hung up the phone and raised her brows at me. "Your lucky day. He seems to have someone already."

She plopped her pen on her desk and spun it. "You're free, but honey, you know we have cameras all over this here school, right?"

What was she getting at?

"I do now."

"Just be mindful of that darlin, you follow me?" Her Texas drawl was more evident on the word 'darlin'.

I nodded. "Yes ma'am. Got it."

"Oh, before you go, I also wanted to tell you about my nephew who just enrolled. His name is Ben."

"Ben? The same Ben that started working at Tacky Tacos?"

She gave me her best motherly grin. "That's right. He did say something about that now that I think about it. Isn't that where you work?

"Yes."

She winked at me. "Isn't he a catch?"

I didn't reply.

"Anyway, he's a good kid. He's just had a lot happen in his young years. God rest my sister-in-law's soul and her sweet daughter. So, my point is, if he comes off brutish, just ignore it."

I nodded and went to exit when another worried student came in. Ms. Jolly lit up on him in no time flat.

"Mr. Reynolds! This is going to get fun, today!" she said with a big cherry lipped smile. Did that woman have nothing better to do?

I walked briskly to third period and finally felt some relief when I took my seat in the back row. For the past year, I have worried every time I was called down to that office. How many more times would I be able to dodge that bullet?

CHAPTER 8

If Only

Third period was painstakingly slow and boring today. My mind drifted between scholarship news and foster care woes. Suddenly the boy with the cool eyes at work popped into my mind. Ben. I regretted my stray thoughts over those things. When class was over, Mrs. Franks requested a summary of what we learned. I hadn't learned a thing.

"Exit tickets must be written in complete sentences. Don't come to the door if you're still really a first grader and not a twelve grader," Mrs. Franks said while standing to turn the projector off with her remote. The batteries must have been dead because she slapped the back of the remote and grimaced before giving up to take her spot by the door.

She stood there partly into the hall with her SBF look and watched shrewdly as other classmates walked up with their sticky notes in hand. She reveled in being a tough teacher.

"K … k … k … you all may go. Next … " she said moving her glasses to her head. If you ran into her outside of school, you would think she was the cutest Asian woman you had ever seen. Here at Sterling High, she was Hitler in a skirt.

"Old shrew." Kiki snuck up beside me.

"I know," I replied with my back to Mrs. Franks while putting my notebook and iPad in my backpack.

"Hey, why don't we go prom dress shopping and you can tell me all about *Antiques Roadshow?*" Kiki asked.

This was the only class we took together so besides work, we didn't get to talk to each other much. However, she knew me well enough to know that I had no plans of going to prom.

"Kiki, prom's not happening. And sadly, the charm isn't worth anything."

"Oh, sorry."

I headed to the door with my yellow sticky in hand. Mrs. Franks didn't make eye contact with me. She just glimpsed at my sentences and nodded for me to exit. Kiki, on the other hand, was given the evil eye. I felt for her. She never gave her full effort in school. I didn't know how she ever passed anything. But Kiki didn't have to worry about an education. Her family was rich.

I stood in the hall and listened to Mrs. Franks tear into Kiki again. "Nikki Michaels, of all the … "

The shuffling of feet through the halls made it impossible to hear the whole tongue lashing. I stepped as close to the action as I could to hear, but then I saw *him*. Or at least I thought it was him. That intense stare that made me uneasy at Tacky Tacos couldn't have been but fifty feet from me down the hall. More and more students moved around that spot making it hard to confirm what I saw. After a few moments of searching, I gave up and turned my attention back to Kiki's demise.

I still couldn't hear everything, so I went off body language. Kiki's brown hair was pulled back in a high ponytail, so I could see the blood vessels in her long neck pulsing. I looked at the floor willing Kiki to just shut up and take it. That way, we could rush off to our next class without being late.

Finally, Kiki was released from Mrs. Franks and came out with bulging eyes. "That horrid woman," she whispered. "She's always busting my chops."

"You're an easy target, Kiki. If you would just do your work, you could slide through these next few months unscathed."

"Touché."

Her thin eyebrows lifted slightly as her eyes hooked themselves on our school's soccer star that was coming down the hall towards us.

"Hey, Ralph!"

Ralph replied immediately, "Hey." He was always happy to see Kiki. He walked closer to us wearing one of his usual black Metallica t-shirts, cargo shorts, and Converse sneakers. The boy loved American styles, even the ones that were no longer trendy.

Under long eyelashes, I scanned the halls in Ralph's direction wondering about Ben again. Oh no, all I saw was Brady. Brady Harris. Ugh! I swear he took up the entire hallway. The huge and brutish baseball team catcher briskly caught up to Ralph. Brady stood almost a foot taller than his Hispanic friend. He was the one I detested more than any of those sports' boys. As he got closer, he let out his ear ringing laugh at us and pointed at Kiki.

"You got hammered by the queen hag teacher."

He didn't care how loud he said it or whether or not Mrs. Franks heard because he knew he was bullet proof. No one sent those guys to ISS. Not when our baseball team was going to State.

Kiki's brown eyes turned black. "Screw you, Brad."

Brady flared back, "*Brady* not Brad, sweets." They did this to each other often, but everyone knew he had a crush on Kiki.

He wiggled his eyebrows at me. "Hey, blondie."

I rolled my eyes. "Don't call me that."

I knew he looked down on me. I didn't fit into his perfect-women only world. He made fun of me last year about the gap between my top two front teeth. As if a foster care girl had parents with money to put braces on her. Granted he didn't know that, but either way, it hurt.

"Oh, sorry," he said sarcastically and eyed my chest. See? Wrong attention. I covered the neckline of my pink cotton t-shirt quickly with my discounted Letterman jacket. I didn't have a big chest, so I never knew why boys bothered.

He smiled. "I liked that picture on Instagram, by the way."

Kiki came to my aid, "Brad, do I need to slam you on Twitter again? Was that goofy baseball player meme I likened you to not enough?"

I grabbed Kiki's elbow. "Come on Kiki, we're going to be late for fourth period."

"Yep," she said and turned toward me with a smile. She knew he aggravated me and she always had my back. Once upon a time, Kiki didn't have anything to do with me either.

I was the outcast of the school, and I didn't wear hip, expensive clothes. However, I think she took to me because I was everything her mom couldn't stand.

Kiki turned quickly and waved at sweet Ralph. "See you around."

Ralph gave her a timid smile and said, "I may come get some of that taco tonight."

His English was still iffy. He knew he made a huge slip up because he immediately dropped his eyes to the floor. By his side, Brady burst into an even louder laugh as Kiki and I turned to walk away from the perverts. Kiki took a hard left for music. I headed up the stairs to computer class with one thought on my mind: boys are immature and pathetic, and that's why I don't date.

❀ ❀ ❀ ❀

The final bell of the day rang, and I slowly packed up. I preferred going to work after school because it gave me something to do for the rest of the day. I was off today though, so I wasn't in any rush to leave school. Kiki, my dear Kiki, came running into my classroom like she had the biggest news since tampons. After she waved at Ana walking by, she grabbed my arm.

"Come see!"

I cringed. "Oh God, what?"

She steered me out and down the hall to the exit. We both squinted when we left the dim building into the bright sunshine. Before I could question her more, she pulled me over to the student's parking lot.

"Look at that hot number." She pointed ahead. All I saw were spoiled teenagers getting into their fancy cars.

"What am I looking at?"

She took my chin and turned it a little more to the left. "See him? Ben!"

He wasn't far away, but I noticed him when he turned to shake another boy's hand. "Yeah, I saw him earlier today. Ms. Jolly said he just enrolled. He's her nephew. But why is this such a big deal?" I challenged her.

"Look at his car."

I looked over and saw him lean back against a black Audi A-6. "And?"

"That's an expensive car! How does a dishwasher afford that?"

"Kiki, that is rude."

"Oh, Téa. You know what I mean. And he's Ms. Jolly's nephew. So, how can he afford that?"

She had a point about the car, but I actually liked Ms. Jolly. Maybe Ben wasn't so bad after all. I stared off across the parking lot and saw him conversing with Aiden Sawyers, another senior. Ben stood out among the crowd with his tall stance and dark coloring.

"So, Ben's our age," I said.

At the least, he was most likely. Could he have a jaded past like me? Something more than just a deceased mother and sister? More importantly, why did I care? I told Kiki goodbye and jumped on my bike to head to work without looking anymore at Ben. However, as I headed to work, I continued wondering all about that new guy. I was usually able to read every human being I came into contact with. I could not read him.

That wasn't all that puzzled me that day and for the next week. The strange things the lady from the show, Alex, said in that hotel still bothered me, too. She had looked so serious. All of her belongings were high quality, so she came from or made good money. She was surely a smart lady. Therefore, I just reasoned out that the charm was a special artifact that I needed to take care of. Surprisingly deep down, I hoped I was wrong.

Either way, I was very distracted all week.

CHAPTER 9

Trust

"More rain?" I said to Kiki while standing outside on the steps of our school again. It was Friday of that same week. I was so relieved I survived until another weekend..

"Yucky, huh?" she replied and tapped her fake nails on her bottom lip.

"Yes. I really could use some sun and relaxation after the kind of week I had."

I was mentally stressed after all the odd things I had been witnessing. On Tuesday, an insane amount of cop cars kept me up all night. On Wednesday morning, the campus counselor had made an off-handed comment about calling my foster mom that had me scrambling for more excuses. And during third period, that same day, I had looked down at my charm and thought I saw it glow.

On Thursday at work, the charm suddenly seemed heavy. I pulled the whole thing off and rubbed my neck. But when I put it back on, it felt fine. The other odd thing about it was that it drew Ben's attention. He didn't usually talk to me. However, when I messed with the charm that day, he actually spoke to me. It wasn't anything spectacular, just a compliment on how special the charm must be to me.

Kiki coughed next to me and broke through my thoughts. "I hate this weather. Be glad you're off tonight." She wiped her nose with a tissue and turned towards me. "Sinus hell. Hey, you need a ride?"

I didn't really answer. I just shook my head and watched the school bus drive onto the street.

"This weather is yucky. It better clear up for spring break."

Kiki looked so cute with her red button nose. Spring break officially started today. Kiki being sick and all the rain was not a good sign.

"So, what about that ride?"

I was tempted to take her up on her offer, but then she'd know way too much. She'd never drop me off far enough from my home and not want to inquire more. No way would she fall for that.

"No. There's not any lightening, so it will be fine."

Her mouth gaped open. "What?"

I stepped out into the cool drizzle and fired back, "I'll be fine. See, it's not even raining much?" Too many rainy days were making it harder to keep my secret from everyone. I wished the rain would stop.

As I got to my bike, I heard her yell over the wind, "Yet!"

I took the chain off my bike quickly and with my backpack secure, I took off riding down the road. I didn't need any more questions from Kiki about the *Antiques Roadshow* tonight either. I would have to lie to Kiki again about the unofficial private meeting that took place after the show.

Remembering Alex's words, I tucked the charm into my shirt just in case. Stinging my face like several pins sticking into my flesh, the rain came down in hard waves as I pushed on to make it at least halfway home.

I was so busy fighting the rain that I didn't notice how hard pedaling got all of the sudden. Maybe it was because the last few streets were smooth. However, when I crossed onto Sheppard St., the older street began to work against me. It seemed really odd, though. I had never had trouble here before. I kept struggling to pedal until I realized something was wrong. Stopping in front of Chase bank on the corner and out of the way of traffic, I got off to examine my bike.

My tires were flat. Both!

How could this happen?! I didn't ride over anything. The hood on my raincoat was keeping some of the harder rain off of me while I examined the situation closely. There wasn't any sign of a puncture. And if I ran over something how could it have affected both tires? Which led me to one conclusion, someone did this.

Steam was escaping the drainage holes on both sides of the street and cars rushed by me one by one without delay. There was no one on foot behind or around me either. I thought back in my head wondering if anyone at school hung around my bike after dismissal or if anyone acted strangely. The faces in the diner next to me had innocent enough expressions and paid me no mind.

It was no matter; something didn't sit right with me. My gut churned and a cold wave of dread passed under my skin and down my spine making me incredibly uneasy. My breathing slowed and the pace of the rain seemed to speed up. I exhaled again and froze. It felt too much like that dark night a few days ago when I ran without looking back.

Another car, bigger than most, came around the corner and sped closer to me. This time the man looked at me before he finally sped by me. I was thankful he went on. Then, I saw a fancy car with four rings on the front bumper. It started to slow as it came down the road.

"Oh crap!" It couldn't be.

I wasn't standing around to make sure. I pulled my bike down the adjacent alley and hid the best I could behind a tall trash can overflowing with boxes and old fabrics. A few long seconds passed before I stood up completely to go and check the scene. When I stepped back into view, there were no cars stopped. I sighed and started the hard trek home by foot.

An older couple walked by me with a tiny white dog cradled in one of their arms. The little thing kept his attention on me until they too disappeared around the corner. His sweet curiosity reminded me of the dog I found when I first landed on the streets. My dog was a stray and mixed breed dog similar to that one. I named him Otto after Otto Hahn, the father of nuclear chemistry, because I was fascinated with nuclear fission at the time. Otto kept me company every night until the day he ran off.

When the Murray Tower came into sight, I knew I had only a few more blocks to go. The strange feeling that passed over me earlier had dissipated, and I began to feel better. I started to debate stopping at the Mexican café coming up. I could have some tamales and do my ELA homework there. A smooth sounding car pulled up beside me. I reluctantly looked over to see that the window was rolling down. It was a black sedan, and inside was the elusive dishwasher from Tacky Tacos with his dark hair laying messy over his forehead.

"Téa?"

I stopped. "Yes? Ben?"

"That's right. Now get in," Ben said in a demanding tone that didn't sit well with me. Surprisingly, he flinched right after he said it. He then took a breath and smiled revealing dimples on each cheek.

"Let me give you a ride," he said now genuinely.

"What? No," I replied. Ain't happening. Sexy guy here could be an ax murderer. Ms. Jolly's nephew or not.

"Look, it's pouring out here. You'll get sick." He looked behind at the street and back up at me with soft eyes.

"I'm not far from home. Go on. Have a good night." I noticed a younger couple watching us.

"Why are you over here anyway?"

He looked around again. "It's only a few blocks from work. Why wouldn't I be?"

"It's still out of the way going this direction."

"Honestly, Ms. Jolly is my aunt. She asked me to start giving you rides home."

I had known that woman for years. What was her end game here?

"I know she is, and I'll be sure to tell her that I don't need your help. I'll be fine," I exclaimed and started walking.

He maintained a slow speed beside me. "Téa, look at you. You're soaked. No way in hell I'm leaving you out here.

Just come eat some dinner with me. I'm cooking burgers. I'll take you home afterwards."

He faltered. "It would be good to get to know each other since, you know, we work together and all."

I stopped walking. My hair was flat against my face and my clothes were sticking to me. I felt disgusting. Either I walk into a freezing cold restaurant soaked, or I go with him to a warm home where I could towel dry myself off. The latter was so tempting but so stupid. Then, I felt it. The same sensation I felt when Alex picked me up after the antique show. And that didn't turn out bad. The feeling was more instantaneous this time, almost unnerving.

"Okay." What has gotten into me?

With that, Ben completely stopped the car. He jumped out and put my soaking wet bike in the back of his fancy, girl magnet vehicle. The tendons in his muscular forearms bulged out when he lifted it making my mouth go dry.

I got into his car and immediately felt claustrophobic. He had the heater turned way too high. I had to close my vent quickly before he slid into the driver's seat beside me. The black interior was spotless, and I was immediately enamored with the rush of a manly spice scent. I couldn't help but smile.

"Really, thanks. But I would have been fine. I'm used to this."

I pressed my hands down on my thighs and took a deep breath. A sudden bead of sweat moved from my hairline to my brow. Ben ran his hand through his wet hair and looked over at me.

"Why are you so against getting help?" he asked and licked the rain drops that had fallen on his lips.

I unconsciously parted my own lips. I'd never been this close to him. He really had the coolest colored eyes. They looked like they had a hue of transparent silver laid softly above his brown irises. Being that I studied and read book after book on human anatomy, I couldn't help but wonder what genetics could have mixed to make such mesmerizing eyes. I was getting way too lost in those eyes. Then, I turned to take in the blistering rain that seemed to pick up as soon as I had relief from it.

"I'm used to doing things on my own. It's best that way."

Ben sat there, and I presumed he was still watching me. "Best how?"

I shrugged. "No strings attached." I turned back towards him. "I don't like to owe anybody *anything*." I emphasized 'anything' and he nodded. With that, he put the car in gear and headed off.

I watched his profile. He had a long nose above soft lips. His clear complexion was only tarnished by one or two small scratches along his neck and upper cheek. I wanted to ask why but held back. Even though the silence was awkward, he kept his eyes on the road, and I kept mine on his jaw watching it clench as if he was in deep thought. The town streaked by out the window, and I had time to consider what it was about him that has had me so conflicted ever since I met him ... What was it about *him*?

The scenery of the city from inside of the vehicle was nice. Many people were out and about, even though the rain was persistent. Umbrella after umbrella lined the next block as patrons marched into the hotels and restaurants while we left the business section of downtown. The next street over was another hot spot for the homeless.

This area, though, was not the friendliest. They were more territorial there. The ring leader, Cyrus, stood out in the rain collecting donations from bystanders and smiling with his big gold toothed grin. I sunk into Ben's car seat to hide my face just in case. No way would Cyrus recognize me. However, I was a little self-conscious.

Ben's deep voice startled me. "So … how is school going for you? I heard about you getting Best of Show in the Regional Science Fair. Now, are you—"

He stopped mid sentence and turned up the volume on the radio to listen to what Shirley Q news anchor was reporting.

"… and police say they do have a few leads they are investigating. Right now, they are advising young women in the Houston and surrounding areas to not stay out too late and for everyone to immediately report any suspicious behavior to the local authorities. This is Shirley Quam reporting from Sugar Land."

Ben rubbed the back of his neck and breathed in slowly.

I reached across to the round black knob to turn down the volume. "What's all that about?"

He didn't seem to react. His eyes were steady on the road. "You hadn't heard about the serial killer?"

"I heard something about three girls killed in Corpus Christi. That's about it. Is it related?"

He started rubbing the steering wheel with the pads of his thumbs. "Yes, they think so. But they reported this morning that two more girls went missing in Sugar Land."

"Oh, I didn't realize." Was I being too daft? But I never kept up with the news.

"You *should* pay attention."

Ugh!

"Preach much?" I asked raising my voice a hair.

I also didn't want to entertain the thought that the uneasiness I've had lately could be related to a serial killer that I may have or may not have come into contact with.

He didn't reply.

CHAPTER 10

For Real?

A few minutes later, we pulled into an ultra-sleek neighborhood. If I wasn't intimidated before, I was now. The houses that sat off the street were immensely decadent and grandiose. I shook my head in disbelief.

"Is this where your house is? Surely not."

My chauffeur didn't answer but kept driving until we came to a driveway blocked by a huge iron gate. As soon as he pulled up, the gate opened revealing a beautiful two-story stone home with oversized windows. Gas lanterns by the wooden front door flickered. Tall perfectly cut shrubbery offset the simple porch, and gorgeous wooden beams welcomed us.

"You're a dishwasher. What's the catch?"

"It's my family's home."

"Oh, that explains it. Are they here?"

He peered over at me. "No. It's the house that's used more for business. I moved in just a few weeks ago."

"What kind of business?"

He put the car in park and huffed with aggravation. "You ask too many questions." Then, he jumped out and came around to my side to let me out.

"You coming?"

Slowly I rose to my feet while still taking in the structure. I didn't belong here. What was he thinking? Or am I some charity case for him?

"Look, I didn't take you as a rich boy. I guess ..."

"What?"

"This is too extravagant," my voice inaudible.

He reached out his hand for mine. "You're more like me than you know."

I highly doubted that, but I took his warm, firm hand and followed him into the mansion anyway. His hand engulfed mine almost completely. But what I noticed more was his strength. I imagined all kinds of things he could do with just one hand. He tugged my hand gently as if in some rush.

When we walked into his house, paintings of earth toned scenes aroused my senses. Adaptations of Native American Indians from free range times to more modern times graced each oversized canvas. "Your family is in to Indians, aren't they?"

He eyed me and then followed my gaze to the engrossing pieces. "I guess you could say that."

Through the foyer, there were two odd looking totem pole statues topped with huge eyes glaring back at me. Behind them, there was a spectacular water fountain. It had to stand at least eight feet tall with an eagle's body swirled around it like a soft serve ice cream cone. I developed an appreciation for art going to galleries with Ms. Adele. This piece was up there with those famous ones I used to admire.

"Wow! This is breathtaking!"

I was talking to myself, I guess, because Ben had disappeared while I admired the piece. The water cascading down was warm to the touch and had a soft viscous texture like honey dripping from a honeycomb. I closed my eyes to better enjoy the feel and hear the smooth splashing sounds reverberating from the pool at the base.

Out of the corner of my now opened eyes, I noticed Ben was standing not five feet away from me holding some folded garments. He spoke with a velvety, soft voice. "Clothes for you. You'll feel better once you have a bath. My treat."

His hair was barely damp from outside and looked jet black against his dark olive skin. The grey shirt he was wearing brought out the silver glow in his eyes even more. I couldn't help but stare. He stepped forward closer to me.

"What?" he asked.

I frowned up at him. "Oh, nothing. Look, I'm fine."

"I insist. Two doors down the hall and to the right."

He set the clothes on the couch table next to me and proceeded to an adjoining room. The clothes were a matching set, a white and tan t-shirt with a tan pair of pants. I picked them up and followed the directions he gave me. The whole time I walked down the hall and into the bathroom, I cursed myself quietly for it.

What was I doing? I didn't even know him. Was it the stress of the last few days over worrying about going to State? I wasn't sure, but battling people that were trying to help me, took too much energy right now. There was no way I was going to pass up the bathtub I found behind the white-washed oak door either.

OMG! It was amazing!

I excitedly shimmied out of my wet sweater and skintight jeans. I was running the hot luxurious water in no time and began dropping the light blue bath balls into the bath with no cares in the world. I couldn't remember the last time I had experienced such opulence. The marble tub filled up with suds, and I dipped one toe in to check the temperature. It was perfect! Then, my whole foot, next my second foot, to my rear end, and then all the way up to my chest.

"This is heaven," I moaned up to the ceiling above me.

The recessed lights were scattered all above and dimly shining down offering just enough light to see sparkles on the bubbles that were embracing my upper torso. I wanted to fall asleep and never wake up. Forget the dinner being prepared for me or the impending odd conversation that was likely to come between Ben and me. Forget the troubles of foster care or the upcoming science fair. Forget all my woes and past mistakes. I wanted peace. If even for just a few minutes in a strange house with a strange guy.

Tap, tap, tap.

So much for that. Ben spoke through the door lightly, "Dinner is ready, Téa."

"I'll be right out."

A few minutes later, we sat at the breakfast bar made of solid grey slate. The burgers smelled so good. He had even fried up some wide cut fries and placed them on a huge platter between us. I picked one up and dipped it into the small glass bowl of ketchup beside me. My host didn't say anything. He just took a few bites of his burger and kept his eyes low.

I smiled at him. "Hey, thank you for the bath. It was really nice."

Ben didn't look up. "No problem. You needed it."

"What I stunk?"

He said nothing.

"Well, what did you expect?"

Still nothing.

I was surprised that it was me trying to get the conversation going. Usually, I'm the one who can't stand to talk to people. But something about him interested me.

"You really don't say much," I said and pulled my almost too small shirt down a little more in an attempt to close off the midriff showing. If this shirt was originally his, it sure had shrunk.

He glanced down at my efforts and back at me with a surprised expression flitting across his face. It disappeared quickly.

"I'm trying to eat," he said frigidly.

I abruptly added, "I knew this conversation would be odd, but I didn't expect that we wouldn't have one at all. What is your deal?"

Ben stopped eating and put his burger down. He never smiled or acted like he cared about anything. His clothes were always simple, too. Nothing was ever name brand or overly nice looking. He was just a simple guy with simple ways. In this moment, he was also very reserved too. I felt the cold shoulder was going to get worse.

He looked up. "You can't just 'be', can you?"

"I guess not, but you know you are the one that picked *me* up. At least tell me why besides the whole my aunt wants me to do it."

His full lips moved slightly and then stopped while he folded his arms in defiance showing surprisingly large biceps and sculpted forearms. "So you can't just be thankful. Figures."

"Excuse me!" I was starting to rev up.

"City girls," he said and stood with his plate to head to the oversized kitchen.

"Oh no, you don't."

I burst to my feet and followed him right on his heels. "City girl?"

He turned back towards me. He touched the cubic zirconia stud earring in my left nostril and frowned. I didn't hold back. No one was going to mistake me for someone I was not.

"What is your deal? You come to school in a fancy car, live in a mansion, act like a hermit who needs a job washing dishes, and then you pick me up just to be nice! Something doesn't add up. Not that I'm not thankful, but what's your game?"

I was angry. The spoiled city girl comment did me in. Ben was legions off with that statement. His usually soft grey, brown eyes were now squinting under his furrowed brows.

"Step back!"

He had the audacity to point his finger at me. He looked at his finger, dropped it, and tilted his head at me.

"Sorry."

"Why? Were you going to hurt me too? Not many men can hurt me anymore. Those days are over, asshole."

He countered, "Maybe not men, but what I brought you here for has nothing to do with humans."

I stepped back then. Humans?

He added, "Sit."

"So now you're going to talk?"

He looked around before glaring back at me. "When I'm done talking, you'll wish I never opened my mouth."

I sat on the stool closest to me feeling a laugh coming on any moment. "Lay it on me. What's your story?"

Did I really want to know? I guess I did. Beneath that reserved and intense exterior was someone who was very intriguing, and I finally got him talking.

"Nothing like what you're going to expect. Téa, I'm not a real high school student anymore."

He leaned back against the kitchen counter and crossed his legs at the ankles revealing military style boots I had not seen yet. I sat there stunned. Crap, time to run.

"And I have a second job," he said while effortlessly lifting himself up onto the countertop behind him. He took a deep breath and eyed me steadily.

"Do you believe there are beings here that aren't human? Aliens?" he asked.

I snorted and eyed the exit. "What? No. Are you some kind of freak or something? Nothing like that has been discovered yet. Although, my mom would be all over this if she were still alive," I said with a sarcastic voice.

"A freak?" he asked. Was that a hurt expression?

"And what about your mom?"

I didn't respond. Not going there.

He sat up straight. "Let me show you something."

With that he motioned for me to follow him down a narrow hall off the kitchen. Why did I still trust him? Every hair on my body was standing on end, but I was drawn to him in a peculiar way. Then, he stopped and did not turn around. He just stared at the floor, and shook his head.

"This doesn't make sense. Someone so intrigued by science yet you're not open to believe."

"What's going on, Ben?"

Without warning, he grabbed my arm and threw me into a room before I could take evasive maneuvers. A shockwave traveled up my body almost choking me. I failed. I was too trusting of him and I'd let my guard down.

CHAPTER 11

Leap of Faith

The door behind me clicked, signaling a locking action. Immediately, I dove into it trying to open it.

"Ben! Open this door! Ben! What are you doing?"

There was no answer on the other end. I knocked again and again with no response. Suddenly, my heart started to race. The darkness in the room was suffocating me as I tried to breathe in and out slowly. Is Ben the serial killer? The slow, steady breathing technique wasn't helping. The flashback came before I could calm down.

"Téa, get back here! You messed up and now you're going to pay," my foster father yelled with a slur. The burly man caught me and raised up his belt before slamming it into my flesh again and again.

"No! Please, stop!!!" I screamed.

"I warned you, Téa. Ten-year-olds are no good and need more discipline than most. I warned you," he said between swings.

"I won't do it again!"

I was now crying. Larry Hadley hated girls. The other foster kids were boys, and they never got beaten. Their eyes were peering at me from around the corner while Larry swung over and over. I hated them. I hated him.

"Now, to detention."

"NO!!!"

I knew what that meant. I kicked and screamed all the way to the basement. It would be the twentieth time I had to go into that dark isolated existence. In one fell swoop, he shoved me in and latched the door. Tears came like a hot summer day rain. I wasn't sad anymore. It was no longer those kind of tears. No, something new was growing inside me.

Anger.

Anger so deep and terrifying that it scared even me. I slammed my head onto the door panel once, twice, and then a third time. The blood immediately dripped down my face, and I didn't care anymore. Something had snapped inside me. I was like a machine with no care at all. To my surprise, on the fourth slam, my head went right through the door.

My breathing was now slowing as the panic attack passed. I was sitting on a hard surface and was going through all my coping strategies that I was taught. Even the one from the therapist, Dr. McKay, from when I was with Ms. Adele. I couldn't stand that doctor. She had been paid well by Ms. Adele, but I thought it was a waste of money. Tonight, I was relying on those techniques and the others I learned. I needed to regain my composure in order to find a way out of this mess.

Then just as I was coming back down from it, I heard something. It was a swishing sound. Something was sliding across the floor. A dog maybe? I squinted my eyes to take in my surroundings that were barely lit by the only recessed light that still worked in here. I was trying hard to see if the movement was from a dog that maybe Ben had. But when the thing in question came closer, I could tell it wasn't a dog. Moving slowly towards me was what looked to be a man dragging himself across the tile floor.

"Hey, are you okay?" I asked and was about to jump up to help him when he lunged at me and grabbed my arms with superhuman strength. I screamed and then managed to get a kick directly into his gut. He released me and staggered back. It was then that I noticed his face. It was grotesque and disfigured.

He had knife wounds all over his body but was miraculously still alive. A strange colored liquid had stained his clothes and skin. It was pouring out of his body like blood, though.

The odd man breathed heavily and made hissing sounds like a snake. His fingers were spread out revealing long nails similar to claws. I had to look passed the monstrous features to be able to tell that he was a human. As he got up to his full height, he grimaced revealing sharp teeth. Two of which were longer than the rest, giving him a vampire-like appearance.

I spoke unevenly, "I don't know what is wrong with you but you better pipe down."

He shook his head ridiculously slow and kept his eyes locked on me. There was no talking him down. As he again moved towards me, I looked around and saw a broken lamp stand. Quickly grabbing it, I slammed it into one side of his head. He barely faltered. Then I slammed him on the other side and still no relenting. Finally, I knew I had no choice. He was going to kill me if I didn't get more violent. I took the broken end of the lamp and shoved it into his abdomen.

It went in like a hot knife through butter. I let the lamp go and watched him collapse onto the ground.

I spun around on my heels and started banging on the door again. When there was no answer, I sank back down to my knees. I didn't know what to do. Looking back at the dying man, I tried to reason out that *that* wasn't going to be me. Ben was not going to leave me locked in a room dying like this man before me. Then, to my amazement, my roommate started to move again.

"No way," I said just above a whisper. "No way you can still be alive!"

He kept moving to get up, so I knew my time was short. I had no idea how I was going to kill him. Sitting there against the door with much of my energy drained, I fought another panic attack. No way was I going down like that. If I had to, I was going to fight like a mad woman. Suddenly, the charm around my neck started burning my chest right beneath my collarbone.

Was I imagining the heat? I started thinking back. Could the lady from the *Antiques Roadshow* be telling the truth? Even if it's partly true. Could the dream have meant something too? Could the charm be the connection?

I looked down at my necklace again and thought back to that dream I kept having. I remembered the little boy sticking the charm into his friend's mouth.

"No, that's crazy," I yelled out into the room.

The superhuman man was now almost completely standing. I had no choice. I grabbed the lamp stand again in one hand and took a leap of faith with the other hand that now held the acorn.

"Screw it!" I yelled, popped the gold topper off of the artifact, and threw the rest of it in my mouth while swinging the lamp at the villain coming at me. I swung again when he shielded my first swing.

Reacting exactly like Uncle Bob had taught me, I kicked my attacker's legs. It was just enough to throw him off balance. Thankfully, I had the enemy on the ground using that old Green Beret move. I ran to the other end of the room to bang on more doors when I remembered the object in my mouth. It wasn't hard anymore. I wasn't choking on it, though. So, maybe I'd spit it out while fighting.

I then felt an empowering feeling pass over me like a warm blanket. With it came stinging pulses through my veins.

"What the … ?"

Up one arm and then down another until the pain in my joints disappeared. My legs throbbed with an incredible amount of energy. The monstrous man behind me was now being registered in my brain as a viable threat. It was like a radar had just turned on. I didn't need to turn to gauge the distance between us. I took the lamp and without turning around, I shoved it in a downward direction under my right arm and into his knee cap causing him to fall.

I took the metal rod again while facing him and thrust it directly into his chest. He fell to the ground. Realizing that it was the blow that finally stopped the monster, I dropped the weapon and looked at my hands. There was something thick pulsing through the veins on the tops of my hands. I began to shake when a bright light intruded into the room.

CHAPTER 12

Trust

"Do you believe me now?" Ben asked after we left the room. He had his hands out in front of him signaling for me to calm down.

"You bastard! You locked me in that room and with a maniac!"

"I had to do it, Téa. I had to see …"

"See what?"

"That you were really a chosen one."

I laughed. "You're insane. I'm calling the police." I headed towards my backpack and he didn't stop me.

"Go ahead. But you must know. They won't help you. Some of them will want to do just the opposite."

Like what they did to my mom? Still, I defiantly turned around towards him. "How long did you trap that poor guy down there to make him become like that?"

"I trapped him but that was not what made him like that. He's not from your world, Téa."

I laughed again.

He actually smiled a half smile. "You feel the seed in your veins now. You feel it running deep within your core. I saw you swallow it and since you didn't spit it out, it means it was really meant for you. Now, it's inside you, alive and thriving."

I spit at him. "Freak. I can't believe you just sat there and watched me fight for my life. What, did you have a camera in that room?"

He wiped my spit off his now stoic face and pushed on. "Stop fighting me, Téa. You need to calm down and listen. I'm sorry I did that to you, but you are in so much denial. I knew it would take something life threatening to convince you. But he was too weak to really harm you. And I swear I wouldn't have let him."

Chocolate brown eyes seeped with … sincerity?

"I'm not convinced."

"You have no choice but to be convinced now. You feel the strength and the awareness of everything around you? You're hyper-sensitive to all beings now."

I couldn't deny that something had changed. I could feel his neighbors from fifty feet away moving through their house in preparation for bedtime.

"No, no, this is crazy!"

"You'll get more comfortable with it as your body adapts. But Téa, you need training to use it right. If not, they will find you and kill you before you get to your full potential."

"Who?"

"I'll explain that later, now you need to come with me," he said and reached his hand out to grab mine.

I turned and kicked him hard in the chest. He fell down easily, which surprised me. Then, I jumped on top of him and punched him. He didn't put up as much of a fight as I thought he would. I was able to grab his keys and get out the door before he could stop me. I ran to his car, popped the trunk, and pulled my bike out. Ben still wasn't chasing me, so I pushed 'lock' on his key, threw the keys in the trunk, and closed it up before running off on foot while pushing my bike.

When I was a few blocks away and felt that I was in the clear. I pulled out my cell to order an Uber. I wanted to call the police. I really did. But then they would figure out my situation and I'd be back in foster care. The only thing I knew to do was tell my boss and the school officials. Oh no! What if Ben is responsible for the deaths of those girls in Corpus? He came around not too long after those reports. I've got to go to the police, but how?

I was dropped off by my Uber driver a few blocks from home. I was relieved to be out of Ben's reach. He'd never find me here on a street corner. I saw Uncle Bob as soon as I rounded the corner from my parked bike.

"Uncle Bob, I'm turning in early."

He looked at me quizzically, "You okay, Téa?"

"Yep." I slid into my sleeping bag.

"You look like you been fighting some demons tonight?"

I froze. "What?"

"Demons. You really need to take that lady up on her offer. You're starting to look too much like us here on this street. I know what having demons inside looks like."

I sat up straight. "You believe in demons? What about aliens?"

"Of course I do. My savior removed demons from several poor souls back when He walked among us. If I can believe in that, then I can believe in aliens too."

"Not the same thing," I thought and laid back to watch cars sputtering by while thinking of the horrific events of the night. My anger had become unleashed. I killed that man in Ben's house, and I wanted to kill Ben for doing that to me. I hated when my anger came out. That is the emotion that I knew all too well.

When anger takes hold it is all encompassing. Everything turns dark like clouds moving gingerly in front of the sun while you work your best to keep it at bay. But then hope is completely snuffed out and you're on autopilot moving only to the aim of self-preservation. A hint of sunlight may pop in for just a second and trick you with glints of crystal warmth, but then it's gone. You're pulled back into oblivion, the calm before the rage. It had been years since I went that far. If I ever got to that point again, I'd be lost for good.

After talking to Uncle Bob, I remembered going to sleep and having another strange dream. It was a new kind of nightmare. I was being chased by people without faces. They all had a mark on their arms in the shape of something like a snake. When they caught up with me, they clawed and screamed at me. It just made me fight harder and harder. I was always fighting something, during the day and in my dreams. But this time, I didn't know who or what I was fighting. I screamed out, "Stop!" and woke up to furrowed eyebrows over soft chocolate eyes.

"Téa! Are you all right?" he asked.

I squinted. Leaning over me was the person I didn't think I'd have to see again for a long while. But instead of being upset, he looked worried. He was kneeling beside me with his hands up in a show of surrender and asked, "Why are you out here?"

"Ben? Get away from me, or I'll finish what I started!" I slapped at him as he did the unthinkable and pulled me up into his arms.

"I'm sorry, Téa." My face was pressed against his hard chest. The smell of Cool Ice aftershave filled my senses. He was hugging me?

"Don't fight me. I don't want to hurt you. We need to talk."

I pulled my head back to look up into his eyes. I was fuming. "I should kill you."

He held me by my upper arms and smiled down at me. "Yeah, you should. But not until you tell me one thing."

"What?"

Uncle Bob walked up beside us. "Téa, you okay?"

I jetted my chin out at Ben. "It depends on what he has to say."

Ben released me before asking, "What was that dream about that I just woke you up from?

I stepped back. "How long have you been watching me sleep?"

"Long enough. Tell me the truth, Téa."

Looking down at the cement, I tried to recollect it. "Just a nightmare. I get them a lot."

"But this one was different, right?"

Uncle Bob inquired, "Is this a friend from school, Téa?"

"Yes, sir. I'm okay."

With that Bob stepped back and went back to his rounds, and I focused on the nightmare.

"Yes, it was different."

Ben touched my shoulder and for the life of me, I didn't know why his touch felt safe. "Did they have the Adart mark?"

"The what?"

He frowned and shook his head. "No, I mean something that looks like a snake. On their arms. Did they have it?"

I about jumped back in shock. "How did you know?"

"Because I dreamed it too."

❋ ❋ ❋ ❋

Two or so hours later, I was sitting in a car traveling next to the man I hated just ten hours before. Ben had convinced me to take a ride with him to speak with someone who would better explain to me what was going on. I couldn't deny that our similar dreams piqued my interest. As the car took us farther and farther north, Ben actually made small talk about school. He even had me laughing at one point when he talked about his crazy aunt, Ms. Jolly.

Then, his friendly demeanor disappeared when a radio announcement came on about the lady found in the manhole that was in Houston on a business trip. Police still had no leads. They did say that she was a fifty-year old lady of native heritage. I didn't understand Ben's change in mood.

"What is wrong?"

"Nothing," he said sharply.

"Did you know that lady?" I inquired back.

"Maybe."

"Oh, how?"

He gave me a hard look. "That's enough talk for now."

I squeezed my hands into fists trying to control my angst. I didn't like when someone told me it was not time to talk. Then, I reflected on what he said. He knew her? I wondered if that was a coincidence or not. He didn't talk to me at all after that. He would stiffen up when I tried to make small talk. I was still doing everything I could to try to like him against my better judgment. There was just something about him.

"Why don't you like me?" I had to ask.

He frowned. "I do." Both of his hands on the steering wheel squeezed tighter.

"It's because I'm homeless trash to you, isn't it?"

"I don't think like that, Téa. But it did take me off guard."

"It's okay, I'm used to it. But you know what, I know more about the real world than your rich spoiled self could ever comprehend."

"Whatever," he said, keeping his eyes on the road.

"See, that's what I mean."

"Just be quiet," he now glared at me.

"Fine then." Why did I bother to bicker with this boy? It was crazy what he brought out in me.

"Fine," he said with a resolute mouth.

I couldn't help it. "So where are you taking me?" I deserved to know.

His knuckles on the steering wheel turned white. "Away."

"I know you already said that, but specifically, where? I have a right to know. I'm trusting you, remember?"

He fizzled down. "Outside of Livingston."

I continued to pry, "Who is there?"

"The others. I'm bringing you to train with them." Looking over at me, I saw his face was now open, friendly.

"Train? And the others? What others?"

"Adrian's."

"What is that?"

"The others that are connected with a Kabar."

"A what?"

"Seeds from our tree of life." He gestured to my chest where my necklace previously hung.

I looked down. "That acorn?"

"Yep."

CHAPTER 13

Legend

Another two hours passed and we came upon a huge section of land off of the highway that was surrounded by a tall fence with barbed wire on top. The men at the checkpoint opened the gate without inquiring. The more I took in my surroundings, the more I realized where I was.

"This is an Indian Reservation, isn't it?"

Ben kept his eyes forward. "Yes."

I was about to ask more questions, but he put his hand up. "Look. Just wait. All will be revealed soon enough."

We rode on a winding driveway through richly colored glade into the thrall of the woods. Light barely escaped the canopy above. Then, it opened up again revealing rows and rows of tiny houses. We passed through what seemed like several acres before we came up on a huge cement wall.

"Another gated area?"

His pretty boy face struck me suddenly when he fought a smile. "You could say that."

He nodded at the gate attendant who opened the second gate for us. Upon entering, I noticed that the houses were more cookie cutter and spread out. He parked the car by some trees outside the small neighborhood and turned towards me.

"Stay in the car. I will be right back, got it?"

"Yes." I lied.

He rubbed his hands on his faded jeans, took a deep breath, and exited the car towards the woods. I quickly jumped out, shut the door quietly, and followed him at a distance. He moved through the shrubs as if on a mission. The tall grass gave way to a small clearing where he stopped in front of an older lady. She wasn't grey yet, but had a few laugh lines and was a bit curvy. I hunkered down in the shrubs just close enough where I could hear but not too close for them to notice me.

Ben nodded with respect to the lady in front of him. "Cheyenne."

Cheyenne responded, "Benjamin". Then she tilted her grey head to the side. "What is wrong? You said on the phone that it was a success."

"I thought I was sent down there to retrieve the Kabar for me. A woman is not supposed to do this. Especially not a *human* one that does not believe in anything but herself."

Cheyenne looked around. "Shhh … keep your voice down. But I don't know, Benjamin. What I do know is that she *was* chosen."

"An Ederian human? This is crazy. Something is not right. All the Kabar wielders have always been men. There is so much at stake right now. And you'll see when you meet her. She only believes in what humans have proved. She doesn't think outside that realm, at all."

"Give her time. She's still in her infancy. All she has ever known is struggling and relying on herself."

"An Ederian, that is human, with a heart full of hate? You'll see. She's so angry."

"And you aren't?" she asked and Ben took a step back.

He continued, "You said it yourself that she helps people. Helps others when no one has really ever helped her. That is powerful. And the things she has seen while living around such a spoiled self-indulged world. Can you imagine? She has defied the odds and survived without help. There must be something special about her."

"I don't know."

Ben slid his hand into his pocket and pulled out something that was hard to make out and handed it to the lady.

She smiled. "You two are a lot alike. You both carry anger from your childhood. Give her time."

He nodded and turned to walk back towards his car. Hunched on my legs, I fell back on my butt and floundered for a second trying to escape without being detected. I jumped behind a tree and cursed under my breath because he had already passed me and was heading back to the empty car.

I didn't know what to do. I didn't want him to know I overheard the conversation. I was still trying to figure out why they kept saying *human*. He really believed that alien thing. And so did everyone here. They were crazy like my mom was. But I wasn't concealing that I heard it because I was embarrassed, but because I was going to try and use it to my benefit when the right time came.

I darted back and forth between trees trying to rush around out of sight but still in the direction of the car. However, I was unsuccessful in my endeavor of getting back. The landscape did not look familiar now. I was lost. I sunk down by a tree trunk trying to figure out what to do next. Putting my hands through my hair, I fought my frustration.

"Lost?" an unfamiliar man's voice asked bringing me out of my pity party. He was wearing a long beige tunic style garment with fringes all along the arms. Definitely Indian formal attire. His wavy brown hair falling down passed his shoulders would make any woman envious.

I quickly rose to my feet. "Maybe. I'm Téa."

He frowned. "I know that."

I reached out my hand for a possible shake. "And you?"

"Dasan, but most call me Des," he replied but did not take my hand. His beady, deep set brown eyes studied me under a tall and wide forehead.

I dropped my hand slowly. "Hello Des. So you must know that I'm Ben's friend?"

He didn't reply this time. Instead he reached up his broad, dark skinned hand and placed it on my forehead. Then, he stepped back and gave me a disturbing look. I could tell that he didn't like me before he even spoke again.

"Human, woman, and raised with the white people," he said and shook his head. "You'll disgrace us." Then, before I could counter to question why Indians referred to us as *humans*, he turned to walk away.

I hated to, but I knew I had to follow him in order to find my way back.

"Wait!" I yelled out and the jerk did not stop. When I got up closer to him, I added, "Are you always a turd? Wait!"

I reached my hand up to touch his shoulder in hopes he would slow down. Before I knew it, he had swung around, grabbed my wrist, twisted me around, and pinned both my hands behind my back. I fought to free myself but his strength was unyielding.

He leaned in behind me and whispered into my ear annunciating each word slowly, "You ... are ... worthless."

I was shocked. "Is this how you Indians show hospitality?"

He squeezed my wrists tighter.

I struggled and seethed, "F-you."

The burning behind my eyes started immediately. I was about to lose it and this time, I didn't care. If I got free, he was gonna see some major wrath from what he considered a simple white girl.

"Des!" a familiar voice yelled out from behind us. "Let her go!"

Des didn't abide, but I could tell he was turning to address Ben. "Ha, there he is. The man maid servant."

"Screw you Des. Now let her go or else."

I stretched my neck to peer back over my shoulder and noticed Ben standing with his fists clenching in and out. He was in a fighting stance and did not take his eyes off of Des.

Des laughed. "Makes sense. She is a pretty thing. I can't say I blame you."

Des turned back to me and sniffed my hair. "Sorry about that though, Ben. Some things you just can't have, man. But nothing would stop *me* from having her, human or not."

Then, he slowly released my hands. I swung around and kicked him in the shin causing me to drop to the ground hard with him not far behind me. On my elbows, I moved back as fast as I could, but he grabbed my ankles and slid me back towards him.

"Feisty little thing, isn't she?" he said and pinned me under him.

I saw Ben's foot kick Des in the stomach causing Des to roll off of me. When I was free of the heavy body, I scooted back and watched Ben jump on top of Des. The two began punching each other relentlessly.

"Boys!" a woman yelled out across the scuffle. Not five feet away and looking down at me was the woman from earlier that Ben had been talking to.

"Miss Cheyenne," Ben and Des both said in unison and then got to their feet.

"It is a shame that they both still want to act like children." She reached out her hand and helped me up. "I'm sorry you had to see that. My name is Cheyenne Locklear."

"I'm Téa. Téa Lane."

She smiled sweetly at me. "Yes, I know." She stood about my height and had dark knowing eyes.

"Come. Walk with me, Téa."

CHAPTER 14

Hidden Treasures

We walked for a few minutes passing through shrouds of huge oak trees farther into the woods. The tangled branches above me reminded me of the pain in my arms and legs. My body was still humming from the assault, but something new and different was creeping in. Ben was going to fight that guy for me.

Cheyenne finally spoke breaking into my thoughts, "We're so glad to have you here, Téa. You've probably guessed that I'm Indian."

"Feather not dot I presume, since we're on an Indian reservation, right?"

"Excuse me?"

She stopped and sat on an oversized rock. She was wearing Levis jeans and a plaid shirt. Her long grey hair was pulled back in a low ponytail.

I sat on the ground next to her. "Feather is what we refer to as an American Indian. Dot refers to a person from the country of India."

"Hmm. You are opinionated and brash, aren't you?"

"I've been told worse."

"Do you know the only reason we American Indians were called Indians in the first place?"

"Something about how America was discovered."

I had such a smartass tone, even I didn't like me at that moment.

"Yes, it's because the Spanish explorers that originally encountered Native Americans on this continent thought that they had landed in India. That is why they called us Indians to begin with. So, I'm not sure if I should be offended or not. You tell me."

She pointedly called me out.

I shook my head. "No, sorry, but why am I here?"

She picked up a stick. "You are science minded. Do you believe in another race of beings? Ones that could come from another world?"

"It's possible. Not proven, but possible."

She eyed me. "Do you believe in aliens?"

"I don't know."

"Even after seeing an alien first hand?" She rubbed her bronze thumb across the side of the stick.

I shrugged. "He was sick with some sort of virus. That's all that was."

"Doubting Thomas after all you've seen?"

"What?"

"Nothing."

She brushed the leaves away revealing soft dirt. "How about I just talk and you listen without judgment until I'm done? I won't go into too many details. In fact, I'm going to tell you this in the simplest form. A child's version if you will. Sound good?"

"Sure."

She waved her free hand around us. "Most of us here … are not human."

"Now, come on. Stop." I scratched my left arm feeling nervous.

"I'm telling the truth, Téa. We are from a planet called Aepi. It's the next star system over from Earth but still within the Milky Way."

I smirked, "Do what?"

I had to laugh. How coincidental that this Indian was talking like my insane mom? The same mom that was institutionalized for schizophrenia and later killed herself. I shivered.

Cheyenne huffed. "I guess science minded or not, this is going to be more difficult than I originally thought. Please hold your comments until I'm done."

I nodded. I'll let her go on and on the way my mom did. It won't change anything.

"Our world was being attacked by another alien race from the planet of Epex. It had been going on for a long time. These beings not only destroyed everything in their path, they had also sought to steal our treasured seeds for what they could do with them."

She continued on, "Téa, we are the last of our people. The Epex had finally become too strong for us and broke through our last defenses. Only a handful of us got away."

"Let's just say that I believe you, when did this happen?"

"The exact date will not match your sun's calendar. But I do know that when our ancestors arrived, it was around the year 1802 here."

She sure did sound convincing. "Y'all have been here that long? How come we don't know about you? And how is it that you look just like us?"

"For one thing, everyone in this galaxy is a humanoid. We all look about the same. We just have different adaptations depending on the planet we hailed from. Secondly, when our ancestors first arrived here, they examined your oceans, lands, and inhabitants. What you call the Native American Indians, had a culture that was the closest to what we were. For a while, our ancestors hid in the water and studied the Indians when they came down to the beach. Then, with the help of your sun's energy, we were slowly able to adapt to look and act more like them. But it also changed our bodies to where we could live primarily on land. It was a paramount change because we couldn't survive in Earth's water."

I raised my hand. "Wait, wait! The Aepi are water aliens? Where is your huge fin?"

"On our planet, we spent about half of our lives in water and the other out. Even our spacecrafts were built underwater. We've always had two legs like you. But what we can do with those two legs in unison will surprise you."

"Underwater? So, Aepi can breathe underwater?"

My mouth was gaped open.

Cheyenne ignored the question. "As the years went on, your sun continued to change us in an evolutionary manner to where we are now almost identical except for a few differences genetically. But yes, we can still breathe underwater."

She winked at me and continued, "The changes made it easier for our race to adapt. We could let down our guard more. Even our organs are now more similar. All internal workings were close to begin with but have evolved to better placement. Which is good timing since humans today have the equipment that would expose us if our bodies hadn't changed. We also stayed on the reservations so to not attract attention. And that is important?"

"Why?"

"My friend, Maul, her son wanted to compete in the Summer Olympics one year for swimming. Bet you can figure out why. But the council ruled against it, especially since they do physical checks."

"Because he's part mermaid and would have crushed the competition drawing attention to him?"

She laughed. "That and to enter any sporting event on that level requires blood work. Our hydra levels, which you call blood, is one of the biggest things that has not changed about us. It's also the reason why we only mate within our own kind. Those that don't follow the rules we've set, lose the child in utero. Any human doctors that may have happened to stumble on that just blamed the miscarriage on blood incompatibility when the couple denied lab work."

She took a small switchblade knife out of her pocket and cut a tiny spot on the inside of her elbow. I cringed until I saw it. The blood that should have come out bluish red and then light red when it hit oxygen, stayed deep blue.

I froze. "How did you do that?"

"I cut myself."

Cheyenne took a small rag out of her pocket and held it to the wound.

I shook my head. "I mean, how did you make your blood stay blue?"

"I told you, Téa."

I started to stand, shaking my head. "This can't be. My own mother believed this and took her life when no one else believed her. This can't be happening."

I then sank to the ground fighting the sudden rush of emotions. Was I losing it like my mom?

Cheyenne kneeled next to me. "I'm sorry about your mom. But we *are* real."

I wiped the beads of sweat off my brows. Ben slowly moved towards me and with his pocket knife made a tiny slit in his arm as well. Blue blood was seeping out. So, was it true? He stopped within ten feet to give me space. He had a pained gaze, almost like he was worried about what I'd think of him. My mind began to race, but found its way back to … the seed.

"So, what I swallowed was not a Native American Indian seed?"

"Yes and no. We managed to bring with us a very important plant from our world. It produced seeds that we call Kabars. These are the seeds the Epex have been trying to steal from us for generations. Your Kabar was actually meant for one of our ancestors."

She leaned forward and touched my left hand pulling me back down to sit.

"The recipients of the seeds were called the Protectors on Aepi. The Protectors were the ones who protected the

Aepi people from the Epex and will now protect us here. All of us."

"What do you mean?" I asked and saw Ben bite his nails. Nervous tick?

Cheyenne removed the rag and checked her cut. "When we blended in among the Indians, we separated into seven tribes and planted our sacred tree under the water. Then, we took turns traveling back to keep watch over it and waited. We waited for it to shed so there could be new Protectors here since ours stayed behind to give us time to escape."

"What tribes?"

"From all over America. The tribes we mixed in with were the Modoc, Shoshone, Ponca, Yakama, Sioux, Navajo, and Coushatta."

She placed her hands in her lap.

"When the tree grew to full capacity again, it started to shed its seven seeds that would be given to the first born of each of the Aepi in each of these tribes. But only when he had passed puberty and was still a virgin. After the seed was given, the family line had to stay pure blooded Aepi for the seed's influence to remain from generation to generation and with first born sons. And this is very important to note because the tree was not able to survive here on Earth. Earth's waters are too acidic. The tree was only able to produce during the first season. No more. So your seed was the seventh, and the last seed it shed. Back on Aepi, we had thousands of Protectors."

I swallowed hard. "Okay, okay, so let me get this straight. Your surviving ancestors brought the sacred tree of Aepi to Earth and replanted it underwater?"

"Yes. Basically."

"How did y'all get here?"

"Only one spacecraft made it out of the Epex space barricade. Only one. It carried the Aepi royal family here. Des, me, and Ben are distant cousins of that family."

Spaceship? That interested me, but I had more questions.

"So no more Protectors?"

My tired eyes caught Ben's intense stare. I cleared my throat and she noticed.

She shook her head. "Six of the tribes' boys did successfully ingest the seeds. And we'll need all the help we can get."

"What exactly are Epex?"

"Where we are a peaceful race, the Epex are not. They don't ask, they just take. See, they are a dying race. They can no longer reproduce. They thought our Kabars could help them cure that infliction. When we wouldn't give up our only means of protection, they went to plan B."

"Plan B?"

She eyed me cautiously. "They started abducting Aepi women and taking their reproductive eggs."

"What?"

"They cut into their wombs which killed them, and then they reengineered the eggs to make them viable for male gamete fertilization in their labs."

"Oh, God." I let her words sink passed my rational side.

She lifted her thin brows at me.

"Did all that even work?" I bit my lip almost breaking the skin. This was a lot to take in.

Cheyenne paused. "Unfortunately, yes. They were able to make hundreds in their labs and quickly. But just males. And that is why they kept coming back."

Her stare drifted towards the tree line. "Before we knew it, we were outnumbered. Even our Protectors were not strong enough when the Epex came back with their huge hybrid army. And some of these Epex are already here on Earth. These are the Epex from the original mission that found Earth."

I shifted. "Here too? Then we must tell the authorities. What do they look like? How do we find them? How many?"

"They're humanoids too, just a different race. And you've seen one. You fought one at Ben's dad's house."

My heart palpitated. "That is an Epex?"

I started to wonder if Jack the Ripper was Epex. His killings were horrific and similar to what she was describing. The police never found him.

"Yes, they actually look a lot more like land dwelling beings than we did. Just a few differences as you've seen."

"That man. It was odd. He reminded me of the vampires from the books around 1800 like the Bram Stoker stories."

"Yes. They do appear like that when they are desperate. That is because their food source, which is a little different from ours and humans, are large cattle. They eat and devour bigger animals whole."

"They don't eat humans, huh?"

"No, not humans. Or at least not that we know of."

"So that really was what I killed in Ben's house? Is that what you're telling me?"

I rubbed my head to stop the building headache. I couldn't reason out what Cheyenne was telling me. It was too strange, but I always believed there could be aliens out there. In a way, I had hoped.

"Yes, an Epex. When Benjamin started having the dreams, we sent him over to find the last Kabar before the Epex did. It was supposed to have been consumed by his great-great-grandfather when he reached puberty. Tragically, it was lost in the 1800s when the rogue Epex sect came here following our ancestors. They attacked the old Spanish mission where Ben's ancestor was living at the time and tried to obtain it then. But in light of our newest discovery, we see they failed. The Kabar resurfaced for you."

"Is that why he doesn't like me?" I asked quietly hoping Ben didn't hear.

"Doesn't like you?" she asked smiling now. Her bright teeth contrasting against her dark skin was lovely. "I wouldn't say that. I think you are a lot like his mother in some ways. But I think he acts the way he does around you because he doesn't understand you. The Kabar sees something in you, Téa. You are the first Ederian and human that one has connected with. Also, the first not raised under the Indian values and traditions. Overall, Ben is just concerned about your loyalty and how your training will go."

She giggled. "Talk about a shock for Ben when he went looking for it only to find you with it."

It all started to make sense. Ben wasn't in his element as he was on his reservation with the Indians and other aliens. Did he cut his hair to try to blend in with us while he was in

Houston? In the city? That's something he must have hated to do. But why did I care?

"Okay, and what is an Ederian? Woman, right?"

"Yes."

"All the fighters have been Adrian's, not Ederians. Benjamin thought he'd be the Protector. But you can tell you both are connected, right?"

"What do you mean?"

"He is your Watcher, which means he will be by your side all the way."

Cheyenne grinned and reached to move my hair off my face. "Something is different and none of us know why yet. You are a puzzle that will later be revealed."

CHAPTER 15

The Res

We approached another clearing lined with little frame houses and two playgrounds. People dressed in everyday clothes were standing around talking until they saw us.

Cheyenne was the first to speak, "Everyone gather round. I have an announcement to make." She winked at me and took my arm as the crowd of about twenty came in closer. "This is Téa Lane. She will be with us for a few weeks of training."

She turned to me again. "Téa, these are some of the good people of Timber's Village. We are a small sect of our bigger tribe, the Coushatta, which live on this reservation as well. They are also the only ones that are aware that a few of us are Aepi."

Just then, Ben walked up making me feel a little intimidated as he towered over me. He took my hand, nodded at me, and turned with me to the crowd. His hand was strong and covered my entire hand. I was sweating from my nerves making my hands extra clammy. I did not like being in front of people. The science fair about did me in. And the information I just received from Cheyenne was starting to freak me out. Ben seemed to pay no mind to my excessive sweating, though.

As the men and women stared at us silently, I became even more incredibly self-conscious making me sweat profusely. I hated this. I hated the spotlight and this attention. I fought back the next panic attack.

Ben looked down at me and squeezed my hand in a reassuring gesture. Did he know what I was about to succumb to? Next, he raised my left hand with his right over our heads and spoke, "Téa will be under my care. Please help me give her a warm welcome."

Under his care? I was just about to question that when the villagers broke out in cheers. He slowly let my hand down before letting it go and walking off. I stood there alone as everyone disappeared into their homes. No questions, no more introductions, everyone just left.

Cheyenne was standing beside me then. "They seem to like you."

"Seriously?"

"Yes. All the Aepi are accustomed to being with humans now, and they with us. In fact, this afternoon we are doing one of our joint tribal ceremonies. I see you met Des who is already dressed for it. We will find you something more suitable to wear, too."

"Oh, that explains the traditional clothing. I was wondering. Everyone else is dressed like ordinary people."

"Téa, dear, we *are* ordinary people."

"Sorry, I have just never been on an alien reservation before. So, did Ben grow up on this reservation? Man, I have so many more questions than just that."

I followed behind Cheyenne as she led me to a small, perfectly square house. It measured probably just twenty by twenty feet.

"In time, we will answer all your questions. I know you are extra curious, you being a scientist and all."

"Scientist in training."

She smiled. "To answer your first question, yes and no. His father, Buck, parted ways with us not long after Ben's sister died. Everyone feels like Buck sold out."

"What do you mean?"

"Some big business men came to the casino and struck a bargain with him. He started doing work for them. After his daughter's death, he just left. He was gone."

She pulled out keys and opened the door to the house. "Casino?"

"Yes, the Emerald Casino a few miles from here. That's where we get our funding for our schools and other needs. Gambling is a big industry for reservations."

"Is that how Ben's dad has that expensive house in Houston?"

"House in Houston? That sounds right. His dad is doing extremely well from what I hear. He sort of has to now that he's banned from the reservation. However, not the Aepi. You can never be banned from us. We must stick together under the circumstances. But we are partly peaceful too. Maybe part of the reason the Epex could so easily sneak up on us."

"I see. But banned from even a reservation? That bad?"

"Long story. I will tell you that Ben and his father do not get along. Ben resents him."

Cheyenne switched on the lights to the house, and I followed her in.

"What about Ben's mom?"

"She died when he was just a few years old."

"Oh."

The house had a cute living room with the bedroom directly off the kitchen. It reminded me of an apartment. "This will be where you stay while you are with us. I hope it is nice enough. I know it is small." Her dark eyes implied a question.

"Too nice," I returned.

"Good. Here is your key." She handed me a two-inch key on a key ring in the shape of a fish.

"Thank you." I wanted to know more about Ben's dad without seeming too nosey. "So banned, huh? I can see why Ben may resent him. I'm sure that was hard for Ben."

"Ben is a family man who believes in traditions. He doesn't talk to his father hardly at all, but he carries the torch of his ancestors in his father's place."

She turned back to the door to head out. I flicked off the lights and met her outside. I noticed Ben standing off at a distance talking to someone with his back to me. I couldn't help but feel for him. I didn't have parents but the one he had left, disgraced him. The enigma that was Ben started to unravel before my eyes, and I started to see him in a new light. As if reading my mind, Cheyenne spoke, "Ben has the potential to be a great Aepi. Aepi men are strong and powerful men by nature. You will appreciate that one day. You will need him more than anyone, one day."

"Look, about that Cheyenne. I'm honored that y'all think of me as something special, but I'm really not. Sure, I was able to swallow an extremely old artifact. And sure, I feel something has changed inside me. But I'm not a fighter."

"You will be. Ben brought you here to train. This is one of our best training outposts. He will help prepare you. He is your Watcher."

"So how bad is it now that the Epex are here?"

She moved to a nearby bench, sat down, and reached her hands up to me. "Bad enough that two Protectors have been killed."

I took her hands and sat next to her. "What? And what if they all come here like they did on the Aepi planet?"

"Let's not go into all the particulars yet. Tomorrow, you will start your training. Then, I believe you will be ready for the harsh details."

She held both my hands in hers. "Téa, I believe you are more ready for this fight than you can even imagine."

She used her thumb to slide under my sleeve at the wrist and then removed it. I cringed at what she might have found. However, her face revealed nothing.

"I just need you to believe in yourself. When was the last time you believed in yourself? It's been awhile, hasn't it?"

I shrugged.

"Ben tells me you won the science fair. I imagine you worked extra hard thinking there was no way you could win."

I nodded. She seemed to know a lot more about me than I thought.

I turned towards Ben who was in conversation with what looked like a young lady that had walked over to him. She was really pretty with long brown hair and dark tan skin. She smiled big at him and at one point even made him laugh. I was taken aback by it. Someone could make him laugh? Him? But it didn't matter at that point. She made him laugh. So, maybe there is a cool side to him. Maybe he won't be so bad to work with.

I kicked the dirt at my feet. I still wasn't happy at the day's events. I should be honored, but I was mad and felt trapped. No one asked me if I'd like to be some great Protector who would work side by side with aliens. And did this mean that there is a chance these aliens could take over Earth like they did Aepi? The Epex didn't look that bad. A little scary, but they didn't seem to be too much of a threat to us, right?

And I had plans of going to college and ...

Heck, I had all these plans of rising above my street life and, one day, living in a beautiful home while training to be an astronaut. Will this new revelation stand in my way? Could I just walk away and pretend I didn't know what I knew? Live out my days till the end of the world. It may not be too many days, but at least I'd finally have happy ones before the end. But was that good enough?

Hmmm. The Aepi spaceship lingered on my mind long after Cheyenne walked away.

Am I closer to my dream than I ever imagined?

CHAPTER 16

Traditions and Heart

The dance ceremony they put on that afternoon was called a pow wow. It started just a few hours later. They dressed me in a huge gown with bright colors of orange and yellow. My hair was pulled back into a braid, and I was given a simple foldout chair to watch the show.

The ceremony was actually exciting to see. The Indian men, some possibly aliens, came into the clearing like they were on parade. Each had feathers in colors of brown, black, white, and grey all around their heads, on their ankles, and strapped to their arms. They were moving their feet to the music of the drummers nearby. Arms were flapping, feet were tapping, and heads were ducking in and out while they spun around and around.

Many of the men were a little plump, which I wasn't expecting, until the younger Indian men came out. Those guys really livened up the show then because they moved their feet and arms quicker than the older men. It was a spectacular dance. The more I sat and watched, the more the arm and leg movements began to look like birds playing in the air. After a while, I didn't see people under those feathers. It all blended together harmoniously in an act of pure entertainment.

Wow!

Every now and then a little tyke or two would wander off into the fray. They wore modern clothes but with maybe a crochet belt or cap with a single feather. At age five or so, they were quickly absorbed into the stampede. No one looked concerned. No screaming moms or overprotective grandparents. Everyone proceeded like it was the normal thing to happen.

I clapped along with the music and dancers until I noticed Ben staring at me from across the parade. Shyly, I looked away and hoped I could disappear behind the dancing men. Just then, a young woman came and unfolded her chair to sit next to me. Her hair was pulled back in a thick braid highlighting her high forehead and lovely hair line. She clapped along with everyone else and turned to me.

"Hi, I'm Shia."

"I'm—"

She interrupted me. "Stop, I know who you are. Anyway, I'm so glad to see another girl in this fight."

She smiled with bright white, perfect teeth contrasting against her dark skin and hair like Cheyenne's. However, Shia was the most beautiful Indian woman I had ever seen.

"What do you mean?"

"I'm Des' Watcher," she said.

I smiled at that. "Really?"

I liked her instantly.

She nodded. "Des comes out towards the end of the line."

"Oh?"

"Yes. The traditional dancers are the Warriors, Storytellers, and Protectors from the tribes. One day maybe you could be the first woman to dance alongside them. You know, since you are a Protector."

I almost broke out into a cold sweat. "Um, I don't ever see me doing that."

"Never say never. So what is your story?"

"My story?"

"Yes. I'll go first." She leaned back to cross her legs at her ankles. "I was born to two loving parents. It wasn't until I was ten before they figured out my struggles in school were because I was dyslexic."

Shia was a sharer, for sure!

"Dyslexic? That is something the schools notice when we're five or so. What took your school so long to diagnose you?"

"Our schools are different on the reservation. But to make a long story short, the struggle killed my confidence. Being a Watcher has helped me a lot in that area. I still have a ways to go."

"Oh, I'm sorry."

"Don't be. Now, tell me about you."

"No. I'm not open like that."

"I didn't figure you were." She laughed. A different kind of laugh. It was crazy loud. Then, she rested her chin on one hand.

"Want something to drink?"

"Do y'all have Cokes?"

"Well, of course. I'll be right back."

She got up and ventured off leaving me alone again. It wasn't long until someone sat down in Shia's chair that was not Shia. It was Ben. I cringed.

"How do you like it so far?" he asked while leaning over with his elbows on his knees. His intense stare took me off guard.

"It's neat."

"Are you starting to be okay with everything?"

"Not really. I'm still mad at you."

He leaned back in the chair. "Look, I never got to tell you I was sorry. I am sorry. I know that was a little harsh what I did back in Houston. I promise I was not going to let that thing hurt you, though."

"Now, you tell me?!"

"I'm your Watcher, Téa. You are now the most important thing in my life."

I got chills when he said that. I had never had anyone besides my parents tell me that before. I couldn't lie, it felt so good to hear whether I fully believed him or not. Dang, it felt good to hear.

"Thanks."

I caught myself watching his profile while his words sunk in. He was really a good looking guy for an alien. If what he was saying was true, I lucked out because he was really hot. What was I thinking? But he was also scary to me in a way. I still didn't know what *they* really were.

Ben turned those cool dark eyes back on me and frowned. "What?"

He was wearing the traditional Indian garb. If it wasn't for his short hair, I would have forgotten that he was the

Ben that I met in Houston or an alien. He looked just like any Indian here. Funny how clothing and accessories can alter someone's look instantaneously.

"Nothing. You really love it here, don't you?" I asked.

He studied me. "Yes, it's my home. These are my people, my culture, and my life."

Obvious pride exuded from his tone. I admired that side of him. A warm feeling radiated through my belly. It was nice being around family-oriented people. Years I dreamt of something like that.

"Well, it seems like a pretty cool place. It's quiet and peaceful. The people here seem so in touch with nature." Surprisingly, all of this and him were really starting to grow on me until he spoke again.

"Listen, you're on your own on with surviving the training. It's going to be tough for you," he said, ruining the good jives.

"Thanks for the vote of confidence," I said and rolled my eyes.

He shifted in his seat. "Take this seriously, Téa."

"I am, jerk."

I pressed my fists into the chair. Why did I let my guard down again just to get hurt again? He didn't like me at all.

Ben rubbed the back of his neck. "What the hell is your deal?"

"What is your deal?"

He got up without another word and walked off. I guessed he was done with me.

CHAPTER 17

Octaves above Crazy

Shia must have noticed because when he walked passed her, she started back towards me right away.

"Everything all right?"

"Just when I thought I could finally start to stand him, he shows his true self again. Has he always been a jerk?"

"Ben? No, Ben is great. A little rough around the edges but all in all a good guy."

"So, he's just a pain to me? Do you think he's still jealous?" I asked without showing too much emotion in my voice.

"Of what?"

"That I'm the one the Kabar chose."

"Téa, if you think like that then you really don't know Ben yet. He is loyal to the cause and his people no matter the call. He may have questioned your effectiveness at first, but he will do what he needs to do. That is not what's bothering him."

"What is it then?"

She squinted her dark eyes under thick brows and turned back biting her cheek.

"I wonder if in some way you remind him of his sister."

"His sister?"

"Yes. Her name was Tayla. You are built similar to her, petite body and features. And you are feisty like she was," my new friend said. "She and I were close. Good friends."

"What happened to her? Cheyenne said something about her passing away."

"Things are tough and complicated on Indian reservations. Even though, we are Americans, we are still treated a little differently."

"What do you mean?"

She looked at me point blank. "Tayla was murdered and her killer or killers got away."

"Oh no, by Epex?"

"No. I'd rather Ben tell you this one day, but it may take him forever. I'll tell you what I know."

"Okay."

I shifted in my seat to take all the information in. I wanted to know what made Ben tick, but my heart was already starting to break for him.

"Late one Thursday night four years ago, Tayla was headed to the store across the highway, Abbot's, to get Ben medicine. He was fourteen and she was sixteen. She had just started driving. Ben's dad was out of town on his new business venture, but Ben was sick so Tayla had to care for him. Anyway, Abbot's is located off of the reservation, but they were the only ones that had cough medicine on supply. We don't know what fully happened. Ben had gone to Cheyenne later that night worried about Tayla not coming home. Cheyenne went out looking for her and called Buck. Buck did not answer the phone, so she contacted the reservation police. Reservation police found Tayla's body and truck a few days later."

"Oh God. How did she die?"

"It gets worse. The autopsy ruled it as a car accident meaning that she wasn't murdered. But they found evidence that she had been assaulted."

I dropped my eyes to the ground. "By whom?"

"No one knows. She wasn't dating anyone. But listen, not many know the truth about her assailants. Most just think it was a car accident and that's it. My dad was on the reservation police. He told me the details to warn me, I guess. Don't tell anyone, okay?"

"Okay."

"I just think you should know since Ben's your Watcher."

"Got it."

"Anyway, the store owner said there were men talking to Tayla at the store. It may have been one of them that assaulted her."

I wanted to vomit. I started shaking like a leaf as the anger brewed. And I didn't even know Tayla. "What did they do to the men?"

"Nothing. Since it was ruled death by a car accident, there was nothing they could do. Reservation police have no jurisdiction to white men off the res."

"What the hell?"

She shrugged. "It is the law, and it happens all the time. Cheyenne's aunt was raped by truckers traveling through a long time ago. They got off. This is how things are on reservations across the country. American Indian women are sexually assaulted at a rate four times the national average."

"The law protects against rape."

"The law is different on reservations and a lot of non-natives know this."

"How is it different?"

The music around us died down while laughter filled the night air. I ignored it. I wanted to know what the hell was going on.

"A non-native can come onto a reservation, rape a woman, but if he's caught off the reservation, he doesn't get charged," Shia said.

"So basically the rapist has to be caught by reservation police while the attackers are here on the land. If off the land, they get off?"

"Yes."

"The Epex are one kind of threat, but this is ..." My cheeks and ears were burning. How could it be like that? I looked into the crowd trying to see Ben.

"What about the Protectors?"

"What about them?" Shia asked.

"Why can't they hunt the rapists down?"

She frowned. "We have to follow man's law. Plus we can't get discovered."

"This is ridiculous. Poor Ben. So does Ben resent his father because his father wasn't around when this happened?"

Shia took a sip of her Coke. "Most likely. But who knows."

"I can't say I blame him."

"It's no one's fault but the men that did it to her."

"It still doesn't excuse him being so harsh with me."

She smiled her pretty smile. "Let me ask you something."

"What?"

"What is really bothering you? What is your story?"

I set my own Coke down on the sandy ground. "There is so much about me that you all don't understand yet."

"Téa, I think we know you better than you think we do. Give us a chance. Talk to us. Return the favor to us."

I didn't know if I liked her comments. I tried to let it go and make more small talk. So, I turned to her and asked the question I had been dying to ask, "So how do you work with someone like Des? If Ben is going to be like that to me, I need to know your secret."

"He's not all that bad either. We grew up together. We are like brother and sister."

"Oh, I thought maybe y'all were a couple."

Her eyes got wide. "No. That is out of the question."

I followed the crowd and noticed Ben was leaving the gathering. I wanted to go to him. Talk to him. Maybe not tell him what Shia told me, but just talk. However, following behind him was that young girl from earlier.

"Téa?" Shia broke into my thoughts.

"Yeah. Sorry, I got distracted."

Her gaze followed mine, and she didn't say anything else. We both just sat there. She watched the activities with excitement, while I took in all the new information.

No matter how traumatic the reality was for women on these reservations, I still couldn't shake my own despair. I sat there stewing over my own new reality here trying to make sense of it all. I still didn't like that someone or something was deciding my fate again. I didn't like that at all. I felt trapped like I was back in a foster home waiting on the next shoe to drop.

The scars on my wrists began to itch, so I rubbed them inconspicuously. Those self-inflicted battle scars were long since healed. It was all mental. After all the latest developments and my unease over what was happening on these reservations, I began to feel like I was losing control again. I hated everyone and everything. There would be no peace in my mind tonight.

CHAPTER 18

Freedom

That night, I went to sleep in what they referred to as overly simple. To me, it was immensely elegant. The last time I slept inside four walls and felt safe was twelve years ago. If they only knew. This was a treat for me not a deterrent as Ben would like it to be or not a test as Cheyenne eluded to. I still felt that they mistakenly viewed me as the spoiled human. A typical American. That's okay. I'd take it. I needed the nice hospitality for a change, and I lavished in it as I went to sleep.

Then a few hours later, an intense pounding woke me up. The splatter of Slurpee-like sucking sounds filled my senses. I opened my eyes and realized I was still on the reservation but trapped inside, removed. I knew everyone was asleep so what would it hurt? I was too stressed to go back to sleep. I slipped out of my shell of a room and stepped into the cool breezy rain. Within seconds my blonde hair was drenched with elemental pride and my spirit had come back alive. The lack of freedom had been piercing my soul these last few days, and I needed a release. Now, standing out here in this powerful storm, I never felt so alive.

I closed my eyes and tilted my face up to the heavens as the clouds released all they had over and over onto me. Fiercely trying to return me to the Earth drop by drop. And then lyrical sounds filled my ears as the wind picked up again. An andante beginning mixed with fire and passion. I spun around with its movement and swirled as a dirt devil free of my confines. Free of my scared, miserable heart. The puddles under my feet flattened as slick ice aiding in my speed. I was cavorting with her. She and I were moving in agreement and nothing was going to take her away from me.

Then, something did. A trapping of blankets and hands grabbed and pulled at me. Before I knew it, I was confined back in a room and sitting on a bed. I kept my eyes low as the cursing began. He was angry. I could tell, but I didn't want to allow him to see me cry. Ben would never be able to understand me. He would always be distantly watching me in doubt. But I knew who I was.

I knew who I was.

Rough fingertips lifted my chin, and I reluctantly gazed into those caramel eyes with a silvery glow. Ben had a pained gaze and something else. That something else was even more puzzling. He stared at me and was no longer speaking. His breathing had slowed and his jaw clenched as if he was fighting something or someone other than me. His warm breath danced over my face in an unsure manner. The moment froze us in time.

This puzzling man now reached down and grabbed a warm and soft hand towel to wipe my cheeks and mouth with it. I watched his eyes as he stared at my lips through the slow ministrations until my face was all dry. He cleared his throat and rose from the bed. The loss of his body heat bothered me for some reason as I watched him head for a wicker style dresser. He pulled out a blue shirt and jogging pants.

"Change into these."

He handed me the clothes and walked out into the next room. My old blue jeans and thin tank top were drenched. My backpack with all my own clothes in it was back at my own lodging. My hands were still shaking as I dropped my wet clothes to the floor and pulled on his clothes. Immediately, there was the fragrance of spice. Sitting back on the bed, I shivered uncontrollably still.

When Ben walked back in and saw me, he wasted no time pulling me into his arms and wrapping us up in his warm wool blanket. He scooted to sit up against the headboard with me in front of him. His long legs out on both sides of me. I laid back with my head on his chest and the steady beat of his heart slowly helped me drift off to sleep. I remembered the thumping sound and the comfort of his embrace, then I was out.

✾ ✾ ✾ ✾

"Téa, run!" People were chasing us down a cobblestone street. Those same people without faces. They had the snake-like tattoos again and could run extremely fast. I was so scared of what they were going to do to us. Ben managed to open a door off the road and pulled me in with him. He locked the door behind us and turned to me taking my face in his hands. "Téa, you need to go the rest of the way by yourself. I'll stay here and fight them off to give you time."

"No, I'm not leaving you. You're supposed to watch over me, remember? We can't do this."

"I'll be fine. If we don't separate, then we both die. It has to be this way."

"No!" I yelled and cried into his shoulder.

"I'm sorry, Téa. I failed you," he said to me and did the most out-of-character thing next.

He kissed me. And it was an amazing kiss. I'd never felt another's lips on mine before. And his were amazing. They were soft and warm and moved over my mouth like they were tasting every part of me. Even though I was upset and scared, I let myself drown in that flaming hot kiss lit by pinned up passion and need.

"Téa, wake up!" Standing above me now were those same lips, but they weren't trying to kiss me.

I sat up. "What's going on?"

"You were having a bad dream."

I rubbed my eyes and noticed the warm sun coming through the windows. It was well passed morning. I wondered if he knew what I was dreaming. I felt my usual cool exterior turn blood red. I knew my cheeks were burning.

"Oh! What time is it?"

"Ten."

"Why did you let me sleep so long?"

More importantly, why did he have to wake me up? It was a yummy dream. But why did I dream about him at all? I couldn't figure out what all that was about.

"You needed your rest. Remember, you were out in the freezing rain last night. I need you well. Here, I got your backpack from the other house."

He stepped out while I changed. I put on my Tacky Taco's t-shirt and some yoga pants. Then, I realized something.

"Wait! I slept in your room all night?"

He walked back in rubbing his face and replied, "Since I can't trust you to act right, I had to keep an eye on you all night." I noticed him play with his earlobe again like he did the morning he found me on the streets.

"What do you mean?"

"I'm your Watcher. I make sure you are doing right."

That did it. Images of sexy lips were gone. "Are you kidding me? I am not a child. You will not treat me like a child."

He pointed to the ground by me but kept his intense eyes on me. "As long as you do stupid things like that, I will."

"Hell no! I've been surviving on my own for years."

"Téa, things have changed. You have a job to do now. People need you. Get over it."

"I won't get over it. This is stupid. I'm going home." I jumped up to grab my backpack. That was the final push I needed.

He stepped in front of me. "Is that how it is? You're a quitter? Glad to know that now before we get into a real fight with the Epex."

I was smoldering in anger now. "I am not a quitter. But I will not let someone like *you* tell me what to do." I pointed and poked as hard as I could into his almost steel chest.

He didn't even flinch. "It doesn't work on me."

"What doesn't work on you?"

"Your new abilities. That's a safety protocol, I guess you could say. Protectors can't hurt their Watchers. I am immune to your powers."

I swung around and diverted my anger toward something else by punching the wall. I didn't believe him about my strength until I saw what I was now able to do to his wall. My fist went clean through it. When I pulled my shaky hand back, there was not any blood or scratches.

"Oh my God. I knew I easily killed that man at your house, but I really thought it was because he had been weak. I can't believe this."

He just snickered. "Thanks for the hole in the wall."

I just stood there in shock staring at the damage. "I'll fix it, I promise."

"Now do you believe that you're special?" He turned and headed out the door.

I didn't know what to say. I dropped my backpack under his painting of a huge grizzly bear and measly followed him outside.

As we were walking down the hill, I played out everything in my mind. I still decided to stay. Then Ben finally spoke, "You know you have some serious anger issues, right?"

I just kept my eyes forward. "You know you bring them out in me, right?"

CHAPTER 19

Jedi?

A huge sumo-looking Indian man met us at the bottom of the hill. He stood at least six five and had to weigh in at 300 pounds. His long hair, painted face, and necklaces were authentically Indian. All he was missing were some feathers. He looked down at me and said, "I'm Paul."

I fought the laugh that surely showed in my eyes. "Paul?"

Ben nudged me, and Paul glared at both of us.

I frowned at Ben before turning back to Paul.

"Nice to meet you, Paul."

I was not thrilled about being trained by such a big guy. He would definitely kick my butt.

"So what moves will you show me first?"

He gave Ben a funny look then turned back to me. He spoke with a pudgy cheeked voice, "I'm not the one that will teach you hand to hand combat, that's Ben's job."

I stepped back. "What?" Could this get any worse?

"Yeah, Ben's the combat trainer here. Watcher or not, he's our best. No, I'm here to train you mentally for what you will come across. A cross between mind and body exercises. Similar to yoga."

My jaw dropped. That big guy was responsible for that? This is getting really interesting.

"So what do we do first?"

He nodded at Ben. Before I knew it, Ben had his hands around my neck. I fought against his hands and gasped for breath. Then I kicked and kicked with no contact made to my target. Tears filled my eyes as I watched the white of Ben's eyes almost turn black. I was blacking out.

I remember Paul walking up next to me.

"Téa, stop fighting."

I couldn't believe it. He wanted me to stop? Then something must have distracted Ben. He loosened up for just a second, and I yanked myself loose. Falling to the ground coughing, I grabbed his ankles and yanked back. He fell to the ground next to me and tried to come back at my neck.

"That's enough!" Paul yelled above the commotion.

Ben stopped and stood up brushing off his pants. He offered me his hand to help me up.

I coughed some more while touching my neck. "Screw you!"

Ben stepped back, and I heard him and Paul talking. I could make out Paul's voice saying, "She doesn't trust you?"

"You don't understand. She doesn't trust anyone."

"No, I think you feel inferior to her. And nothing is further from the truth, Ben."

"Not true."

"Yes. You have always been my best pupil, fastest and smartest. However, you never seem to believe in yourself. I don't get it."

"You done?"

"No. You have to get her to trust you. She will if you will just trust yourself. And if she can't trust you, how will we get her to where we need her?"

Ben put his hands on his hips.

"That's your problem," he said and then walked off.

When I could finally talk, I aimed my rage at Paul. "What was that about?"

"You ever watch *Star Wars*?"

Star Wars?

This big ole Indian is a huge contradiction. First yoga and now he's asking me about *Star Wars*.

"You kidding me, right?"

"I take that as a yes. It's not very different from that. A Jedi cannot have anger or doubt in their kitchen. It would render them useless. Ben and you seem to have both. What a pair!"

I ignored the last comment. "In their kitchen?"

"African American idiom."

"Don't know it." I brushed the dirt off of me.

"You can't get distracted. Can't let anything in your head."

"This is the part where you tell me I will turn to the dark side if I don't control it," I said, but I was already there.

"Good, you have seen it."

I rolled my eyes. "Anyone being choked to death would fight back. It's survival instincts."

Then, he leaned in towards me. "Someone who carries the seed would not react the way you did. The seed brings awareness of all situations. All other trainees have handled that correctly until you."

I put my hands in my pockets.

"See, this is all a mistake."

"Seriously, stop the self-doubt. Don't you want this? Don't you want to protect your family and friends?

I sassed. "I don't have family and hardly any friends."

"Do you not care about anyone but yourself?"

"Yes, but they're doing just fine."

He slowly went to sit Indian style in front of me on his tiny yoga mat. It appeared to not be an easy feat for him. I fought the urge to help him down. When he ungracefully got to the ground, he looked up at me.

"Sit."

I did as instructed but with flair.

"Cheyenne told you the seriousness of the situation, right?"

"Sort of," I said looking around unamused. Any moment now they'll fire me, and I'll be on my way back to my life.

"Did she tell you that the new threat killed two Protectors? We only have five left including you."

That comment gained my attention. "Yes and no, but there are only five of us?"

"Only seven tribes were anointed. Both deceased men, Balk and Chris, have male offsprings, but it won't be for years until they are operational. That leaves Des, his father and a few other fathers, and three sons. All of them have exceptional teams."

"Their teams?"

"All Protectors assemble a team. You can't do it all alone, Téa. You have to learn to work well with others."

I cringed. The little group work I did in school was about all I had in me. I had even asked teachers before if I could just work alone.

"I'll keep that under consideration. So, who was able to kill Balk and Chris?"

"His name is Borax. He is the Chieftain of the group of Epex that are here.

"What about the military. Can they stop them?"

"No one can stop them but a Protector. The Epex are incredibly strong and tricky to kill. It would be like bringing a knife to a gunfight. Get my drift?"

I nodded.

"On top of that, we are a shadow operation. The mass public can't know what's going on for real, they'll freak and start killing anyone that looks suspicious. Remember, Epex can disguise themselves just enough to go unnoticed too."

I understood.

Paul's face paint was beading up on his neck from the sun's heat.

"And Téa, another tidbit you should know. Borax has already figured out that you have the last viable seed."

I froze. "What do you mean he figured me out? Or viable seed?"

"We don't know how yet. But we do know that he could still harvest the seed from you for their purposes."

I shivered. I did not want to ask how.

He continued, "The other Protectors are a few generations from the first Protector that digested the Kabar. You are the first generation. You are of high value to Borax.

You don't know how much Ben has been politicking to just hide you away. Not train you to fight. He was out voted."

"Oh."

The breeze picked up giving me an ominous feeling. I scratched at my wrists under my Tacky Taco long sleeved shirt in order to steady myself. I should have been scared. However, all I thought about was that Ben wanted to hide me?

CHAPTER 20

No *I* in Team

Mental training was more rigorous than I thought it was going to be. I calmed back down after everything Paul told me sunk in and we were able to continue with the day's activities. When I got back to my room, I dropped onto the bed laying across it with my eyes on the ceiling. I was taking in all that I had just learned. I jolted when I heard movement in my room. I sprang up and saw Ben sitting in the chair across from me. How did I miss him?

I spoke first, "What do you want?"

"Still sore over what happened?"

"Well, duh."

"I'm not going to apologize for things done during training. I told you it would be hard. It's only going to get worse when we spar."

I wasn't sure what to say. I didn't want to fight tonight. I was really tired and the dinner I had just finished wasn't sitting right on my stomach. He got up and moved to sit next to me on the bed. I gave him an evil eye.

"That's close enough. I'm not in the mood."

"Let's not fight. Let's talk. We haven't gotten to talk much. Maybe that is what is wrong." He fidgeted with his large hands.

The fact that he was making an effort coupled with his woodsy smell, all instantly simmered me down.

"We've talked. We don't get along. It just is what it is."

"Tell me about yourself."

"No."

He pushed through my ornery comments. "Why did I find you asleep on the street the other day?"

I sighed. "Do you really want to know all of this?"

"Yes."

I leaned back on the palms of my hands. "Will you tell me about yourself too?"

Then I paused and wanted to ask about his sister, but thought better of it.

"Maybe."

I crossed my arms over my chest. Talking about myself was not something I did often. "I'm a foster care child, as you probably already know."

"Yes, so why not sleep at your foster parent's house?"

"Because she had a stroke and the state would deem her unable to care for me if they found out."

"How would they find out?"

"Because now her children send a caregiver that would question things if she saw me. Ms. Adele never told her grown kids that she took me in. She knew they would disapprove."

Ben leaned in. "So, what would it matter if the state found out?"

"I'd end up sent to another foster home."

"What's wrong with that? At least you'd have a home." Surprisingly, this strong man's posture was now relaxed.

I shook my head and raised my voice a hair. "A house is not always a home, Ben."

For some reason I wanted to share more with him. I've never wanted to share with anyone. The way he sat there listening intently with those entrancing eyes. I abhorred him but felt drawn to him. Watching his calm face made me simmer me back down.

"Do you really want to hear this?"

"Yes, Téa, I do."

I rubbed my thighs with my hands to prepare for this disclosure. I wouldn't say too much. Just what needed to be said. "I've lived with three different families before Ms. Adele. Each of the three before her had its share of problems. No way was I going to chance going back to another of those situations."

"What kind of problems?"

I started to unbutton my shirt when I saw him shift and hold in a breath. "What are you doing?"

I pulled one side of my shirt down from off my shoulder to reveal the scar from my early childhood. "This is what my second foster parent said needed to be done to get me in line."

He grimaced. "Geez, what did they do that with?"

"A cigarette lighter."

He reached up to touch the hideous scar and his fingers lingered.

"There is more. But it's too hard to talk about. I prefer to just share that with my therapist. And that information was not easy for her to get out me." I eyed him harshly.

Ben didn't get the warning. "Okay, but any of this is good to know, Téa. The Epex will use this abuse against you. Anything else that you can share?"

"No, that's enough!"

"Téa, you have to believe me. We are now connected. No way around it." He slid closer to me, and I began to drown in his manly scent. Along his jawline I could make out stubble starting to grow giving him a rougher look around those soft, full lips.

Then he whispered, "Open up to me."

As he reached up and touched my face so tenderly, I flinched.

"Téa, I promise for now on during our training and in everything we do, I will warn you ahead of time before I attack you. I won't surprise you like that again. I didn't know, Téa. I didn't know." His last words a whisper.

His face was now inches from mine and the feel of his hand caressing my cheek was intoxicating. The dream from last night came to mind and my mouth went dry. I honestly had never kissed a guy before. In that dream was the first time I had even come close. I wasn't sure if that was where this was leading, but I willingly leaned into his touch and closed my eyes. He slowly moved his thumb across my bottom lip causing me to slightly open my mouth.

My chest began expanding with each breath. When nothing happened, I opened my eyes to find him staring at me with a wrinkled brow. I pulled back embarrassed and looked down at my tingling hands. My body was craving something, someone. I could see from my peripheral vision that he was still staring at me. He swallowed twice and was about to say something.

I helped him out, "It's okay. I'm emotionally drained. Your touch just felt really good. No one ever touches me like that, I …"

Before I could finish my sentence, he grabbed my face with his strong hands and pulled me to his mouth. It was better than in my dream. He took my whole mouth inside his rendering me speechless. Then, he shoved his hands through my hair to pull me in closer. I breathed in between each kiss shocked at the feel of his tongue.

Shocked at the need made obvious by his ravishing lips, and his hands that were now making their way down my back. I put my unsteady palms on his chest and felt his breathing intensify. He broke away and slid his wet lips slowly down my neck and to my collar bone. Then, he pulled my shirt down off my shoulder exposing my scar. He kissed it tenderly. It made my mind whirl.

I couldn't help but let out a small moan as he kissed the hideous scar so gently and affectionately. Why hadn't I ever kissed someone before? If I only knew it felt this good. Stopping abruptly, he pulled back and grabbed my face again.

"We can't do this Téa."

He paused to swallowed and study my flushed face. "But man I want to. I didn't realize it would be this hard."

His voice came low. Then, he pressed his forehead against mine, and I yearned for the return of his amazing lips. Is that some alien thing, that they have the most sensuous lips?

"What do you mean?" I asked almost inarticulate.

He didn't answer. He swallowed several times between his own heavy breaths. Then, all he said was, "Dammit!" and stood to head out the door.

"Ben? What's wrong?" I got out just as he closed the door between us.

CHAPTER 21

Face-off

"You're up early Téa." Shia stood before me with a big smile and a cup of steaming hot coffee.

"Want some?"

I shook my head. "No, I'm fine. I'm not a coffee drinker."

She grinned again. "Not yet."

The sun was just coming up over the line of trees. It reached out to me warming my face and arms. A new day was beginning. Another day that was not promised should make me thankful, but I was still apprehensive. With that emotion, I closed off again feeling the slight chill in the air.

Shia frowned at me. "What's on your mind?"

"Lots."

I fiddled with my fingers. "I just got off the phone with my boss where I work. I had to explain my absence. It wasn't easy. I am doing this at a time that he needs me the most."

"What did you tell him?"

I looked easily at her. "What could I tell him? I just lied. I told him I had a lead on the possibility of finding my maternal grandmother."

"How did he take it?"

"Bitter at first, but he warmed back up. He understands my plight. He's a good boss." Poor Kiki. She's bearing the brunt of my absence by working more shifts. She's going to kill me.

I sat down on the beach house style chair next to Shia. "So, what all is involved in this training today?"

She set her coffee down on the table between us. "It's not easy. My first training was years ago."

"I've learned some moves from my friend who is a military vet. Is it similar to that?" I finished tying the boots she loaned me and stretched my back.

She nodded. "Somewhat, but you train with a weapon."

"A gun?"

"A gun can't stop an Epex. We fight with these."

She stood up and pulled out from behind her back two knife-shaped weapons. They were both as long as my forearm with c-shaped handles and a hooked pointy edge.

"We call them spiked daggers. Ben will show you why the need for the funny tip. It won't be what you think."

Holstering them back behind her back, her eyes were now fixed on something behind me. "Hey, Ben."

I turned to see him decked out all in black. Today, he was sporting a short strand of colorful beads made out of a variety of small stones. He came closer to us and asked me, "Are you ready?" His eyes slowly scanned my face. I got nervous under his stare.

"Yes," was all I could say. Making eye contact with him after yesterday was tough. But dang me, he looked good. I got up and followed him into the trees until we were alone with no sounds but the birds and the breeze.

He stopped and looked around. I stood behind him watching his broad back move up and down with each breath. He was listening for something but didn't tell me what. I just stood there waiting for him to speak. A few moments later, he turned towards me and my heart skipped a beat. That was when I realized, I had a problem. I had fallen for him.

"Did you hear that?" he asked with a tilt of his head. He licked his bottom lip distracting me. Sadly, I couldn't hear anything after that.

"What?"

He frowned. "How did you not hear that?"

I didn't know what to say.

"Listen, it's making a hovering sound above the trees. Close your eyes."

I did as instructed, and he stepped up close to me. My heart was now racing to where all I could hear was the thumping in my chest.

"Hear it now?" he asked just a breath from my face.

I opened my eyes to his mouth right above mine. I didn't want to admit that I couldn't hear it. I didn't know what to say.

"You don't, do you?" He leaned back and looked upset.

I stepped back and saw the dirt shift under my feet. It was a little strange, but I ignored it. "No."

He turned away and sighed. "I knew it."

"Knew what?"

"You're distracted."

Can you blame me?

"No."

He turned back and nodded. "I messed up. Protectors and Watchers can hear even the tiniest animals and insects from around their surroundings. We're the only ones that can. We follow these creatures to gauge if there is a threat."

"You mean like when birds fly away before a tidal wave?"

"Something like that. When you hear them, you will know what I mean. And you will be ready for what is to come."

I couldn't help myself. "You told me you would tell me about you after I shared about me."

"We don't have time for that. We've got to push through this roadblock and train."

"Not until you hold up your end of the bargain."

He folded his arms across his chest. It was the first time I noticed his impressive tattoo across his forearm.

"What do you want to know?"

"How did your sister die?" I asked without thinking. It was a rhetorical question but I didn't want him to know I knew already. I wanted him to talk to me about it himself.

He dragged his hand over his jaw. "She was killed."

"How?"

"By an Epex."

I felt my jaw drop, and I didn't know what to say. That was not what I was told. Who lied to him?

"She was going to the store for me and he attacked her. Do you see why this is important to me and to so many? Is that what you needed to hear to get you engaged?"

"I'm sorry." I still felt he was holding something back.

"It's alright. Are you ready to focus?"

"Yes."

"Good."

And just like that, I was back to business. I wasn't sure but something else snapped inside. It was like I wanted to be great to honor him for what happened to his sister. I had a new kind of purpose. I couldn't believe this guy's effect. A match was lit that started a fire. I also decided that I wouldn't bring it up again. If that was how he coped, I'd leave it at that.

"Where do we start?"

He stood there for a second not responding. I bit my lip and wondered what was holding him up. Then, he slowly erased the distance between us and grabbed a few strands of my hair. His eyes softened.

"First off, you need to pull all this up," he said softly.

His attention was now on my hair in his hands. Then, painstakingly slow, he released each blonde strand from his fingers.

I frowned. "How?"

"In a ponytail like you girls do." He had a 'duh' look on his face.

"I can't wear a ponytail. They give me headaches."

He put his hands on his hips, looked away with a sigh, and demanded, "Run from me."

"What?"

"Try to run from me. I'm warning you, I will catch and restrain you."

Well good. He's holding up his end of the bargain. He's warning me like he said he would.

"Okay."

I took a step back and bolted off. I didn't get five feet before he grabbed me by the hair and pulled me back into a choke hold.

"Ouch!! Stop!!!" I squealed.

He hesitated for just a moment and spoke into my right ear. "Now do you see why you need to keep that hair pulled up, Goldilocks?"

"Okay, let me go!"

"And also rolled into a bun. None hanging down. Got it?" Then, he released me.

I rubbed the back of my head where he about pulled out all my hair.

"Got it."

After that, all we did for that first day was jog around the perimeter of the reservation. He told me that stamina was the most important thing in physical combat. That was pretty much the entire conversation for the day. We got back to the houses around six when dinner was served. I was so hungry. I sat at the banquet table under a huge tent style awning and began indulging myself in smoked venison and fried hush puppies. It was so good.

"How was your first day of training?" Shia sat down next to me and dug into her meal. "These Southerners really know how to cook, don't they?"

I just nodded with a mouth full.

"I always liked coming down here for the ceremonies. I hated when we had to rotate between tribes and go somewhere else. I've been coming down here enjoying this since I was a kid."

I stopped to really look at her. "You had a life as a kid? I figured your whole life revolved around your Protector."

She giggled sweetly and her almost too flat face became more feminine with each smile. Like me, she didn't wear any makeup. We were both simple girls, but she was beautiful. She didn't need it. Sitting there with her I realized that I really needed a girl to talk to. She smiled again.

"No, silly. That didn't start till I was thirteen when Des gained his abilities. But we were both friends forever that it seemed like nothing really changed."

I saw that as my chance to ask, "You said that you couldn't have a relationship with Des. Tell me why."

She finished chewing a piece of her meat. "Protector and Watcher are not allowed to be intimate."

My heart sank.

"Why?"

"Legend says that it makes them both weak. It depletes their abilities to almost nothing. Why do you ask?"

Then, her eyes opened wide, "Oh no, you like Ben?"

I looked down quickly, "NO!"

"Yes, you do. I knew it. The way you two look at each other."

I perked up. "He looks at me like that?"

Her smile faded, and she looked to be thinking of the best words. "Maybe. But listen, just let it go. You shouldn't even entertain that thought, Téa. But I'm not going to lie, if I was partnered with him, I'd be in trouble. He is good looking. Although, I preferred his hair long."

Just then, she looked up across the tables and back at me. Ben had just walked in with his tray and glanced over at us. I just left him thirty minutes ago but having him there in front of me again took my breath away. His presence dominated the whole area by the way he moved and reacted to everyone. I couldn't help but stare.

"I … I've never really liked any boy. This is all new to me. In fact, I hated him at first. Now, I don't know what is going on. Is that really true about the legend? Is he really off limits to me?"

Hope was fading as I watched Shia continue to falter.

"I don't know of anyone who has chanced it. I just know it is strictly forbidden and the other Protectors have male Watchers."

She looked back at Ben, who now was talking to that young Indian girl from the last time.

"Besides, Chloe has been after him for years. You haven't noticed how she flocks to him every chance she gets? The last time I was down here over the summer, was when it became really obvious."

I followed Shia's gaze back to Ben. Chloe touched his hand while talking to him like they were extremely close friends. A pain shot through my gut when I saw him smile back. Geez, he had a great smile. He had never flashed that grin at me before. I went to stand.

"I think I'm done eating."

Shia frowned up at me. "You need substance. All you've eaten was part of your meat. That's not enough protein."

"Yeah, I guess the running today did me in."

I didn't know why I was suddenly angry and no longer hungry. "See you tomorrow."

I threw away my tray into the trash can not too far from Ben but tried to keep my eyes down low. "Hey!" I ran into someone. Staring down at me was an older Indian man.

"Watch where you go," he told me in a stern voice and held a serious look for a few seconds.

I stepped back. "I'm sorry. I'm just tired."

His long, dark face peered down at me and then broke into laughter. "That is fine. You, young ones. If you are not on your phones, then your heads are in the clouds. No one is grounded anymore." Harsh words but he was laughing. I wasn't sure what to think. He reached out his wrinkled hand.

"I'm Soal. I keep the grounds up."

I returned the shake. "Téa. Téa Lane."

"Yes, I know. I know of all the young Protectors. I don't envy you, though."

Out of the corner of my eye, I noticed Ben and Chloe get up with their trays to carry them into the woods alone. What the hell? Go on and make it obvious!

"Téa?"

"Yes?"

"I was asking about your family. You are obviously not Indian. I think everyone is curious about where you came from and how this came to be."

"Oh, um … my parents died when I was young. Look, sir … Mr. Soal, I prefer not to talk about it. But it was nice to meet you."

And with that I waved bye and made haste to my little house to rest. I never really liked people nor conversation. I for sure didn't like it right now. Opening the door to silence was what I needed after everything lately. I walked in and closed the door immediately. The air was already on so the cool chill in the air felt really nice. I sat on a chair by the small dining table and let my shoulders relax. No, I didn't like too much conversation. Now, I could sit and unwind.

CHAPTER 22

Envy

I slipped into the warm sudsy water in the tub back a few minutes later and sighed. I couldn't help but think about the last few days. Besides learning about the existence of another world and evil aliens, I discovered that I could have feelings for a guy. Not a boy kind of guy. A man kind of guy. Even after everything I went through at the hands of one of my foster fathers, I could still like men. I guess the happy memories with my real dad helped me to see men in a good light and not a horrid one.

I laid back and allowed the warmth of the water to spread all over my body. Laying my head on the side of the tub, all I could see was Ben's sly grin. If only he would smile at me like that. I looked down at my chest, belly and legs. I caught myself comparing them to Chloe. Where she was tall, I was short. However, I was thinner and prettier. My skin was clear, my lips fuller … Ugh! I had never compared myself to another girl. I never had time nor want to do that. What was happening to me?

It didn't matter anyway, Ben had his mind on her. Or was it because of the rules between Protectors and Watchers? No, surely not. How could they expect anyone to work so closely together and not develop feelings? That couldn't be what it was.

So, then maybe it was my worst fear, I wasn't good enough for him. Especially now that he knew I was homeless. A human, homeless reject. I wasn't a pure blooded Indian either like that little tart, Chloe with her raven hair. Once again, I was forced to look upon people that had what I could not have. The story of my life. The story of my miserable life. The only thing I was ever good at was science. Yet here I was, playing like I could save the world from fantasy land with brute force only.

I sat up in the tub and shook my head. "This is insane, Téa. You have to get back to work," I told myself and got out of the tub to dress. Afterwards, I walked around the room antsy when I should have been worn out. I didn't know what to do. It was obvious that there was something going on here. I did have these new insane abilities. But did I really believe them? And was there an alien spaceship in our ocean?

With every step, I struggled with the decision more and more. I know I called work to inform them of my absence for *family* reasons, but did they believe me? Would it jeopardize what I had worked so hard for? If it did, then this new reality as a Protector would be all I had. What if I am a bad Protector?

What would I do and how would I support myself? And then I thought of my brother. What if these abilities or these people could one day help me find him? They seemed to know more than the average police or authorities. And could I train myself to use my new powers to find him with their help?

Falling onto the bed, I reasoned that I would give it just two more days. No way was I going to be able to stay training when school resumed, though. Missing school was not an option. If so, the foster care system would get a call. I couldn't chance that. Ben had no clue what I was risking by being here.

He brought me here, said it's important that I train, and then ignored me when we were not training. I felt like I was somebody's worker bee with no fringe benefits. What was I supposed to do, take it on faith that this was so important? That I was supposed to be someone important here but not treated like it?

"Ugh!!"

I groaned and jumped out of bed. I put on my jogging suit and grabbed my flashlight before I escaped outside to get fresh air. Everyone was done eating and were retired to their homes. The darkness had set in quickly, so I followed the moon into the trees. When I got to a huge oak tree, I slid down its trunk and pressed my back up against it. I could hear an owl not too far off. Its hooting was crisp and relented only against the wind.

The sounds of the forest took a back seat to a man's voice. I stood up and looked around. All around me were trees and darkness. I shined my flashlight between each tree and squinted as far as I could see. The voice tapered off and then came back louder.

That was when I recognized the voice. It was Ben. I turned off the flashlight before I was detected and sat in the darkness listening. A part of me didn't want to hear what Ben was saying, but my curiosity held me in place. I stood up against the tree trying to slow my breathing, so I could make out his words.

"What about her?" I heard him say.

Then a woman's voice spoke, but it was too soft to make out.

"Don't worry about her," he returned.

Then, there was silence before a funny sounding giggle. So Ben was still with Chloe and out in the dark alone with her. Figures. I couldn't take it. I took off back towards the houses dodging tree after tree the best I could without light. Sadly, I passed more and more trees that kept telling me that I was lost. Again. I turned on the flashlight and shined it around. I really messed up. I turned off the flashlight, to take a breath and calm myself.

"Okay, Téa. Get it together. Go back the way you came and try this again," I told myself to steady my mind. Just as I was about to turn around I heard footsteps crackling the dead leaves not ten feet from me. I paused, too scared to move.

"Oh, no, what have I done?" I thought to myself. "If I turn on the flashlight, they'll know exactly where I'm at."

I took a few slow steps in the opposite direction of the sound and heard them move closer to me. With that, I took off running away from the sounds. Another few hundred feet and I stopped to hide behind a tree. I got the same strange feeling I had when I was back in Houston thinking I was being followed. That was twice in only a matter of weeks. I sat on the ground willing myself to remain calm, as the perpetrator ran by me.

I couldn't make out its form, size, or if it was even a person or an animal. I sat there frozen counting in my head until I thought the coast was clear. Now that I was lost in the forest at night, I had no other choice but to sleep there until morning. I had slept in the cold outdoors before without a fire. I could do it again. But if it was an animal, could it sniff me out? Oh, no, there are coyotes out here. I couldn't stay. I had to figure out a way back.

Slowly standing onto my two feet, I started to walk backwards the way I came but kept my eyes forward where that thing went. Just as I took five or so steps, I ran into a hard chest. Spinning on my heels with my flashlight in hand, I slammed the side of its face with my flashlight. Countering back, it pushed me to the ground and forced its body weight on top of me. Then, I smelled him and knew without seeing, it was Ben.

He hissed at me, "Téa, it's me, Ben. What are you doing out here?"

"Get off me!" I yelled back.

He didn't move. He had me weighted down with his pelvis over my legs and his hands shoving my wrists into the ground beside me. "Haven't we discussed how important it is for you to stay inside at night?"

"Ben, I'm going to say it one last time, GET OFF OF ME!"

"Fine," he snapped back and jumped back to his feet pulling me up with him so hard my face slammed into his exposed, bare chest. He wasn't wearing a shirt! The feel of his skin beneath my cheek was going to be my undoing.

I stepped away to regain my composure and turned the flashlight to shine it on him. All I could take in was a nicely sculpted chest and shoulders before he squinted and grabbed the flashlight from me. I reached out to grab the flashlight back.

"Give that back to me."

"Not until you tell me why you are sneaking around in the woods in the middle of the dang night?"

Sneaking? What did he think I was doing, spying on him? Are you kidding me?

"I was not sneaking. I came out to get some fresh air. But speaking of being out in the woods in the middle of the night, why are you out here?" I motioned to his body. "And without a shirt on?"

He shined the flashlight at me. "None of your business. Now it's time to go to bed." He grabbed my arm forcefully.

I winced. "Hey, that hurts."

"If anyone is going to be able to man handle you into submission, it's me. I'm the only one that can."

"Submission?"

He kept walking, pulling me along. To my surprise, it was not the direction I thought the houses were. I was going to get even more lost if he didn't come along when he did.

"Yes, Téa. That's another lesson you have to learn."

"I'm not the submissive type."

He stopped. I could tell from the little bit of light that was coming from the flashlight pointed ahead that he was thinking of what to say. Then, he turned to me with a mischievous smile that took my breath away.

"Yes, little one, I think you are."

I about died. "What?"

"No more talk. Let's go," he said and started dragging me along behind him again.

"And who are you calling little?"

"You are smaller than me. Special abilities or not, I could take you down in a second."

"No, you can't."

He stopped and smiled back at me again. "Oh, you wanna play?"

Oh crap. What was his deal tonight? It was really not like him. And there was only one reason why he was shirtless with another girl in the dark. So, did I disturb their fun? Is that what this is? I stood there debating. His calloused hand grasped mine, and his eyes intensely bore into mine. For some reason, I actually became shy. I didn't know what to do. I cowered down.

"No, I'm tired." Then, I shoved by him to head in the direction he was taking me. "I'm going to bed."

Ben followed closely behind and grabbed my hand again. "Téa, wait."

I stopped but did not turn around. "What?"

He was now standing right behind me. I didn't know what he wanted to say, but I felt what could have only been a few strands of my hair lift slightly off my back for a second. Then, those same strands drifted back down onto my shoulder.

"Nothing," he said softly behind me.

I preceded to head home, one step in front of the other.
I wasn't sure if he followed me or not. I didn't want to
know. However, the whole way back and for most of the
night, I thought of him.

<h1 style="text-align:center"><u>CHAPTER 23</u></h1>

Abilities

The next morning, we continued my training like nothing ever happened. Nothing with that other girl, nothing with me, and I still didn't know if it was him who first followed me in the woods are not. I chose not to bring anything up to him unless asked.

"Stand with your legs apart and your arms by your side," Ben said all business like.

I moved my feet into position.

"It's obvious that you know some moves already. The main thing physically is that you can control the moves while holding the daggers."

"Yeah, Shia showed me those."

He handed me two and put one in each hand. "Do you feel the weight?"

"I can tell it has mass. Of course, they're not heavy to me."

"Give it a second."

I did just as asked and within moments, the daggers felt heavy. Not too heavy but heavy enough that I had to grip tighter.

"How did that happen?"

"Your strength adjusts to objects when needed."

"But how is that good?"

"Cause you need to be able to control them. If they're too light, you will be all over the place with them. Now take one in your right hand and draw circles in the air."

"Circles?"

"Yep."

I rolled my eyes. "Okay."

I moved the knife to chest level and with my arm extended, drew circles into thin air.

"Now with your left hand, do the same at the same time."

I moved my left hand up and started trying to work in unison without the blades touching.

He took the knives from me and connected them at the points. "Epex come in many forms. Most describe them like vampires, and some like zombies, depending on how well they camouflage themselves. But all of them share one thing in common."

"What is that?"

"Two hearts. That's also why they appear so much bigger than us."

"Really?"

"That and the fact that they possess special abilities like you. They are an incredible, formidable threat. The Epex are stronger than humans and regular Aepi. They can heal quicker and don't feel pain like we do, even you."

"So how do we kill them? And why can't we just use a gun?"

"You kill them like you'd kill any human, stab them in the heart. But it has to be done simultaneously to both hearts or they will heal back too quickly. Each heart has the ability to pump enough blood to regenerate the other heart in just one second."

"Like salamanders?"

He nodded. "That is why you have to stab both hearts at the same time. The next part is even trickier. You have to hook up into the hearts from underneath."

He demonstrated with both hands holding the pointy side up on the blades and jabbing straight up.

"Sounds easy enough." I was joking. "So how did I kill the Apex at your house then?"

"You didn't. He was healing when I let you out. I went in later and did it."

"Really?"

He preceded without delay, "The other thing. Your abilities help you pinpoint the weak spot in their hearts. Watchers estimate. Protectors hit dead on. You're more efficient."

"Oh. So if we have to keep their existence a secret, how do we handle their dead bodies? Hasn't anyone autopsied one yet?"

He reached into a pocket off his belt and pulled out cigarette matches, of all things.

"Good question. You see, Epex are also highly combustible. It is something in their chemical makeup. Every time you kill one, you have to go back and light them up."

"What? You make it sound like they're fireworks."

He frowned. "They don't explode, Téa. They just burn up really quickly like when you set paper on fire. They turn to ashes in a matter of seconds."

"Really?"

He put the matches back in his belt pouch.

I put my hands on my hips. "Ben, if your great-great-grandfather was attacked by Epex, are those the ones that are here now?"

"No. We don't think that group stayed. The ones that are here haven't been here that long."

"Are they staying in their ship?"

"We don't know. But most likely, they are hiding out in mountainous terrain."

"Why?"

Ben cleared his throat. "To hunt big game and stay off our radar. They make calculated attacks. That is how we know that they have come alone."

I nodded.

He raised his hands. "Now come towards me and with your bare hands. Show me how you would attack me if you were holding the daggers."

I felt like a moron as I moved in and struck his chest with my balled up small fists. I swear I think he laughed at me. I kept my eyes down and just stared at his chest. He pushed one of my fists away.

"That's okay. Now, step back, close your eyes, and see if you can see my heart."

"I ... how would I do that?"

"Close your eyes and think about the heart muscle, listen for it, and picture it in your mind. Then, open your eyes and you should be able to make out the outline of my heart."

When my vision went dark, I pictured a heart like what he said. Then I heard it. The steady beat that was paced slower than mine but loud and clear, rung in my mind like church bells. I had to put my hand over my racing heart to confirm that it was in fact not my own that I heard. His eyes were focused on mine when I lifted my lids.

I could see the blood vessels in the whites of Ben's eyes pulsing with his heart beat. It was freaky but seemed so natural. I followed the vessels down his shoulder and into his chest. As if just a veil of skin and bones separated his heart from me. I got chills. The outline of his heart was now clearly visible to me. I began to shake uncontrollably.

He ran up to me and held me up by my elbows. "Are you okay?"

"Yeah, just taking it all in."

Truthfully, I didn't like seeing him so vulnerable. I didn't like it at all.

"So did you see it?"

"Yes."

"Great!" he said and moved to pick up the daggers. "This is great!" It felt good knowing I made him happy.

We moved to the nearest oak tree, and he modeled how to strike the tree with the daggers in an upward thrust. I took them and tried to move similarly to what he did. After a few tries and critiques from him, I got it!

"Good job!" he said in an excited tone. Before I could enjoy that moment, he eyed me funny. "Now, take that diamond out of your nose."

"What?"

"The piercing in your nose. You can't wear things like that anymore."

I frowned. "Why?"

"Because I said so," he said coyly.

That set me off. Good mood over. "You know, this is bull. First, you make me pull all my hair into this hideous bun, now you can't stand piercings."

I was on a roll and couldn't stop.

"What's next, you want me to color my hair brown and get a tan? Oh, I know, how about I get some brown contacts to cover my blue eyes so I can look like the perfect little Indian girl. What's her name? Chloe? Would that make you happy?"

I didn't know why I made this personal. I was breathing hard after spewing all that venom. I was expecting another quarrel in return for that.

Surprisingly, he just shook his head. "Fine, keep the piercing. Don't say I didn't warn you."

I didn't get any rebuttal? It was odd.

"That's it."

He said nothing, just collected the weapons. Now, I was embarrassed. I couldn't believe I brought up Chloe. He knew I was jealous now. Me, jealous? Over a guy with another girl? What is going on with me?!

Then, he stood back up and squared up his shoulders. "Now, we try it on the real thing."

"What!? Already?"

He lifted one side of his mouth in a half smile. "You're fired up. I think you're ready."

We started walking farther from the living quarters. "Where are we going?"

"You'll see."

I tried to keep up with his long strides. "So, how long have you been out of school for real?"

He looked over at me. "Just one year."

"One year?" He was older than me.

"Yep, and I heard you skipped a grade. That you are only seventeen and the youngest senior at that school."

"Yes. I do okay at science and math. I tested out of certain classes to get high school credit early."

"You do okay? You have to do more than okay to test out of a class you never took."

"Yeah, whatever."

"You don't like compliments, do you?"

"Not really. I do better just thinking I'm worthless and that nobody likes me. Makes it easier."

He looked shocked. "Makes what easier?"

"Reality. The worse thing I can do is get my hopes up for them only to be shot down. It's happened too much in my life."

I rubbed the back of my neck. "Well, that's enough sharing for today."

"I guess." He looked up ahead. "We're not far now."

About five minutes later, we stopped in front of a huge black and metal building. A white man stood in front dressed in all black too with a rifle handy. He nodded at Ben. Ben introduced us. "Téa, this is Carson. Carson, this is Téa."

Carson stared at me. "The new Protector?" he asked and looked at my hands. "She's tiny."

"She's mighty, though."

Carson laughed and slid his rifle behind his back to shake my hand. His features were rougher making me think he was older than Ben. His bushy eyebrows and beard made him look a little scary, too. However, he wore a cool baseball cap with lime green borders and a bright orange bib. It toned down the 'rough around the edges' look. I loved contradictions.

"Nice to meet you, Téa."

Carson opened the door for us that led to a corridor not bigger than six feet wide. I followed Ben not knowing what was in store. It was freezing inside. I brought my shaky hands up to blow warm air into them. Ben stopped by the fifth door to the right and stopped before opening it.

"I will release the Epex from its shackles. This will leave you with just a few seconds to pinpoint its hearts. Once you see it, react. No delays. Also, don't let him at your neck. He'll tear your jugular out to render you defenseless like a pit bull does to its prey. Got it, Téa?"

I took a gulp of cold air into my lungs. "Yes."

"If you do hesitate, then you'll have a fight on your hands. You're strong and have some good moves, but it only takes one slip up for this thing to overpower you. Don't hesitate."

He reached into his bag and pulled out the two long daggers. I took them from him and positioned them in my hands exactly as I was taught. Then, I closed my eyes to steady my heart for what laid behind that door. After chanting a motivational mantra in my head, I opened my eyes.

"I'm ready."

Even cooler air hit my face as I followed Ben into a low lit room. I fought the anxiety that was building after remembering what Ben did to me back in Houston.

"I can do this. I can do this," I said to myself as he walked over to what looked like a young man cowering in the corner of the room. I was about to feel pity for him until I got close enough to see those eyes. I knew anger well, but I had never seen the kind of anger in someone's eyes like I was seeing in that creature. He hissed at me with a gruesome bloody mouth and went to lunge when the chains caught him abruptly.

Ben had a saber in front of the alien's chest and looked back at me.

"Let's do this."

Ben released the chain and before he stepped even a foot away, the massive alien lunged for Ben. I watched terrified while Ben shoved his wooden saber up the Epex's chin knocking that thing back a hair. Then, Ben struck the Epex with one end of his stick and advanced by shoving the Epex to the ground. Spinning almost effortlessly with the saber, Ben turned to head towards me. I'd never seen someone fight so amazingly. Ben's muscles worked in perfect unison with each of his moves. It was flawless. He was real trained.

When Ben moved to stand by me, the alien was already up and heading towards me now. It stopped when it looked in my eyes and its brows rose. That gave me the rookie moment I needed to perfect my perusal of his hearts. The outlines of the alien's hearts showed immediately. I lifted the knives up with both hands and stepped forward. When the black spot underneath the two hearts revealed itself, I struck. However, it was not hard enough.

The Epex charged me instantly forcing me to fall back. Once on the ground, I looked up. Sharp teeth were right above me while he viciously yanked at me. He was trying to get his teeth on my neck.

I heard Ben in the background. "Téa, protect your neck!"

I struggled for a second and felt its foul breath cover my face. Blood was dripping on my chest as I turned my head and pushed on the alien's chest.

"Ben!" I yelled, but he did not come to my rescue.

"Fight Téa, fight!" was all I heard Ben say.

I looked back up at the evil being above me and saw him smile with glee. "This is the new Protector?" he asked with a deep voice.

When he started laughing, I swung the blunt end of the knife upside his head knocking him off of me. Then I jumped to my feet to tower over him. When he regained his composure, he jumped up on his feet preparing to throttle me. I saw the dark spots immediately and this time, I shoved with all my might directly into them.

The Epex fell to the ground below me with both the knives still buried in its chest. I dropped to the ground beside it and kneeled there to catch my breath. I felt a warm hand brush my cheek and then it was offered to me.

"Give me your hand Téa." I looked up to find Ben standing over me with approving eyes. "You did well."

I took his hand to stand back up and watched him remove the blades from the alien's chest. I worked to catch my breath. The Epex's face was contorted and covered in dirt. My stomach turned. Alien or not, I just killed someone.

"I don't feel like I did well."

"I knew you could do it. I didn't want to intervene because I wanted to see how you would react when things went wrong. That is the moment that we can tell what you are really made of. Nothing else is more important."

I was really shaking now from the adrenaline. So bad that I didn't want to be more than a few feet from Ben. I felt like a puppy when I followed him out of the building and to the protection of the trees. Carson said something to Ben on the way out, but I didn't bother to tune into it. I was trying to recoup.

Ben took my hand when we got to the woods and led me to the bank of a small stream. The water was sparkling from the beautiful day. I just couldn't enjoy it in that moment. Ben pulled a blue blanket out of his bag and laid it down on the sandy shore. He sat to one side and guided me down right beside him. His musky, manly smell caught my attention. It was enough for me to notice that I was still with him. That reassurance helped. I wasn't sure that anything else could ground me like him.

CHAPTER 24

Helpless

"Are you alright?" Ben finally spoke first.

In the distance a huge white bird drifted above the breeze. Its wings arched up and back down pulling my attention away. My breath ceased.

"I'm scared."

Ben reached over and touched my back. "It's not always going to be like that."

I liked Ben's touch, but my thoughts were on the winged creature above who was absorbing my air with every turn in the sky. I was suffocating.

"Téa, talk to me!" There was urgency in Ben's voice now.

All I remember next was laying on my back on the ground with Ben above me. His mouth moving but no sounds reached my ears. Something warm slid down my cheeks. When the drops descended onto my lips, I could then hear a faint voice and make out that it was Ben's.

"Ben?"

"Hey, it's okay. I'm here." He was right above my face wiping my tears away with the pads of his thumbs. Soft lips graced my forehead and then sad eyes met mine.

"Are you alright?"

All I could manage was a nod of my head.

"You scared the crap out of me," he whispered over me. Then his rough palms slid over the side of my face.

Finally, my vocal chords began to work. "I do that sometimes." I laid there watching him.

He had a dumbfounded look. "Do what? What was that?"

"They're like panic attacks."

My heart was now returning to its normal pace. "I just freaked. Is it always going to be like that when I fight the Epex?"

"It gets easier. I swear," he paused. "Maybe I shouldn't have brought you in there so soon. I thought you were ready. I didn't realize it would affect you like that."

His molten brown eyes encircled my face. "I'm sorry, Téa. I did it again. I don't know why ..."

His words broke off, and he turned his head slightly away.

I reached up with my own hands and moved his face back over mine.

"It's okay, Ben. I was just overwhelmed. I never expected it to be like that. Now, I know. Now, I'm prepared. You didn't do anything wrong."

He shook his head. "I disagree. I'm supposed to know you more than you know yourself. That is my job. I don't know why I'm messing all this up."

Then, he broke eye contact with me and grimaced. "Left and right, I'm always messing up with you."

He was self-deprecating, and it was breaking my heart. I hooked my hands around his wide neck and pulled him down within inches of my face. I *was* jealous of Chloe. I couldn't stand that she could have him, and I couldn't. Ben already knew I was jealous of her. With that admission earlier and from the stress of the day, I just lost it and gave in to my needs.

Without pause, I connected my mouth with his reluctant soft lips and felt my universe shift and spin all around me. The Epex, my past, my future, all of my fears blew away. The torture of wanting Ben and not having him swept through my body as I lifted up towards him. He responded with returning a fierce kiss sending me into amazing ecstasy with just that one mere act. I moaned and slithered around on the grass under him.

Ben pulled away from the kiss leaving me frazzled, and then he sat me up. Reaching behind my head, he yanked at my pony tail holder releasing cascading blonde hair down over my shoulders. I was captivated as he lifted strands of my hair the same way he did last night and smelled of them like they were some kind of rare flower that was more fragrant than he'd ever smelled.

"God, don't ever dye your hair. Don't ever change anything about you."

I didn't know what to say.

He picked a blue bonnet next to us and handed it to me. "And your eyes are as blue as this flower. I've never seen anything like it."

I laughed. The comment, so proper and not like him, took me off guard.

He wasn't fazed by my reaction. In a surprisingly possessive act, he pushed me back down and moved both my hands above my head pinning them to the ground. The action rendered me all his. I didn't fight it. Now holding my hands there with just his right hand, he moved his exploring mouth through my hair, over my neck, and to my collarbone. His left hand caressed my right hip passionately, and his breath pounced onto the delicate skin below my neck.

"I want you, Téa. Just like you are," he said under hoarse breath.

I looked up to the clouds and slowly blinked in bliss. The soft azure and sunny sky above mimicked the new found happiness reverberating through my core. Before I knew it, I was floating on a sea of dreams like I never thought would be possible. To be so close to someone so incredible, was definitely more than I dreamed. Now that I was becoming more lucid with each of his touches, I saw the vision of him fighting effortlessly up against that beast.

It was such an erotic sight. My heart started beating out of my chest as Ben said my name again so softly that it made my mind go wild. Then suddenly, it all just stopped. The kisses, the caresses, and hearing my name seductively pass through his lips just disappeared. His steamy eyes were back above mine.

"Dang it ... not like this."

He pulled me up to sit again with moistened hands and brushed my now escaping blonde locks back off my forehead. Turning to sit next to me and facing away with his knees up, he sunk his face into his hands.

"What am I doing?"

I was still speechless and trying to catch my breath.

He was obviously irritated at something. He looked back at me with a childish stare and said with indignation, "With you ... with you, I have no sense. I can't think straight. Maybe that's why I keep making these mistakes."

His stare got intense. "Maybe *that* is why you are afraid and hesitant in these trainings."

I started to shake my head stunned.

"We can't do this, Téa."

He stood with his lips in a thin line looking back down at me. "No matter how bad I want you. I can't have you."

And then before I could counter, he walked around by the water. I sat there shaking and remained almost breathless. The moment we had just shared was amazing, yet it had to end. Ben basically said, it can't happen ever again.

We can't happen.

I didn't know what to do or how to think. Everything in my life had ended like this. I'd get my hopes up and then it would all fall apart. I had forgotten that was why I never wanted to date. I broke my own rule and fell for someone that I couldn't have. I watched that someone pick up rocks and toss them over the water.

He was struggling too. Tears built in my eyes as I thought of every horrible let down in my life. Would I ever be truly happy? At a time when I should be thankful for being chosen to have this special gift of being a Protector, I hated it.

With everything great comes strings attached.

Why can't anything in my damn life be easy? I wanted to scream. But I just sat there taking in every ounce of air

while my old friend, anger, continued to build at the back
door of my consciousness.

CHAPTER 25

Bodies at Play

I woke to seek out Cheyenne the next morning. I needed to talk to someone. I needed to know if it was true about relationships between Protectors and Watchers or if Ben was just telling me that. The night before, I had already been questioning how someone like Ben could like me. Before I fell asleep, I decided that he was just making an excuse. That it really was Chloe that he preferred. I was just a convenient pawn and he was playing the field like all guys did.

I found Cheyenne surprisingly in front of her television watching *Good Morning America*. Her grandson had let me in and brought me to her.

"Téa!" Cheyenne said and muted her television before approaching me. "How is your training going?"

"Good. Do you have a moment?"

She studied me for a second. "Yes, come have a seat."

I sat in a mocha colored, suede chair and rubbed my now sweaty hands on my pants. The living room was decorated in Victorian style paintings and fixtures. Nothing in there was like I expected.

"So what do you do when you are not helping us Protectors that are passing through?"

Cheyenne sat in front of me on her floral couch and crossed her legs gracefully under a long blue periwinkle skirt.

"I'm the local beautician, seamstress, and florist. In fact, I open at nine o'clock for beauty appointments every day."

"Really?"

"Yes, Téa. Everything on a reservation runs pretty much like things in a regular country town. We're still just country folks."

I nodded. "That's really neat."

"So, let's cut to the chase. What's troubling you?"

I'd rehearsed this intro over and over in my mind and now that I was there about to deliver it, I was speechless.

"Is this about you and Ben?"

I looked up shocked. "What makes you think that?"

"I just have a feeling. That's the hard thing about Watcher and Protectors being of the opposite sex."

"Are we allowed to be together?"

She sucked in her lips. "Probably not. What has been passed down through the generations specifically referenced that anything more than a platonic relationship between a Watcher and Protector is forbidden."

"Has anyone ever broken that rule?"

"Not that I know of. Téa, in times like these, it is not wise to risk it. Ben is a great young man. I can see why you would be falling for him. You must understand that even if you want to chance it, there is no way he would. He's by the book."

I didn't know how to react. My eyes darted from side to side. Then I hung on to my last good thing.

"Cheyenne, how do you know that I am really a chosen Protector? I am not Indian and anyone could have found the Kabar. I mean, what is to stop it from pulling away from me."

She smiled. "You *are* a pessimist just as Ben said."

"He said that?"

"Look, I know we don't know why it chose you. But we do know, from Ben's family line, that the Kabar was left with a friend of Ben's great, great grandfather when he evacuated that Spanish mission back in the early 1800s."

I started to remember the dream I had of the two young kids set back in the 1800s in a Spanish mission.

She continued, "Stories of old say that the mission was called the San Francisco de los Tejas mission. It was originally established around the area in Texas where Ben said you found the Kabar."

"Yes, that is right. After the hurricane, there was a lot of talk about some artifacts being discovered that dated to back then and were from both Spaniards and Indians. Did the hurricane cause the Kabar to surface?"

"There you go again. No. Now, the hurricane could have helped the Kabar to surface and find you. But you are special Téa, whether you want to believe it or not. It *is* devastating what happened to your city, but it would have been worse if you were never anointed. There is a real threat brewing. You have to believe in that. Many lives will be at stake. Many have been already. Like I said before, Epex primarily look for young women for their eggs, so be on the lookout for increased reports of missing women when you return."

"So that is why the one Epex group is here." Shirley Quam's broadcast came to mind.

"That's what we're thinking."

"So why me?"

"We don't know that. I do know that Ben had a dream that his great, great grandfather's friend was a little Spanish girl that was helping Ben's family during troubled times."

"What kind of troubled times?"

"Some kind of conflict between the Spanish farmers in the area and the Indians. The Spanish missions were established to help the Spaniards remember their Christian faith so they would not become too violent. It was a way of keeping their own people to stay tame while also attempting to convert Indians to Christianity."

The dream was really coming back to me now. "Really?"

"Yes, they didn't teach you kids that, did that?"

"No."

"Hmm ... history is written by the victors." Her flat mouth revealed some angst.

"So, did the tales talk of the boy putting the Kabar in that little girl's mouth?"

Her eyes lit up. "No, but that is how Ben dreamed it. I'm guessing you did too."

"Yes."

"Well then, either the little girl ingested it and lived, or that is why the Kabar was buried for over one hundred years around that spot. Have you told Ben about your dream?"

"No."

"You need to. You need to talk to him more ... no matter
how hard it is. You need each other."

I crossed my arms. "Yeah, I can see that."

Cheyenne got up and walked over to sit by me. "Téa, no
matter what happens, you are a part of our family now, our
clan. There is no returning to the emptiness you once
knew."

I fought the tears building behind my eyes.

She touched my shoulder. "And if you know anything
about our culture, you will know that once we take you in,
you are one of us. We don't change our mind, divorce, or get
tired of each other like what you've been exposed to."

I looked up at her with uneasiness. "No culture is like
that anymore. Everyone has changed."

"I promise you that we have not. Yeah sure, you're doing
a job with us. But the truth is, I think we were supposed to
find each other whether you wielded the Kabar or not. I
know this as well as I know my own name. And your
presence here has made that even clearer. We are your
family now."

I couldn't help it. A tear made it out, and I quickly wiped
it. "Thank you."

She then did the unimaginable. She gave me a hug.

CHAPTER 26

Shattered

Stewing over Cheyenne's words, I made my way to our morning meeting spot. Ben was already there dressed in his training fatigues. When he noticed me come into view, he handed off his coffee to a young kid they called, Logan. Logan seemed to idolize Ben. If Ben wasn't training with me or swooning over Chloe, Logan was on his tail. The child had to have been ten with short hair and all Nike logo clothes.

Logan saw me and reacted, "Hey, doll."

Ben elbowed him. "Hey, doll? What kind of talk is that?"

I was still pulling my hair up in my daily bun when they both looked over at me again.

"What?"

I had hoped it wasn't because of the Niagara Falls that just took place over my entire face. I thought I wiped away all the evidence of my neediness in the short walk from Cheyenne's.

Ben moved from sitting on the table to grabbing our gear. "Nothing."

"Always nothing with you, huh?" I countered.

"Have a good day, Ben!" Logan yelled behind us as I followed Ben into the woods.

We weren't far in when I added, "He really looks up to you?"

Ben didn't answer.

"So what will our training consist of today?"

"First, some sparring. Then, back to Paul. Do you think you can trust me now or did I just completely blow it yesterday?"

I stopped walking. "You didn't blow anything. I just don't understand what's going on with you?"

He stopped and turned towards me. "What's going on with me? I don't think you fully appreciate how serious all this is!"

My face was burning. "I don't? My whole life has been serious. I'm not just some valley girl with a crush! When will you ever really know me? Isn't it your job to understand me?"

Crap, I slipped again. He now knew I had a crush. Open mouth, insert foot!

Ben stared down at me.

I added, "I do take this serious. Life, death, end of humanity, all of it. I'm dealing with my own demons that y'all could never imagine. It's hard to juggle all of this. And then there is the anomaly of the Aepi."

"How do you mean?" He folded his arms across his chest.

"I figured out there is more y'all are not telling me. Y'all are worried. You know, since such a *powerful people* like the Aepi couldn't defeat them back home."

When I said *powerful people*, I threw up some air quotes with my fingers. Ben's jaw visibly tightened as I contintued,

"I'm not stupid. You all think that there is no way one little human will be of any help when the Epex all come here. Am I right?"

He looked at me steadily in the face. Dang if I didn't get a shot of excitement every time he did that.

"Let's just get busy doing our job," he smarted off and turned to walk off.

"See, that's the Aepi's problem and maybe weakness." Then, I yelled to his retreating back, "Too prideful."

I had him aggravated again and for some reason on this beautiful sunny day, I loved it.

We approached the sparring area, and I saw that Des was already there with some other guys sparring. I was immediately nervous. Des stopped advancing on his opponent and addressed us, "Look what we have here."

Ben flared up. I could actually see red come through his dark cheeks. "Not now Des, we have work to do."

"Why don't I show her some moves … " Des had the audacity to wink. "… out here and in my room."

Before I could react to that myself, Ben had Des in a choke hold. Des kicked Ben down, and the two of them rolled in the dirt. Des' sparring partner, Rob, pulled Des up off Ben and held him back.

Rob got in front of Des while Ben got up. "Man, control yourself, you're better than this."

Des spit blood from his mouth off to the side. "It's a good thing you stopped us. I would have hurt him bad."

Rob frowned. "You know you have to keep a leash on those abilities around non-Protectors, what's gotten into you?"

I couldn't help myself, "That's okay. We understand that a beast is not capable."

I am who I am.

Des pushed Rob out of the way. "I'll show you capable."

Ben pulled me back and stood toe to toe with Des. Rob bowed out, "I guess you both need to fight it out. But remember, Des, it's an unfair fight."

Des pushed Ben back to the ground, and I stepped in between the two. Des started laughing. "Are you kidding me? You may be another Protector, but you're still a girl."

"Then, fight me."

"Honey, I'd floor you."

I pushed him. All six foot, three inches of him with my feminine five foot, four-inch self. Surprisingly, he went back farther than I thought he would. When he came back at me, he swung fast. I ducked and kicked him in the knee cap the way Uncle Bob taught me. Have you ever seen a grown man go down so hard? That was my first time.

However, my victory was short lived. Des had moves too. From the ground, he grabbed my ankles and laid me down flat on my back. I couldn't breathe. Ben stuck a knife to Des' neck, moving him away from me.

Des spit again and said, "She asked for it, house pet. How do you like the change in gender roles?"

Ben poked into Des' neck. "Sign of the times. Now, don't touch her again."

"Or what?"

"Superman or not, I'll kill you."

Paul showed up at that exact moment. "Ben and Des, I need to see both of you!"

Ben stared Paul down and slowly moved the blade from Des' carotid artery.

"Yes, sir."

I sat up to breathe and watched them go with Paul. Rob came over and helped me up.

"Don't mind Des, he's always been jealous of Ben."

Rob rubbed his lazy eye and smirked.

"Why?"

"Des has the Kabar. Poor Ben had to sit second fiddle to me getting his."

Rob pulled his long Indian locks back into a ponytail while looking over at them with Paul. "They're from different tribes. Des' dad always took to Ben, his nephew. It always got under Des' skin. When Des developed his special abilities at puberty, he backed off Ben for a while. I'm not sure why he's being a jerk to him again."

I wiped the sweat off my upper lip. "Good to know."

Rob smiled down at me. "Where did you learn those moves? I thought you were doing your first sparring lesson today."

"My friend used to be in the military. He taught me some self-defense moves."

"Ah! Well, you are quick on your feet. It'll come in handy."

Paul managed to get Ben and Des to shake hands.

"How did they get over that so quickly?" I asked.

Rob peered back at me. "Men forgive way quicker than women. Women can be petty. On top of that, we've been in alliance and mixed in with the Indians all our lives. Pretty much we have become like the Indians. It is not in their nature to hold grudges. If that was the case, they would still be complaining about the white man and what happened several centuries ago."

"What do you mean?"

"Think about all the atrocities done to the Indians by your ancestors, the white man."

"I guess so."

"But we don't try to remind you. That is not how we are."

"I guess you don't."

He laughed. "Nah, we just open casinos and take all your money!"

I laughed back, it felt nice. I noticed Ben rubbing the back of his neck while talking to Des and Paul. He looked good when he took up for me. I couldn't help but smile.

Rob shrugged while watching me watch Ben. "I can see why he likes you."

"Ben? Oh no, no way."

"Yep. You act tough as nails, but you're a sweetheart underneath. Ben needs that."

"Needs what?"

"Happiness with someone that really cares for others. Someone that will be there for him, too. He told me about what you did with your reward money from the science fair."

"Oh." I didn't know what to say.

Rob was about to say something else when Des approached me. "I'm sorry, Téa. I was out of line."

I was shocked. "It's alright, I guess."

Des turned to Rob, "Round two?"

Rob replied, "Let's do it, brother."

Now that the testosterone was revved up all over the place, I thought I'd join them to release some steam. I walked up to Ben, who just finished his conversation with Paul.

"You ready?"

Ben eyed me. "I don't know if I want to go up against *you*, Ms. Mighty."

"You said you're not affected by my strength, since you *are* my Watcher."

He laughed and tossed me a saber. We took off our shoes and met each other in the middle of the sand pit next to Rob and Des' pit. I tried to maintain my focus on Ben, but I wasn't sure I trusted Des yet.

Ben showed me how to hold the saber with my hands apart. After a few failed hits, we dropped the sabers for hand to hand training.

"You're missing something, and it's showing in your moves. I want you stand here with your feet separate and use your forearms to stop my swings."

I did as instructed. He moved slowly at first, and I was able to block most of his swings until he sped up. With each swing, Ben repeated the words, "Defend, defend, strike."

The last hit missed my blocking arm and nailed me in the shoulder. I leaned over giving him the opportunity he needed to spin me around and take me down to the ground. He jumped on top of me and said, "It's all about catching your opponent off balance."

I was breathing hard with my chest expanding overly obvious under him. At that moment, I cursed myself for wearing Shia's black sports bra. He looked down and back up at my face again.

"Too much exertion?"

"Screw you."

He jumped back up to his feet and helped me up. "Let's try that again. This time you try to strike first."

My hair was wanting to come down out of its bun. I blew it back off my face. Then, I set up in position and went through the moves in my mind. My partner held up his hands out straight, one in front and one behind. Then, he lifted a few fingers of the one pointed towards me signaling for me to try again. That was all fine until I saw the smirk on his face. I moved in quickly. He blocked me, blocked me again, and then blocked me a third time. Utilizing my aggravation with myself, he kicked me in the stomach sending me back to the ground.

I fell on my rear first and kicked out of frustration. Ben was above me with his hand out. I slapped his hand away and got back to my feet. He was quick, but I knew he had to have a weakness. I was going to find it and send his massive self to the ground before this training was over.

Back into position, he advanced on me this time. I blocked, blocked again, another block, and tried to kick him to throw him off balance. However, I was not successful. He caught my leg, pulled it next to his hip, and wrapped his arm around the back of my neck pinning me to him.

"You're trying too hard," he said into my ear. Then he shoved me back, causing me to fall back on my rear.

I stood up even more determined. He wasn't going to best me. I pulled my hair out of the bun and retightened it into just a ponytail. Next, I wiped my hands on my black jogging pants and got into position. Feeling the breeze brush across my face, I took a deep breath and put Ben's gut right in my sight. Strange movement of the sand under my feet caught my attention for a split second. When I looked up, Ben was already advancing. I blocked, blocked, and kicked. Sadly, the momentary distraction led me to lose my chance to strike. Ben was even more engaged. He grabbed me by the waist and sent us both to the ground, again.

"Dammit," I cursed under him.

"Calm down. It's your first official training. You didn't think I'd let you get a hit in today, did you?"

"You don't have to let me. I'll get it."

He shook his head. "Such determination." He popped me up alongside him and reached into his bag to throw me a towel.

"Rest. It's time to go see Paul."

"I want another round," I said and saw Rob and Des look over at us.

Ben looked from them to me. "I'll decide when we continue or when we rest. I'm your trainer."

I walked up to him and peered up into his eyes defiantly. "I'm your Protector."

With that, he grabbed my right arm, swung me around, and pinned my arm up against my back. I couldn't move. A slight laugh came from the other training area and Ben pressed his lips against my ear.

"I don't care who you are."

He nudged up my arm an inch more causing excruciating pain. I wasn't going to cry uncle. I stood there in pain while he dominated the situation. I was beginning to hate him again for it.

"Now, are you ready to go to Paul?"

"Yes, jerk," I said and was immediately released. I turned around rubbing my arm.

"You enjoy doing that to women?"

He picked up our gear and walked back up to me.

"Téa, if I treat you like just a woman, we'd all fail."

Then, he walked by me expecting me to follow. I did.

CHAPTER 27

Fallen

We approached Paul a few minutes later. Ben greeted him with a fist pump.

"Good morning, again."

Ben's hair was getting a little longer. When the wind blew, I saw it spike up in the front slightly. Another dreamy thing about him.

The big Indian replied, "Good morning Ben, Téa. Are we ready?"

I smiled. "Yep."

Paul cleared his throat, "First, I need a moment with Téa."

Ben acted okay with that and took off into the thicket. I turned to Paul. "What's up?"

"Walk with me," Paul said and headed in the opposite direction. I followed and felt the movement of the stirring leaves wanting to dance with me. It was surreal out in the country. So peaceful. I was accustomed to living outside, but out here ... whoa, what could I say? If there was a heaven, it would have to be a lot like this. I could hear early morning insects searching for their breakfast under a vast vegetation. Blue jays were on the move fluttering from limb to limb. I wondered if their falling feathers were what made our state's blue bonnets so blue.

"Téa?"

I snapped back. "Yes?"

"Did you hear me?"

I didn't. "No, come again."

Paul dropped his chin like a sassy teen. If he wasn't a huge man dressed in a long white shirt with a fanny pack around his waist, it could have worked.

"Are you in la la land?"

"Just enjoying the peace."

"So, you do like it here?"

"It's taken some getting used to. You know, having grown up in the city."

"What do you like about it?"

Around me all the beauty of the rich colors of green, brown, and patches of red really enchanted my senses. The smells. They had to have been the best, like the scents of jasmine, azaleas, and black-eyed Susan flowers as they sprayed their pollen sporadically around us to lure in tiny creatures.

How do I put that into words?

"Everything."

"Good. You are starting to really tap into your potential."

"How do you mean?"

"You can't be distracted to do this job."

I frowned. "I'm not distracted. I'll have you know that I am always paying attention to things around me. That is how I have always survived."

He stopped walking and sat slowly onto the plush grass. This man liked to sit.

"I know that, Téa. That may have a little to do with why you were chosen. Your survival skills are amazing. No one is trying to downplay that. What I'm saying is that being too aware of all the negative in your life will destroy you. Things in nature are what's positive and vital to your missions."

"What do you mean?" I sat on the damp grass in front of him.

"You come from a culture that is all about yourself. A *me* culture."

"I can see that."

"So, you are constantly around lots of people that do not care about anyone but themselves."

I splayed my hand over the cool grass to tickle my palms. "What are you getting at?"

"Lay with the dog, you get fleas."

"I don't know how well you think you know me, but I am not like that."

His heavy lids always made me think he was about to doze off at any time. He opened his eyes just enough to look like humor.

"If your survival skills are so important than what will you do if you ever had to choose another over yourself?"

A heart palpitation signaled my rising tension.

"I don't know. Hopefully, it will never come to that."

Once upon a time, I would have gladly thrown myself into any deadly event. I used to hate my life. I was even so bad off that I tried to end it myself. However, now that my feet were more firmly planted on the ground and hope of a normal future was in my sights, I had a different perspective. I wanted to live. I deserved to live. I had fought so hard to get to that point. How could I give it all up for someone else?

"We hope so too. But my point is, your heart has to be in the right place to do this job."

I stewed on those last words as we headed back to our meeting point and found Ben stretching. I walked over to him with my head down. Here was a man that stepped back and let me take his glory. He didn't hate me. He didn't own me.

Is that what it would be like to help someone else when it could ultimately hurt you? He also had stood up for me several times since I had been here. I knew that it wasn't the same as life and death, but besides Kiki, Uncle Bob, and Tommy when he has sense, no one had really done that for me.

Paul began, "Today, we are going to test your reactions to each other. Ben stand over here."

He motioned for Ben to stand right in front of him. "Téa, stand in front of Ben with your back to him."

We both complied.

"Close your eyes."

I closed my eyes and felt the breeze gently lift the ends of my hair.

Paul spoke again disturbing the quiet.

"Listen for the rustling in the leaves."

The soft rattling below my feet made me aware of Ben's body directly behind me.

Paul spoke again, "Téa, we know you can hear Ben's heart, but can you see him moving his hands behind you?"

I thought to myself, "How could I miss that man behind me?"

I frowned while still staring at darkness before answering aloud, "No … wait!"

I could sense movement behind me but it wasn't from the air he was disturbing with his hands. It was a different sense that was engaged besides touch. Almost primal.

"I do," I said with a shocked tone.

Paul asked, "What is he doing with his right hand?"

I stood there trying to read this new sense that was not of the five I had known since birth. It was like an energy that I was picking up all over my body.

"Figure eights."

There wasn't a reply. I opened my eyes and turned back to see both of them nodding their heads.

"Good job," Paul said to me.

Ben just stared at me.

Paul motioned again. "Now, Ben sit down right here."

Then, he motioned to me. "Téa, you and Ben are going to play an old game, hide and seek. Téa, you will hide and in ten seconds, Ben will come to find you. He will have no longer than five minutes to achieve this goal. Make no sounds and do not go far. I hear you get lost in these woods a lot."

I glanced at Ben whose face was void of emotion. Jerk. "Whatever."

Paul brought my attention back to him. "Ben tells me that he's never had a problem finding you before."

My jaw dropped and I looked at Ben. "What ... is that how you've been finding me?"

Ben smiled. "Since the beginning. You were always easy to find. How do you think I found you sleeping on the street in downtown Houston?"

Paul broke our banter. "Yes, but he tells me that it is getting harder for some reason. Téa, it is supposed to get easier for him. Watchers should always know where the Protector is at all times."

I shut my jaw and shuffled my feet slightly. "Are you kidding me? I will never have privacy from him?"

I pointed to the guy sitting crisscrossed on the ground and pulling up grass like he was enjoying this. He looked up at me from under his dark brows and those eyes said it all. He *did* like it.

Paul interrupted us again, "That is a part of their job, Téa."

"But you said it was getting harder. So can I fight it?"

"No."

"Why is it getting harder for *him*?"

I loved asking that rhetorical question and seeing Ben squirm by my feet was priceless.

Ben piped up and demanded, "Can we just get going with this?"

I answered, "Sure Ben, close your eyes, and I'll go run and hide." I said it in a sassy way that made Paul even look at me funny.

Why did I love torturing Ben now? Oh, I know, because he loved torturing me!

Ben glared up at me and said slowly, "Run, run, little sheep."

"Sure thing," I said and winked at him.

Ben crossed his arms over his chest and closed his eyes. My heart started racing before I had even moved a step. I turned and dashed off in a sprint towards the tree line. One pine, two oaks, and one pear tree passed by me within seconds. I found a ditch and swung my legs down first before tumbling down farther. It turned out I was falling into a ravine.

Putting my arms up, I grabbed the first branch I could tether to and held tightly. One more pull of my right bicep and I was able to hook my foot over another branch that led me to a dug out hole. I sat in the small cave like opening cowering with hopes that the hiding spot was good enough. I knew that three minutes had to have passed. Ben only had two minutes to find me.

Then, another minute slid by, and I heard him.

"Can't hide from the wolf."

Crap, he found me already?!

I went to peer out of the hole, and there he was diving in after me. I slid back on my rear as far into the hole as I could go, but he kept coming after me until my back was up against the muddy wall. His hands grabbed my arms and his lips were with inches of mine. I struggled.

"Congratulations," I said, defeated.

"Do I get a prize?" he asked mischievously.

"What?"

Before I knew it, he grabbed my face and kissed me. I wiggled the best I could to get away but his muscled legs were straddling mine making it impossible. I turned my head, breaking our kiss.

"Don't you dare!"

"What? I think I've earned it."

"I thought you said we couldn't do this … "

He kissed me again then stopped with his nose touching mine. "Your teasing is driving me crazy, Téa."

"So, this is my fault?"

He kissed me again more forcefully this time until I could almost not breathe. His hands roamed over my shoulders to my waist pulling my body closer to him. He was vicious in his movements, and it made my body tingle. Then, he tilted my head to the side and licked my neck. I was still fighting it all the best I could. Just as I was about to not be able to take it anymore and surrender, he started to whisper something in my ear and stopped short.

There was movement blocking the sunlight into the cave.

"What's going on here?" asked Paul peering through the hole.

My chest was heaving from the intensity of the moment. Ben pulled back and his firm eye contact made me shiver. He answered without turning back, "I found her."

"I see that, Romeo. That's not what I'm asking."

Ben still kept me pinned down and tilted his head slightly.

"Dammit, dammit." He let me go and moved back out of the hole.

I quickly followed after him. When we got to the opening, I saw a very unhappy Paul.

"We need to talk."

CHAPTER 28

Visitor

Ben didn't look at me as we followed Paul back to Cheyenne's house. Paul disappeared through Cheyenne's back door without saying a word to us. Ben kept his head down and kicked the dirt. We both were guilty.

Cheyenne came out all dressed up in a sunflower dress and fancy flats. I was going to compliment her attire but she was crossing her arms with a tightness to her posture.

"Ben and Téa, you are both pretty much adults. I shouldn't have to advise you on these types of matters. However, you both know how important keeping with tradition in matters of relationships between a Watcher and Protector is."

She eyed Ben as she continued, "Son, you of all people should know that most of all."

Ben ran his hand through his hair. "I know. I don't know what got into me … "

He turned and looked at me then back at her, "... I messed up."

"The locator tactic should take no more than five minutes. Watchers consistently find their Protector in two minutes. Paul said it took you right at five minutes to find her. That's not good, Ben."

Ben replied, "It *is* getting harder to sense her."

Then, a young man came out of Cheyenne's back door. "Tota, you have a phone call." He handed the phone to Cheyenne.

"Thank you." Cheyenne looked away from us and put her attention on the caller.

"Hello. Yes ... really? ... send him in."

She hung up the phone and addressed me now, "Téa, it seems you have a visitor."

"Who?"

"You'll see. They're coming around now. We'll have to finish this conversation later. But Téa ... "

"Yes, ma'am."

"Remember it takes a team. You have to trust that we know better sometimes."

I nodded, but wasn't sure if I agreed. However, in this new world, I had to admit that I didn't know everything. Not even a little.

As I stood there waiting and watching the uncomfortable faces all around me, my heart started to race. What if it was the foster care system? Did someone turn me in? Could they take me away or even take away my new gift? Is that even possible? I heard Cheyenne and Ben conversing for a few moments and wondered if it was about that. But Cheyenne promised that I was a part of this family now. Would she go to bat for me?

I continued to stress about who it was that was coming for me until I heard a familiar voice.

"Téa?"

I turned. "Tommy?!? What are you doing here?"

I walked up to him. I wanted to hug my friend. But was I still mad at him?

Ben walked in closer. "Everything okay?" Ben asked and seemed a little uneasy.

"Yes."

Cheyenne spoke, "Téa, you do, in fact, know him?"

I was dumbfounded. "Yeah, from school. Everyone, this is my friend, Tommy. I've known him for years but ... Tommy what is going on? How did you find me here?"

Tommy had on his usual name brand clothes and pristine hair. He nodded at everyone and then reached out a hand. "Téa, can we talk in private?"

I was a little scared. There were too many of these strange things happening. "No, you can tell me here."

He lowered his arms. "Kiki told me where you were when I checked in on you at Tacky Tacos. She said you called to take off work for family at this reservation. I tried calling your cell."

"Cell service is spotty out here."

"I figured. That is why I drove up to check on you."

This is freaky but great. "Why would you do that?"

He looked around at everyone and then back at me. "We're friends. It's what friends do."

"Well, I'm glad to see you. But ..."

I dropped it. He did drive a long way. And for some reason, I wanted Ben to see and know that. Why?

"How long can you stay?" I asked, grabbing his hand. That was when I noticed Ben frown and leave abruptly. Success!

I turned to Cheyenne. "Can I show Tommy around?"

She gave me a hesitant nod. "Sure."

"Lead the way," Tommy said and squeezed my hand.

I took him to a small red barn just a few hundred feet from where Ben had just found me. I couldn't help but look over to the spot where we'd been enthralled in each other's lips. I shook my head to maintain my focus on Tommy. We sat down on the cool sand with our legs stretched out. The sun was just overhead shining brightly enough to light the neighboring trees around us into a bluish green.

Tommy still had the hood over his head and his hands were now back in his pockets. He was very reserved today, I couldn't say that I blamed him. He wanted answers, but did I owe them to him? I didn't know what to say or where to start. I knew this conversation would be awkward, so I just sat and watched the blue jays and hummingbirds wiz by the barn.

"I'm sorry to drop in on you. I was just worried about you."

He looked over at me and his usually dark green eyes were catching flecks of the sunlight turning them into a sapphire green. My friend was a good looking guy. That was never one of his shortcomings. However, his constant need for perfection was.

"Thank you."

He threw a pebble down the hill in front of us. "How long do you have to be here?"

"I don't know. Maybe a few more days."

"This is odd. Is it some kind of spring break vacation?"

"Maybe. Why are you all of the sudden so protective? And to drive all the way out here." I was flattered all the same.

He shrugged. "You left without telling me or Anna. Listen Téa, again I'm so sorry about what I did."

He was referring to that social media post.

"You shouldn't have done that."

"But you don't think you're beautiful. I wanted to show you from the comments and attention how wrong you were."

I inhaled a deep breath. "Still Tommy, you know how private I am. I hate social media, selfies, and all that crap. But I'm flattered all the same."

He smiled simply and put his arm around me. "You know we go way back? That's why I've always looked out for you, I guess."

"I know. How far back exactly? Fifth grade, right? I just remember seeing you here and there in class through the years. We weren't always at the same school. Depending on which foster home I was in."

"Wait. Fifth grade was as far back as you remember? You don't remember the night my adoptive mother brought you home from the hospital? You were around eight years old."

I bit the side of my cheek. "Hospital?" Flashes of ambulance lights came to mind.

"That's right, Sarah. Mrs. Patterson was Sarah. The night that tall man brought me there. She was there comforting me."

He nodded. "Yeah. She cared for you and your mother in the hospital after your father was killed. I met you later that night. Do you remember that?"

I looked up at him. "No. I can't believe I never realized that. She was my first foster care rep."

Tommy plucked a weed. "She had just taken me in that night too."

"Really? I didn't realize."

"And then we started school together. Parson Elementary."

Ms. Smith and her scary long ruler came to mind. "Parson Elementary? I remember some of that. I guess I have known you longer than I thought."

"You were in and out of different schools. I can see how it would be tough to recollect everything."

I became curious. "What all else do you know? Do you know about my father?"

He bit his lip. "I don't know all that. She didn't tell me anymore."

"Tommy, I knew you were adopted. I just guess I never asked about what happened to your parents."

"Drug overdose. That's all I know."

I looked back at the barn and shook my head. "Sorry. Us and our crazy lives, huh? You turned out better than me." I nudged his arm. "All high society."

"What?" he asked and straightened his sleeve where I wrinkled it with my hand.

"You know what I mean. But it was good that you were adopted by a rich family. You always had to wear and have the best!"

"I value order, rules. It doesn't have anything to do with money."

"Yea, right. I'm glad you're here, though."

He leaned back eyeing me. "Really? The one that never wanted help or anyone hanging around you. I thought you'd berate me, not be happy to see me. But I'm glad you've forgiven me. I'll never do that again."

He leaned back on his hands. "We've gotten in several fights through the years. The older you get, the more hard-headed you are towards me. I was always the one to hold a grudge for too long, not you."

I laughed. He was right. I stood up and gestured him to follow me to my temporary living arrangements. We passed Shia who was doing some afternoon yoga. She popped up and smiled. "Who's this?"

"Shia this is my friend from school, Tommy. Tommy, this is Shia."

They shook hands. Shia tapped her foot. "I heard about you and Ben. Wanna talk about it later?"

Tommy frowned. "You and Ben?"

"Nothing, just broke a rule or two. Nothing big." I told him and responding to Shia, "No, I'm good. But thank you."

"No problem." She smiled up at Tommy. "How long are you staying?"

He paused. "Actually, I don't know. I'm just glad my girl here is okay."

Shia's eyes lit up. "Your girl?"

I shook my head. "No, it's nothing like that."

I took Tommy's hand. "Look, since you drove all this way you should stay the night at least."

Shia jumped in, "That's a great idea. I'll go get the key to our other empty cottage. He can stay there."

I smiled. "Shia, that sounds great. Thank you!"

CHAPTER 29

Stirring up Pain

I walked through the forest after settling Tommy into one of the other cottages by mine. It felt good to take a walk alone. The wind picked up and followed me to an opening in the tree line. I sat down next to a patch of blue bonnets and ran my hands over the top of each blooming beauty. My friend Tommy was here. I was actually a little excited. It felt good to forgive him, too. And we were more connected than I originally thought.

I closed my eyes and thought of my parents. Those were the happiest days of my life. Even though, I couldn't remember first meeting Tommy, I could still remember very vividly how I lost my parents. It was a freezing cold night. The coldest it had been in Houston in twenty years. We had lived in Brenham at the time, but my father's work had us in Houston often. My mom was so excited because we were going to stay at the finest hotel there for the weekend. My father had just closed a big deal with an oil contractor and we were going to celebrate when he got back from his meeting.

"Téa, baby, hand me my phone charger," my mom said and smiled at me with her ruby red lips.

"Yes ma'am." I went over to her smaller suitcase and pulled it out of the small pouch. When I returned to her, she was deep in thought.

"What's wrong?"

She flinched at my voice and shook her head. "Nothing honey. Things are great. Now, turn around and let me brush your hair before dinner. We're going to your dad's favorite restaurant."

"That Japanese place?"

She giggled. "Yea, that one. Now, Téa you have to keep your hair brushed."

"So it will look like yours?"

She sighed behind me. "It already looks like mine, but how a person presents themselves to the public is how they are perceived. No matter how smart, talented, or rich you are, you will look like a bum if you don't keep good hygiene and care about your appearance. Understand?"

"Yes ma'am. Ouch!" She had just gone through a huge tangle and my tender head was screaming because of it.

"Hold still."

"It hurts, mom."

Ding. Ding.

"Hand me my phone, Téa. I just got a text."

I ran to the night stand between the two queen beds and grabbed her phone. Then, I heard a knock at the hotel room door.

"It's daddy!"

"On text?"

"NO! He's at the door! Can I get it?"

Mom got to her feet and her navy dress pants fell briskly over her white pumps.

"Coming!"

She opened the door to our room and let my daddy in. He came in looking absurdly handsome in his grey suit.

"Our reservations are at six. Are y'all ready?"

"Yes, sir," I said running up to him.

My mom smiled over at me. I smiled back. My little brother, Bryce, grinned too from over his Nintendo DS. I loved that little guy. He was going to be my sidekick, like Patrick. I was going to be like SpongeBob. I had big plans for us. We were going to rise from the ocean and save the world. We at the restaurant before dark. As we were walking across the parking lot, I got a really strange feeling before the chaos began.

All I remembered afterwards was screaming and being thrown to the ground. A huge man picked me up and brought me to a truck. His truck's cab was warm. Whimpering came from the front seat of his truck. It was my mom. Her hair was matted. She lifted her hands to cover her face, and I saw the blood.

"Mom, are you okay?"

She didn't answer me. The tall stranger opened the door again and handed me a bottle of water.

"Here. Drink this," he said kindly.

I took it from the dark skinned man. My mom slid over to the window and glared up at him. "Where is my husband?"

"I'm sorry," he told her, and his strange colored eyes caught mine. "Young lady, it is all going to be okay."

"Bryce, where's Bryce? My brother!"

The man shook his head. My mother started sobbing profusely and asked, "They took him, didn't they? Is that what I saw? I know I saw them take him! How long until the police get here? How long?"

The rest seemed like a blur until we got to the hospital and a tall lady came to sit by me. She sat with me for a few hours. She had a

*floral smell and wore pearls. When she brought me chocolate was when
I finally spoke again.*

"Hi."

She smiled, "Hi, Téa. My name is Sarah."

"Nice to meet you, Sarah."

*Over the next few weeks, I stayed with her. She brought me to visit
my mother at the Rusk Mental Hospital. I screamed and cried every
time I had to leave my mom when visitation was over. I didn't
understand it all, and I never got to see my brother again. Happiness,
as I knew it before, was all gone.*

"Téa."

A whisper woke me from my thoughts. Only wispy trees
danced around in the breeze on all sides of me.

"Who's there?"

No response. My stomach growled, but I ignored it. I
still saw no movement but the rustling of the leaves on the
ground. I moved to stand and wiped my hands on my pants.
After standing there for a few minutes, I decided that I must
have imagined the voice. I wasn't ready to go back yet to my
room for the night.It was a nice and warm afternoon, and I
needed more peace. I headed towards the creek thinking
about my memories. Suddenly, Ben popped into my mind.
Him and our erotic encounter in my hiding spot from
earlier.

When I walked through the bushes, I saw ... Ben.

He was standing in the deeper part of the creek with
water up to his waist. I froze and watched. He was bare
from the waist up and had his back towards me. The
tendons in his shoulders and arms poked out as he stretched

them behind his head. I shivered thinking about how *that* man could like *me*.

The sun came out from behind the clouds and shone a bright hue over his golden skinned body and black hair. I had been around many boys before, but never looked at them the way I was looking at Ben in that moment. I was a goner.

I took a few steps backwards and he turned to look right at me. His torso made a perfect, beautiful *v* into the water. What was I thinking? I forgot that he always knew where I was. I let out a quiet, "Hi."

He smiled funny at me.

"What are you doing out here?"

He had an incredulous stare. Was that embarrassment? What does he have to be embarrassed about? "Um, nothing. Just getting some fresh air. It was a warm day, and I thought the cool water would … ummm … help my thoughts."

I started walking towards him. "What thoughts?"

He looked at me dubiously. "I said personal." Then he turned back away from me.

I got bold. "Hey, don't turn away from me. I open up to you and you to me, remember?"

"Not on things like this, Téa," he said over his shoulder.

I took off my shoes and stepped into the water. Pebbles scratched at the pads of my feet. "We need to talk anyway. Come here so I don't get too wet."

He ignored my request. "You come to me."

I pointed out across the water. "Out there?"

"Yep."

"I don't have a bathing suit on, Einstein."

"You don't need a bathing suit. No one is around, especially not your lover boy, Tommy. I saw you leave him at the cottage."

I got furious. "He's not my lover boy."

I stepped back out of the water and took off my jacket, jogging pants, and shirt. I was down to just a tank top and yoga shorts. I briskly waded out into the frigid water before he could turn around. I sunk in the water not far behind him.

"We've been friends for years."

I moved slowly in front of him. The water was to my ribs.

Ben moved in closer. "Okay ..."

"I swear." I shrugged. "So you talk about me to your friends?"

"Like who?"

"Rob."

"Is that a crime?"

"No. I just don't understand why."

"You fascinate me."

I froze. "Why?"

"Everything you've been through yet you still look out for others."

"I thought you said I didn't care about saving anyone."

He didn't reply. The fish began to jump around us and leave me momentarily distracted. Ben's heavy eyes were on me again. "I didn't expect you to come all the way out here. Now, you're too close."

"Too close?"

He ran his hand over his face. "I'm supposed to remain at a distance from you unless we're training."

"Oh. That's right, we got in trouble."

"You can say that. Now, I've been given rules in regards to you."

I wanted him to reach out and touch me anyway. I craved it.

His eyes bounced around me and back over to my face. "But you're like a drug to me now."

In my head I was screaming, *you to me*. But I knew it was wrong.

"What are we going to do about it?" I whispered. His wet torso and hair … oh geez, he was a gorgeous specimen of a man.

He got right up to me and leaned over sniffing my head and down my neck. I closed my eyes and tilted my head for him. I wanted to run my hands up that strong chest he had planted in front of my face.

"How far is too far?" I could barely ask.

He whispered into my ear, "I don't know."

"And I really fascinate you?"

"God yes."

Before I could say another word, he picked me up. I wrapped my legs around his waist as he kissed me again. His lips were laced with carnal need.

"I just don't know. I don't know what to do, Téa. And then you come out here," he said between kisses. "I was trying to get away from you. To have space. To get you out of my head. Just when I get relief, I sense you again and there you are." He pulled back and held my face with his thumb dragging across my bottom lip like he liked to do.

"We are in our own private hell, aren't we?" he said. "I know I can't have you. Help me fight it."

His pleading eyes threw me over the top. I shoved his hand out of the way and grabbed the back of his head to kiss him again and again. I couldn't stop. The water started to get chillier as the sun hid back behind the clouds, but I didn't want to get out. I wanted these moments. Nothing was going to stop me from having him. I had never felt that good with anyone before. God help us.

CHAPTER 30

Not Without Me

Training resumed over the next few days. It was more physical than mental now. I was getting a lot quicker and more confident. I was even getting almost as good as Ben. Today, Ben and I did more laughing than sparring, though. Around noon, we stopped to rest and have a roast beef sandwich and grapes. I sat there on our picnic style blanket watching a few ants try to climb onto our blanket in search of scraps. Ben was laying on his side with a wistful expression on his face.

"You look beautiful," he told me.

I retorted, "I'm sweaty. No way."

"I don't think you could ever not."

"Haven't we established that I'm not comfortable with compliments?"

"No," he sounded amused. "But why?"

"Because I'm not used to getting them," I replied nonchalantly.

"I may have to change that."

"Ben, what did you give Cheyenne when we first got here?"

He looked oblivious.

"Okay, I followed you into the woods when you told me to stay in the car. I followed you to Cheyenne. I didn't hear anything." I lied.

His hand brushed at the blanket. "You're so full of surprises." His eyes looked off distantly. "It was nothing. Just something my dad wanted me to give her."

I rolled my eyes. I felt like I got the brush off. "So, tell me about your dad."

His voice held an edge of derision now. "Good ole dad. What can I say? He turned his back on his tribe." His brows lifted and his lips sucked in.

I nodded. "I heard a little about that. Why?"

Ben shrugged. "After my mom died, he lost faith. He felt we were fighting a losing battle. He wanted what he thought was a better life. I guess what I'm trying to say is that he wanted out of the trenches. He wanted nice things and a nice life. He was tired of sacrificing."

"And you?"

"I thought he was a coward. I resented him … "

His voice trailed off, "I resented him for a long time."

"But he's your dad. I'd give anything to have my dad back."

Ben studied me. "I know. He's not all bad. After my mom and sister died, it was just really hard for him. He leaned on me a lot. I did the best I could to help him, but I was mad too." In the sunlight, Ben's eyes showed more of the caramel flakes. I could get lost in them while I caressed his smooth golden skin, his jaw with small stubble now showing, and his delectable earlobes that he started rubbing while I watched him. What I'd love to do to those ears.

"How's Tommy?"

I frowned. "How's Chloe?"

He reached over and grabbed a ripe grape.

The unspoken agreement hung in the air for a second. "If you have to know, he's fine. I talked to him some more last night."

"I know."

I grabbed the last grape shoving his hand out of the way for it. "Of course, you do. Then why ask?"

Ben's white shirt showed every contour of his arm and chest muscles. I didn't know why I felt the need, but I wanted to be wrapped in those arms.

"He's staying longer than expected."

"Yea, he's having some truck problems."

"Truck problems, huh?"

"Tommy's just a friend, Ben."

I laid down beside him with my head under his chin and breathed in his closeness. I shivered as I lifted my arm over him.

"What's wrong, baby?" he asked just above a whisper.

Did he just call me baby? My heart was singing!

"I don't know, weak moment."

In a chivalrous act, he pulled me in tightly. "I like it when you need me. Tell me what is wrong."

"So, fighting these aliens … will it ever stop?"

His breath brushed a few strands of hair on the top of my head. "I don't know. Depends on if all the Epex come."

I absorbed his words. "Then, I'll just have to be ready."

"Just you?" He squeezed me tightly again. "Typical, but that's what I love about you."

I froze. He said the *love* word now too! What was he implying?

"What do you love about me?"

"Bravery. You think you can take on anything. But your flaw is you also have trouble believing in others."

I tensed in his warm arms. "What do you mean?"

"You have to get to a point here pretty quick where you will rely on another person to help you. You cannot do this alone. Other people are capable too."

I took in a breath. "I know. I'm trying. Just a lot of let downs in my life. I generally don't like people."

"Because of foster care homes?"

"Definitely that and also because of what happened to my family?"

"I heard a little of that. I'm sorry."

Ben lightly pushed my chest to lower me to the ground on my back. I felt his fingertips trace along my jaw. I sucked in my bottom lip. "My brother is still out there. It was always a dead end with police. But I know he's still alive. I gotta find him one day."

Ben now played with a few strands of my hair. "I'll help you when you're ready."

"Ben?"

"Yes."

"I want to know more about what it's like to be an Aepi. How y'all are actually able to survive underwater."

He smiled with just his lips. "Maybe I can show you."

"Show me?" I asked while letting his finger snag my bottom lip and make its way down my neck. It felt heavenly.

He said, "Yes," and lowered his head to brush my lips with his. I reached up and grabbed the back of his head to kiss him harder. He pulled away a bit and just stared into my eyes.

"You are so beautiful."

I smiled as he came down and kissed me again.

CHAPTER 31

Two Starfish

The next day, we headed in Ben's Audi back down South. We passed Houston and traveled down Interstate 45 to Galveston Island. He guided me to a boat the tribe owned at the Sand Dollar Marina on the bay side. It was a nice sized boat, about the size of two SUVs. Ben went to start it at the center console in the middle while I sat on a padded bench seat in front of him. The white fiberglass interior of the boat reflected the sunlight into my eyes making me squint up at him while he went over safety protocol with me. He laughed and handed me a pair of black sunglasses and a hot pink life vest. I watched him put away the bottled waters and Popeyes chicken in the ice chest before he we finally got to head out.

When we exited out of the murky waters of the bay and into the open ocean, what immediately hit me was how vast it was out in the Gulf of Mexico and how small I was compared to it all. I closed my eyes to feel the salty air brush my skin and sing across my ears. Amazing, that was what I called peaceful.

Ben watched the depth finder on the boat closely before stalling it out about two miles from land. He tossed the anchor out and fidgeted with some gear in the deck box. A huge shipping barge trudged by overwhelming me. Men of all different ages stood on that ship's deck waving at us. Another barge followed behind the first but with a French flag flying.

"That's cool."

Ben looked at what I was looking at. "International shipping goes on through this channel."

"Why are we stopping here?"

"Showing you ...our ship is down there." He tilted his chin to the water below us.

"Your spaceship?"

"Yep." He brushed off his hands. "I'll show you." He walked to the side of the boat and stretched and took off his shirt.

I jumped up.

"Wait! Swimming? Out there? I didn't even bring a bathing suit."

"You wanted to see how we lived underwater."

"I thought maybe just see *above* the water."

He smirked. "That doesn't make much sense."

Ben took off his shorts.

"Wait, that wasn't a bathing suit?" I asked.

"Swimsuit? No, we don't swim in anything."

"Nude? You swim nude?" I asked breathlessly.

He laughed and turned around continuing to undress. My mouth gaped open. I had to take my own hand to close the darn thing shut! Right in front of me was the backside of the most beautiful, male body I had ever seen. He dove gracefully into the shimmering water. When he came back up, Ben swiped his hair and winked at me.

"Your turn."

I hugged my stomach. "I told you, I don't have a bathing suit. And Ben, I can't swim!"

"Can't swim? You grew up by the Gulf of Mexico."

I tossed my cell on the deck cushion.

"Hey, don't laugh. Look, I never had anyone teach me. Besides, I'm not part mermaid."

He sighed. "We prefer to be compared to Earth's dolphins. Mermaids are a myth."

"Well, it wasn't long ago that aliens were just a myth too."

Ben shook his head. "Come on. I'll teach you. It's not hard. I won't let anything happen to you, I promise."

He lowered his voice, "Now, strip."

"Strip? Hell no!" Heat flushed through my body.

"Come on. I'll turn around."

He did, but I wasn't about to swim in my birthday suit in the middle of the ocean. But he insisted and spoke over his shoulder, "You wanted to do this. And every pore on your body has to be openly exposed to the water in order to breathe. That's the only way this will work."

"Okay, okay. Give me a second."

I decided I could undress out of my shirt and shorts but that was about it. My shirt was almost off exposing my pale pink bra when all of the sudden, I lost balance and tumbled off the boat. I fell into the salty water in ALL my clothes. Including shoes! When I came up for air, Ben was within arms reach with a twinkle of mischief in his eyes.

"It's not funny," I told him.

"Here, let me help you, clumsy."

He pulled my shirt off, and I immediately sunk down to my neck to hide. Then, I worked on my shoes and shorts myself while he held me under the arm. We threw the soaked clothes into the boat.

"Now, since you have the seed, you will be able to hold your breath for about thirty minutes on average."

"That long?! No way."

"Yep. Just follow my lead. If it gets too much just point up, and we'll come back up. Got it?"

"I guess."

"Okay, baby, let's do this."

"Baby again … ?"

Before I could finish he was pulling me down. I took a huge breath and let him drag me into the abyss of the ocean. As he was pulling me down farther and farther, I started to panic. After a few minutes, I was shaking uncontrollably. I wasn't coherent.

I felt us stop swimming down and the movement of being pulled towards something made me slam right into Ben's arms. The light squeeze reminded me of who had me so tight, so secure. The tension in my shoulders eased and my body relaxed. A gentle touch moved up my back and to my shoulders. Exploring lips grazed my ear and I tilted my head back.

Through the beams of the afternoon sun rays, I could make out Ben's frown as he studied me. He kissed me and I let out the breath I was trying so hard to hold. Salty water moved in and out of my mouth with the feel of his tongue. He pulled away.

"See, you're breathing the water, aren't you?"

I couldn't really hear the words, just felt them. However, bubbles were dancing off his lips.

When I went to try to answer I noticed the exhilarations of heavy fluid flowing down my esophagus. I nodded. I couldn't believe it. But this was what it felt like to be an Aepi. All worries left me, and I could now see the expanse of the ocean all around. He let me float off to the side just holding me by one hand. I gingerly unclasped my previous fisted hands and felt the force of the water push against it.

"Ready?" he asked, and I nodded.

We dove farther down until I could make out some kind of structure through the blurriness ahead. Long beams came up from the ocean floor with a huge platform resting on top. The decay and ocean life growing all over it became more apparent as we swam above it. Ben guided me through an opening on the vessel. We dodged a few yellow fish and fragments of coral on the way in. The entry was very narrow, but I held on to his hand trusting him completely.

After a few corridors, a huge room greeted us. It wasn't like alien ships I had seen in movies. It was almost elegant. Lovely. I touched the walls and felt a velvety texture. Colors other than grey appeared under my hand and spread out below my palm. There were no tables or chairs either. I guess I shouldn't have expected that.

There were belts or restraints attached to the sides where the passengers must have secured themselves during flight. My eyes trailed the roof until I saw something carved and layered in golden colors. It looked like a mural in the shape of Triton's staff. The similarities were eerily close. I rolled onto my back, the best I could underwater, and studied it like a child.

Ben touched my hand. "We've been down here almost thirty, we had better get back up."

I nodded and let him pull me back out of the ship and up towards the surface.

When we got back above water, I was already wanting to go back down. Then, the realization hit me.

I swam.

I swam without knowing how to. Ben climbed the boat ladder with ease and then helped me up. The warmth of the setting sun was so welcome. Ben set out a few towels after putting back on his pants. Thank God. I covered up in one of the towels and laid beside him.

"Ben, that ship was beautiful! I've never seen something so amazing."

He rolled on his side and smiled. "I have."

His salty lips met mine as we kissed and touched among the seagulls and passing barges until I laid back to comprehend what all I had just seen. I didn't know how long I laid there in the shelter of serenity listening to the waves under the boat. I was about to fall asleep when Ben tensed up. I turned to face him and noticed a strange look on his face.

"What's wrong?" I asked.

His stare was distant with a fearful expression. He didn't answer back.

I went to sit up, when his eyes suddenly darted back to me and his face relaxed. I touched his cheek.

"You okay?"

He looked confused and in a weird daze. "Yeah, I'm fine. Hey, it is getting late. Plus we still have so much training left to do."

I let my shoulders sag. "I guess."

He jumped up and reached out his right hand to help me up. "Time to head back."

CHAPTER 32

Times a Tickin'

"Téa, wake up!"

There was a pounding on my door the next morning. I couldn't make out who it was, and I had momentarily forgotten where I was. I rolled over and got to my feet. Ah, that's right. I remember returning to the house after yesterday's swim and feeling extremely exhausted.

I was happy and confused, and maybe a little embarrassed for acting so vulnerable in Ben's arms underwater. I'd entered my quarters last night, grabbed a package of lunch meat from my mini fridge and made a sandwich for dinner. I remembered sitting at the round café style table by the bay window, watching a group of kids come into view and kick a soccer ball. They were about the age that my brother would have been. Tears had soaked my eyes. I went to sleep thinking about my feelings for Ben, the miraculous spaceship his ancestors came here in, and about my missing little brother.

"Who is it?" I asked when I got up.

"It's Carson. Ben sent me. There's trouble."

I made it to the door as quickly as I could and opened it to a distraught Carson.

"What kind of trouble?" I asked and let him in.

"Someone broke through the checkpoint. Des and Ben are on it. Ben sent me to watch over you until he came back. They think it's not human."

"He did what?!? It's my job to fight them, not him! Take me to him now!"

Carson shook his head. "No. I'm under strict orders."

"Get out of my way, or I'll plow right through you."

"No!"

I walked up to him and barely gave him a shove that sent him falling into my clothes basket. I leaned over him.

"Now, point the way."

"Dammit!" He got up off the floor shaking his head. "I can't just point. Come, get in my car."

I followed him to a red Mustang and got in. Carson started the engine and we headed down a winding road towards the huge wall. It reached up twice higher than the houses in the compound. He parked the car a good distance away from the wall and ushered me to what looked like a look out point.

He started up the ladder first with his rifle on his back. I had no choice but to follow. When we got to the top, the vastness of the Indian's lands was revealed. It stretched farther out than I was expecting. I thought I would just see a relaxing stretch of farm land and trees when I looked down, what I actually saw took my breath away. Coming over the wall were droves of people covered in blood and throwing themselves to the ground to get to us. I stepped back in shock and felt Carson grab me.

"See?" he said and settled himself in a sniper like position with his rifle. He began firing.

"Epex? All of them?" My chest tightened.

"Yes," he said between shots.

"I thought bullets didn't hurt them."

"They don't. It's just to slow them down enough to give our guys a fighting chance."

I started to make out the fighters below. They were outnumbered. I couldn't tell who was who, until Des came into view because of the quickness of his knives. He was dropping the enemy in greater numbers than the rest. The others were holding their own but nothing like the Protector. I scanned back and forth looking for Ben until I spotted him drop two Epex simultaneously off to the side.

"Thank God."

I took off back down the ladder with Carson yelling behind me. He didn't chase me though because I could still hear the popping sounds of his rifle. At the bottom of the stairs, I glanced around for the entry into the valley where the fight was taking place. Shia came into view running by me.

"Shia!"

"Téa, go back. You're not ready."

"To hell with that. How do I get in?"

She stopped and turned back towards me tossing me two Protector daggers.

"Here! They need all the help they can get. I've never seen anything like this, Téa."

With that, she took off with me following behind her. We got to what looked like a gate and was immediately let in by one of our guards. He closed the gate right behind us and yelled, "Good luck."

I was about to respond back when something had dropped me to the ground. My knives were gone, just like that. I wiggled under its thrashing and screamed. When I realized it was in the form of a man, I did the only thing I knew to do. I kicked it in the privates. Thankfully, it worked!

It gave me enough time to scurry back over to where my daggers fell. I grabbed them both just as the creature was on top of me again.

"Big mistake," I told it once I saw his weak spots. I thrust the knives right into the sweet meat. He fell on top of me.

I rolled him off and jumped to my feet as another Aepi was fighting the two closest Epex. I didn't recognize him, so I ran passed him hoping to find Ben. Another few Indian or Aepi soldiers were gaining ground against the last of the Epex that came over the wall when something slammed into me again. I couldn't believe I didn't see it. I rolled over and as he was coming down on me, I stabbed him with my daggers.

This time I was not able to hit the right spot. And this Epex was way stronger than the last. He pinned me in place and leaned back just enough that I could see a grey face and huge teeth. It took me off guard giving him the advantage to turn my head and expose my neck. I screamed.

Suddenly, his weight was off me. I went to get up and saw Ben throwing my attacker to the ground. Ben stabbed his daggers into it and killed it instantly. Ben came over and stood above me glaring at me.

"You were supposed to stay behind the wall where you are safe. Why don't you just listen to me?"

He turned quickly and took out the next approaching
Epex with one quick move.

I yelled back, "I am the Protector, not you. That is my
job. You have to let me do my job. If you can't do that, then
dammit Ben, you're in the way!"

I saw Ben's eyes get wide. "Téa! Behind you!"

I threw my body around with daggers at the ready, but it
was too late. This one was quick. He kicked me in the
stomach forcing my body to the ground.

Then, the alien stopped and smiled, "So, this is Téa."

Ben advanced and the combatant easily shoved him off
to the side. The Epex's evil eyes were on me again.

"Good. I've found you," he said while coming towards
me.

Ben had been knocked out from the force of the push
and blood was spilling down his face.

"Ben!" I yelled.

"I've been looking for you, Téa."

I stood back up glaring at him and positioned my knives
at the ready once I saw the creature's hearts become visible.

"Who the hell are you?"

"I'm your salvation, Téa. But you probably know me as
Borax." His voice was dark and raspy. It was so deep that I
thought it echoed all around me.

I stepped back stunned. Instinctively my guts churned.
No way that I could take him out alone. Ben was knocked
out, Des was still pushing back the alien line, and there were
no other Indian/Aepi soldiers around.

Borax knew it and smiled again. "Don't fight me, Téa.
Come with me. You are more like me than you know."

I shook my head and felt my sweat drip down my shoulders. "No, I'm not."

"Yes, you are. The anger in you is so palpable. The human race is so much like Epex. Come, let me show you."

He was up close now and sniffed my skin giving me chills. "Together we'll take this whole planet."

"No!"

I stepped back again and looked over at Ben. He was still not moving.

Borax noticed. "Do you think you can have him? Is that what I've been sensing? You will never have him as long as you are a Protector. But if you come with me, I'll make sure you can. You can have your Ben, and I can eventually have the world."

He spread his arms out giving me a perfect view of his breadth and strength. He was huge, and he didn't bother to wipe his mouth from the blood of his most recent victims. Human and Epex blood, blue and red, was sprayed sporadically all over his face and arms.

"You're evil!"

He shouted back, "No eviler than the humans of this planet!"

I shook my head.

"Look at him, Téa. He is dying. I can make him feel better. The alternative would be that he dies. There is no way you can save him. There is no way you will survive against me. I've killed two of your fellow Protectors already, Téa. Let this go and come with me."

His arms were now reaching out towards me, and he did his best to look sincere. If it wasn't for the blood, his voice, and those monstrous red rimmed eyes, he could have looked similar to us.

"Two more seconds. Decide."

I looked around again. No hope. My survival instincts, that got me this far in life, kicked in. I knew what I had to do. I had to survive.

"Okay," I said and dropped my knives.

Borax clasped his hands in front of him then yelled out, "Mika and Atis!"

Surprisingly these two Epex came out from the compound behind me. They had been inside the whole time.

"Grab the man on the ground. Let's get out of here."

They did as instructed, and Borax took my hand. "I've been wanting you for weeks."

I followed along watching his two men pick up Ben. I looked at Des and the others still in major combat behind us. I was pulled into a crawl space hidden under the compound. It was wet and dark. My heart was going to explode out of my chest. I couldn't believe it had come to this.

When we got through the tunnel, there was a clearing in the meadow with two black SUVs parked off to the side. They were expensive SUVs and both had drivers at the ready. I saw Ben loaded into the back of the first one. Borax tried to pull me in with him into the second one.

"No! I want him with me."

Borax got low and into my face. "You don't bark orders. I'm your king now. I tell *you* how this is going to go."

Blood was still in his saliva and it showered my face adding to the red color growing up my neck. If I didn't hate him before, I hated him now. I promised myself years ago that I wouldn't be another victim to an evil man.

As my fear dissipated and in its place came good ol' anger, I knew I had to relieve it, or I WOULD EXPLODE. Anger surged through my veins quicker than it ever had in my life. I lifted my hand and did the last thing Borax ever expected. I slapped the crap out of him.

He touched his cheek with his meat hands and began to laugh. "Oh, I love a challenge. I'm going to enjoy tearing that thing out of you."

Then, he grabbed my hair and threw me into the side of the truck.

I spit at him. "Oh, you think that is all I got? That's just the venting of my anger. What comes next, is what I'm really capable of."

As he laughed again, clearly enjoying this, I felt the familiar movement of the ground under my feet. It moved like the dirt was shifting around in a circular fashion. It moved almost violently as my anger grew. Closing my eyes trying to meditate as Ben taught me, my senses were still able to clue in to my surroundings.

I saw Ben in the back of the truck surrounded by Epex. I saw the second truck with a driver and two more of the villains. I saw that Borax actually looked *scared*. Before I could gloat, I was being lifted off the ground and left hovering a few feet above small tornado created by the moving sand below me. Borax charged at me, and I lifted my arms to begin a spin in the air that felt as natural as breathing in air. My hair came loose from my ponytail and swirled all around my body aiding in the inertia of the spin.

Borax grabbed at my legs unsuccessfully giving me my chance to laugh. When I came back around facing him, I kicked him in the chest sending him a hundred feet away. Descending back onto the ground, I approached him to give him the final blow. My hands were about to target his kill spots without even the aid of daggers. Yet, it would be flawless. But Borax ordered the unthinkable.

"Kill the man! Kill Ben!"

Out of the corner of my eye, I saw hustling that sent my senses back to the truck that Ben was in. I stopped.

"Wait!"

"Wait? I'm tired of waiting, Téa. I see now that you are not what you seem. However, you have one huge weakness."

I looked back to the truck and felt my energy drain immensely. I couldn't even make out Ben's figure inside the truck now. Borax charged me again and pushed me to the ground. His strength was immeasurably stronger as he yanked my head to the side and thrashed into my neck. I fought with all my might to lessen the severity of the bite as my vision started to blur.

As if out of the heavens, someone crashed into my assailant sending him to the ground next to me. Covering my gushing wound with my hand, it was Tommy.

Tommy yelled out, "Téa, here!" and threw my knives to me.

I released my neck, caught the knives, and jumped on top of Borax. Before Borax could gauge what had just happened, I thrust the daggers up into his chest where I thought I saw his kill spots. His eyes rolled up into his head and his hands dropped by his sides. My body shook immensely as I took several breaths to calm myself after the ordeal.

I felt the blood from my neck continue to run down my chest. I had hardly any strength left so I just simply rolled myself off of Borax. I heard more yelling and thought I saw that Des had made it out there with us now. He was taking out two Epex that were charging after me and Tommy. I didn't remember much else but the smell of my own blood escaping as darkness took me.

CHAPTER 33

Connections

When I was conscious again, I still saw darkness. There were voices all around me, but I couldn't make out who the voices belonged to. I heard, "Téa, Téa," whispered around my head. I felt a warmth touch my hand. I imagined my mother kissing my cheek. My immediate thought was that I was dead.

Gone was the hope of seeing my family upon my death. Gone was the hope of being held by Ben again. I'd never again be able to smart off to him or feel his touch caress my body. The emotion of finally enjoying being wanted ... loved ... would never be felt again.

Suddenly, the sounds stopped. Everything went quiet.

I laid there in darkness hoping to hear something, anything. I must have eventually gone unconscious a second time because when I came back, I was hearing sounds again. But more familiar voices this time. I could tell one was Cheyenne.

She spoke low, "How is she?"

An unfamiliar male's voice spoke, "She's hanging in there. This dog that you say attacked her, he came really close to her carotid artery. I mean, it was crazy close. She has lost a lot of blood, though."

"I understand."

"We're keeping her sedated right now. Are you her mother or family?"

There was a pause. "Of course. This child is my daughter." Cheyenne replied and the response shocked my heart. "Can she hear us?"

"No. She is off in dream land." Retreating footsteps were heard next until a door opened and closed.

Then, I heard Cheyenne again, "Téa, I don't know if you can hear me. If you *can* hear me, stay strong. It's all going to be alright. We're here for you. We'll be here when you wake up. I promise you that."

I was still processing her words to the doctor. Here I was, almost dead, a useless Protector, but she was standing here claiming that I was hers. No matter how much I had failed, she was proud to say I was hers. Then, Ben's scratched up face showed up in my thoughts.

I wanted to cry out, "Ben!? Is Ben okay?"

But I couldn't move my mouth. I couldn't move at all. I drifted off again, as what must have been Cheyenne's lighter footsteps, exited the room as well. When I came back to awareness the next time, I still couldn't open my eyelids. The room was freezing. I felt something lift my hand slightly before it was placed back down by my side.

There was no mistaking his voice when he whispered in my ear, "Téa, come back. Come back, baby."

Soft pressure touched my lips, and I wanted to cry out, "Ben! Ben, I'm here. You're okay. I'm so glad you're okay!"

I couldn't move, talk, or touch him. I was being tortured, a prisoner of my own body. I couldn't stand it.

Ben's voice seemed quieter when I heard him say, "I have to go now. I'm sorry I can't tell you this when you wake up. But it can't wait. We both know this is for the best. I'm sorry, Téa."

I fought harder with my body. Willed myself to wake up, but I couldn't even open my eyes. The door opened and closed, signaling that he was gone. Ben was gone.

❋ ❋ ❋ ❋

There were warm sensations all over my body. Bright flashes surged into my bare eyes causing me to blink sporadically. Were my eyelids finally open? Movement by my side forced me to tilt my head in the direction of I thought I saw it.

I choked on my words, "Tommy?"

He leaned over and smiled. "Téa. I'm so glad to see you awake."

He was dressed in a green t-shirt and jeans like he always wore to school. Just a typical teenage boy. I questioned for a second if everything had been a dream, and if I was just back at school maybe having passed out or something. Had there even been an amazing relationship with Ben, our dishwasher at work? Tears filled my eyes as Tommy took my hand.

"It's okay. It's all going to be okay. You healed just fine. I'm here. Take it easy. You've been in a coma for two weeks."

I shook my head. "It was all real?"

His face was pallid. "What, the attack on the reservation? Yea, that was freaking crazy. Are you not remembering it all?"

It was real!

"What happened?" I opened my dry eyes wider. They stung.

"So, you know about them?"

"Oh yeah. I know everything now. Messed up. I even heard that huge one talk to you. In our language, too." Tommy stretched out his legs adopting a wide, open stance.

"You know I just learned that linguistically, these Epex monsters pick up on foreign languages ten times faster than humans. Oh and the other ones, these Aepi, they know the Indian, Spanish, and English languages? All of them."

He handed me a small plastic cup. "Here, you need to drink some water. You look bad."

"Well thanks. That's what every girl wants to wake up from a coma to hear."

I sipped the cool beverage slowly and felt the liquid slide down my parched throat.

"I don't care about all these dang aliens and their special abilities. All I wanna know is where is Ben?"

Tommy sat down on a stool next to me. His shoulders sagged. "We don't know. The Epex alien that got away, did so in the truck that Ben was held in."

"No!" I felt pain in my neck when I tried to lift up. "What? That can't be!"

Cheyenne walked in almost on cue. She came to my side and grabbed my hand. The new circles under her eyes made her look so much older.

"Téa. I'm so glad to see you awake. You did really well."

I pleaded. "We've got to find Ben. He was here while I was asleep. He talked to me."

She looked at Tommy and back at me. "Are you sure? Ben couldn't have been here. And even then, the doctor said there was no way you could hear anything under sedation. You were just dreaming."

"He is still alive. I know it." Taking a second sip of the water, I almost choked.

"Okay, if that is true. What did he tell you?" Cheyenne asked while taking my cup and pulling up my blanket up over my shoulders for me.

I started to feel like they were placating me. "He told me he had to leave me."

Cheyenne gave Tommy an unhappy expression and turned back to me. "I'm sorry."

I shook my head and the pain on the side of my neck radiated all the way around to the other side of my face.

"Borax. I killed Borax, right?"

She smiled. "Yes. After your brave friend here, Tommy, and the others attacked Borax's minions, a few got away with Borax's body in one of the trucks. But from what I was told, he was down with your daggers in his hearts. Good work!"

"And that was the truck Ben was in?"

Cheyenne answered, "Yes."

Tommy leaned in. "Téa, we will try to find him if that will make you feel better. But you need to get well first. Can we prioritize you right now?"

Hope.

Just that simple statement from Tommy helped my body to calm back down. "Yes, but then we find him. I know it is crazy sounding that I'm saying he survived, but I *feel* he really did."

Cheyenne rubbed my arm and smiled kindly at me. "I know. Now, for some changes. Ben told me about how you had been living on the streets. That stops now. The council has already met again and decided to purchase you a home close to your school and work. You will be able to finish school there."

I froze. Oh no! Now, Tommy knows I live on the streets, too. "I can't accept that, Cheyenne."

"We didn't ask you. We just did it. But it is under two conditions."

"What?"

"You keep in touch with us often. Also, Tommy and Carson will stay there with you to watch your back. They have volunteered to be the first members of your team."

"Oh, no. I'm not living under someone's thumb. And you know what? I never took handouts before. I'm not starting now."

"Téa, there are still some Epex that got away. Your Watcher is gone. You need to accept our help. Carson is a skilled soldier and Tommy's bravery brought Des to you which saved you from Borax. Did you know that your friend, Tommy is also a skilled tech? It really does take a team."

She stepped closer and spoke harshly, "You cannot live on the streets anymore and do this job! You have to do this ..."

He simmered down and continued, "If not for all of that, then at least for Ben."

I glared at Tommy. "Do you understand what you just signed up for?"

"A purpose," he said no longer being comical.

I was shocked. I didn't argue. I knew that stern look from him. He wanted to be better than his deadbeat parents. Maybe he thought that this was his chance.

"How can I go back to life as it was before, Téa, now that I know what I know?"

I relaxed my head on the cool pillow. "Will I have privacy?"

Cheyenne answered, "Oh yes, it is actually a duplex. The men will stay in one unit and you in the other. The center will be shared space for equipment and training."

I lifted up. "A duplex with extra space?"

"Oh yes, the entire thing is over six thousand square feet."

"Are you kidding me?" I asked and started working on moving my legs. The sooner the better.

"I can't wait for you to see it. Right now, Carson and a few others are fixing it up for your homecoming."

"Fixing it up how?"

"Let's just say they are rigging it up right." She grinned and patted my hand.

Thunk, thunk.

A knock at the door brought my attention forward.

"Ms. Téa?" A doctor walked in and approached me. "I'm Doctor Vansant. You gave us all a scare. How are you feeling?"

I nodded. "Okay, I guess. Maybe a little nauseous."

"I expected more. You lost a lot of blood from that dog bite. I'm prescribing you some pain medicine. Are you allergic to anything?"

"Not that I know of."

His white doctor's coat was slightly wrinkled. And the bags under his eyes, confirmed his tiredness.

"Good. I'll also add in something for your stomach and a little something to help you sleep. I'm glad to see you are doing better. You look good. I think I can get you checked out of here sometime tomorrow."

"Thank you," is all I could manage. I was still incredibly tired. "Doctor, you look like you took a double shift."

He looked up from his pad. "We've had a lot of action here lately."

The doctor tore the prescription off and handed it to me with a grim smile before heading out with Cheyenne right behind him.

"Where are we?" I asked Tommy.

"Houston Methodist." Tommy sat down on the stool next to me again.

"Back in Houston?"

"Yes. Hey, Kiki is chomping at the bit to know where you are. I wanted to wait until you were awake and aware before she came barging in."

I looked at Tommy pointedly. "Thank you because I don't want her to know the truth. She doesn't need to know about aliens and all this, okay? I hate that you are involved now."

A beeping sound came from his pocket. He reached in and checked his phone. "You know, I can really be of use to you with all this."

I smiled. "Yes, you are the macho football player and all. Just joking. I know, you can."

There was movement in the hall. Almost like people were running. Cheyenne came back in with a pensive expression. She walked up to me.

"Go on back to sleep. When they bring dinner, we'll wake you."

"Thank you, Cheyenne. I know I haven't seemed appreciative towards you."

"No, don't do that." She patted my hand making me smile again.

Tommy poured me some more water from the plastic hospital pitcher.

"You do need rest. We have lots to do."

School entered my mind. "School? How many days have I missed?"

He looked at his phone a second time. "Just four days since spring break covered a lot of the time that you were here, but they all are excused. Cheyenne took care of that."

"How?"

"Connections," she said and winked at me.

"Oh, thank goodness. I can't be turned into the state. I just can't."

"We're not going to let that happen. Now, get some more rest."

Her face faded from view as I closed my eyes again. It felt good to rest. It is crazy how the body needs so much rest after a traumatic event. I accepted that fact and laid there letting slumber take me away again.

CHAPTER 34

New Beginnings

"This is our place?" I asked standing outside one of the biggest houses I had ever seen next to Ben's dad's house. I was still in denial and waiting for the other shoe to drop. No way, they did something like this for me. No one had ever done anything like this for me.

But then again, I was their new warrior. So as long as I fought, I would live nice. However unpleasant that thought was, I decided now would not be the time to debate it. I wasn't just doing this to help our world; I was doing this for Ben.

"This is it!" Tommy said standing next to me. "Let me show you around."

He seemed to really be enjoying his new life and responsibilities, too. My only requirement for him to work with me was that he stayed behind computers. Under no circumstances would he be able to go out in the field.

The stone structure in front of me was an older home that looked to have been renovated *into* a duplex. But boy did it have such character. The tall wooden front door in the middle greeted us with pale green shutters and square windows. When we entered into the veranda, two staircases were the first things to see. One going to the south wing and the other to the north wing.

They were ornate with rod iron spindles and solid wood banisters. Up above and two stories tall, was a huge skylight shining down on two large magnolia trees that were planted inside the house. Passed the staircases was a huge shared open living room with just one couch and a television.

"It's perfect!" I said.

"You haven't seen it all."

I followed Tommy to the back where the shared kitchen was located. It was a nice sized kitchen with old world dark cabinets and butcher block countertops.

"Come see your unit," he said and grabbed my hand to bring me back to the first set of stairs. We ran up the stairs like we were kids on a playground set again. At the top, there was another entry style door but of normal size. It opened into a smaller living space.

"This is cool."

Tommy squeezed my hand. "You like?"

"Yes."

"Back down stairs off the living is the equipment and supply rooms. I'll show you that in a second. But the plan is to turn one of your closets into a weaponry area as well."

"A supply room? Weaponry?" I pivoted on the balls of my feet taking it all in.

"Oh yeah and we're still stocking it."

"Oh. Okay."

He led me through my living room to a huge master bedroom. It had a four post bed, huge windows, a sitting room, and best of all ... a private bath. I ran and jumped onto the bed. Laying out like a snow angel, I stretched until my neck wound started to hurt again. Tommy stood above me with a charming smile and rubbed the back of his neck.

"What?" I asked giddy.

"Nothing."

I realized my shirt had lifted up just enough to expose my midriff. I quickly pulled it down. "Sorry."

"I'm glad you're happy."

I would be if I could find Ben, marry, and live with him here.

Marry? What the hell.

That word actually exists in my vocabulary? What would I do if I couldn't find him? I jumped from the bed deciding I would dwell on the what ifs later and ran to the bathroom. It had a marble clawfoot tub that looked to have just been cleaned. And man, it looked so inviting.

"Tommy, can you give me a few minutes?"

He smiled and rubbed his jaw, "I sure can."

I closed the door on his retreating form and skipped to the tub. When I first turned on the water, it had a rusty tint to it. After a few seconds, in ran clear. I plugged the tub up, got undressed, and stepped in. It was just what I needed after such a traumatic event. The warm water filled up halfway, and I sank back into it without going too deep that I got my throat bandage wet. The setting sun was coming through the stained glass window and dread hit my gut.

When will I see Ben again? I whispered into the air, "Ben," and floated there thinking of only him. I wanted to tell him all about the house, and how I had dreamed of living in a nice house my whole life. I wanted to share more of my hopes and dreams with him. Then, I imagined his face above mine and his hands running through my hair like he liked to do. I turned my head and willed myself to feel his lips move down from my earlobe to my neck.

"Ben," I whispered again and felt a tear run down my cheek. My heart was broken. I never imagined a man could get that close to my heart.

The rest of the duplex was shown to me the next morning. What I liked the most, besides my bathroom, was the garden area out back. I pictured all kinds of things that could be grown back there from blue bonnets as ground cover to pear trees along the sides. I'd have rose bushes down the middle and even bird baths one day. First I had to go to college and get a better job to buy these plants. I wasn't worried. For the first time in my life, I really thought this dream was obtainable.

Tommy came outside with me carrying two cups of coffee. He tried to hand me one.

"I don't drink coffee," I told him and stuck my tongue out.

"You don't yet. I'll drink both."

For some reason the hot beverage looked really good. "You know what, let me try it."

It was bitter but he put just enough sugar and creamer to offset that. Then, he sat beside me on the garden bench looking out at everything.

"You like?"

"Yes!" I set the cup down on the little round table next to us. "So, the supply room. What all is going in there?"

"Carson is ex-military. I don't ask questions. He seems like he knows what we need. You will have plenty of daggers."

"Of course."

"He's also installing some state of the art monitoring system. I'll be able to monitor the grounds from our unit, the kitchen, and he's planning on putting a monitor for you in your unit."

"That's a good idea."

Tommy kicked the dirt under us. "We're lucky he wanted to come. He's been a vital player on the reservation. Word is that Carson was originally hired to do reconnaissance for them because of his skills. After a while, he signed on permanently for the cause."

"Thankfully, Borax is gone."

"Yeah, the other Epex soldiers won't be as organized now. They'll be easier to fight."

I nodded my head in agreement.

"On a lighter note, school is tomorrow. Ready to go back?"

"Yes, I am. I talked to Kiki this morning. I am still welcomed at work, too."

Tommy sipped his coffee. "Good. I got a job, too."

"Really, doing what?"

He crossed one arm over his chest. "Academy Sports."

"Moving on up, huh?"

"We need the money. My adoptive parents liked the idea of me getting out on my own, so they wouldn't have to be responsible for college expenses and health insurance."

"That's some love, isn't it?"

"They're good people, just money strapped."

He looked over at me with solemn green eyes. "I can't believe you've been living on the streets."

"Tommy, you know I don't like people feeling sorry for me."

He moved his feet across the dirt in an uncomfortable manner.

I raised my coffee cup and noticed it had a winking emoji on the front of it. "Well, here's to life as alien hunters."

He laughed again, and we tapped our coffee mugs together.

CHAPTER 35

Family

"Ms. Jolly, I was told to come see you," I said walking into the dreaded assistant principal's office.

"Yes, hun. Shut the door." She was wearing funny looking glasses today with big black frames.

"You like my new look?"

I wasn't in the mood for small talk. I was nervous. "Yes, looks great!"

She leaned over her desk. The phone began to ring, but she ignored it.

"I got some paperwork in from the foster care system wanting to confirm your graduation status."

"Yes! Everything is going as planned."

"Good."

Ring, ring.

Her desk phone kept going off distracting me. "Is that it?"

She smiled and picked up the handle on the phone before dropping it back down to hang up on the poor soul that was trying to call. "I'm just so proud of you graduating a year early. What colleges did you apply at?"

"Originally, Texas A&M. I changed my mind. I decided to stay closer, so I've applied to Sam Houston and Rice University."

"Rice? That is great!"

I got curious. "Why do you care so much?"

She got somber. "Oh, Téa. I've been caring about you for a long time."

I wanted to say something about Ben since she was his aunt and all, but I was interrupted.

"Hang on, hun. Mr. Magee!" She shouted into the hallway.

The poor freshman came in looking scared. "Yes, ma'am."

"Have a seat. I need a word." The woman ruled the roost here.

Then, she pointed to me with a movement signaling that I could leave. "Okay, you may go now."

"But … "

"Go, we're done," she said with such finality that I was taken aback.

I smiled and jetted off. Maybe it's a good thing that I dropped it. I'll come back in a few weeks maybe. Maybe she'll know something.

I went to last period in great spirits. My hair had been dry all day, my clothes weren't wrinkled, and I wasn't late for a single class. My new life was amazing. I still had trouble sleeping at night. The sounds of the house were different than what I was accustomed to.

Or maybe it was the lack of sounds. I had gotten so used to my mind drowning out the noises of the streets. So much so that I didn't realize I had always had a mental buzzing in my head that had become like a lullaby for me on high traffic nights.

Every class I had gone into had open windows allowing summertime to protrude in. Everyone was getting giddy. I left the school with Tommy after eighth period in anticipation of a fun-filled weekend.

I actually said excitedly, "Where was the latest Epex activity?"

Tommy pulled his truck onto the road. "Since we found the ones responsible for the girls' deaths in Sugar Land, I got a text that a girl in the Woodlands area has gone missing. I'm not sure if it's alien or not."

It had been several weeks since Borax and his army attacked the reservation. We lost quite a few of ours, but we took out almost all of his army. Consequently, activity had seemed to die down lately. At first, I had vengeance on my mind. But I had replaced it with enjoying my new cozy life. I also replaced my therapist with friends. I didn't have any secrets anymore. Tommy and Cheyenne knew pretty much everything about me now. It was nice to know there was someone I could talk to that really knew me.

After school every day, I physically and mentally trained. Carson was adamant about the advancement of my fighting skills. The new levitation ability that I discovered while fighting Borax was sure to come in handy again, too. Every training, we tested and pushed its boundaries to see how much higher I could go. I was the first Protector who could ever do that!

Tommy and I pulled into the driveway of Ben's father's house in the Heights. The same one where I encountered my first alien. It was the first place I wanted to go when I got out of the hospital, but it was fruitless. No one had been home. Neither the day that I left the hospital, nor numerous attempts every week there after that. When we pulled in this time, I saw a BMW.

Tommy touched my leg after he parked. "Don't get your hopes up, okay?"

"Too late," I said and headed straight for the front door.

Someone opened the door after just a few knocks. He stood about Ben's height but wasn't as brawny as Ben. He was in an expensive suit and had his hair cropped short.

"Can I help you?" he asked.

Tommy came up behind me and put his hand on my shoulder for support. I looked up at the man. "Yes, my name is Téa Lane. I'm a friend of Ben's."

He slanted his body away slightly. "Bidzill?"

"Yes."

The older man stood there for a second thinking. Besides the greying at his temples, he looked a lot like Ben. His nose was prominent, and he had the same angular face with a square chin.

"Come in, Téa."

We followed him into the house that I hadn't stepped into since I was with Ben. The fountain caught my attention like it did the last time. My heart ached when I looked over at the kitchen table Ben and I had sat and ate our first meal together. I missed him so much. He's got to be alive. He's just got to be.

I looked back to the man. "I guess you're Ben's father?"

"Yes. My name is Buchannan Rainwater. You may call me Buck."

I smiled up at him. "It is so nice to meet you."

He looked between us two. "How do you both know my son?"

I answered, "We worked together."

Buck gave me a dubious look. "Where?"

"Tacky Taco's off Major."

"What is Tacky Taco's?"

I fought the urge to laugh. "It is a restaurant. It serves tacos."

"My son works *there*?"

"He did for a short amount of time."

"Oh."

"Mr. Rainwater, Buck, when was the last time you saw Ben?"

He then got somber. "It has been a while."

"So not recently?"

My hope was fading.

"No."

We all just stood there not sure what to say next until Buck spoke again, "Bidzill is my only child. He's been through a lot. If you see him before I do, please tell him I love him."

"I will," I said, fighting the tears building in my eyes. "Well, I guess we'll go. Thank you for your time."

"Thank you. I'll show you out." He walked us back to the front door and waved at us as we walked back to

Tommy's truck. When I looked up again, Buck had already gone inside.

Suddenly, it hit me.

"Tommy, Ben kept an Epex trapped in a room in that house. How come he wasn't worried about his dad finding it while it was still alive?"

Tommy thought for a second. "Maybe his dad isn't telling us the whole truth. But you know if Ben is alive, he's doing this so you are at your full potential. Carson told me about your forbidden relationship with Ben. I would do the same as Ben's doing. Staying away. You know, if he is still alive. Hang on to that, okay? It will get you through."

"I know."

I took a deep breath. I knew no one believed me. As time passed, I started to not believe myself either. I was about to load into Tommy's truck when I saw it. Laying on the passenger side windshield wiper was a bluebonnet. I got closer to it to pick it up and noticed that it was tucked under the wiper.

It couldn't have just blown onto the glass. I smiled big and spun around looking all over the driveway and landscaped surroundings. There were no movements and no sounds. Perfectly lining the outside of the driveway were some tall bushes that someone could easily hide behind and not be seen. I walked over to them to look on the other side and found nothing.

Tommy yelled out from behind me, "Téa! What is wrong?"

I walked back to the driveway and looked up at all the windows facing the driveway. I saw no movement or figures.

There was one window that had the curtain slightly moved to the side. Someone could easily peer out from there.

Tommy walked up close to me. "What is it?"

I sniffed the flower and smiled again. "Nothing. It's all good. Ben loved blue bonnets."

"He did?"

"Yes, he did."

"Ready to go?" Tommy asked after smiling at me.

"Yes."

Tommy walked back around to the driver's side and got in.

I looked up at that same window and nodded. In my heart, I believed the flower was from Ben.

❈ ❈ ❈ ❈

We headed back to our house, no ... duplex fortress, thanks to Carson. There was now an electronic bolting system on all exterior doors, cameras all around the perimeter and within, and the equipment room became an armory.

When I walked into our shared living room, I saw Carson on the couch messing with some tech gadget.

"Hey, Téa."

Uncle Bob, who I had convinced to come live with us, was walking around in circles in the kitchen. I pointed to Uncle Bob but asked Carson, "How long?"

"One hour or so."

"What can we do?" I begged. "I know you were in the military, Carson." Uncle Bob paid us no mind.

Carson sighed. "Téa, he needs treatment for his PTSD if you want him closer to normal."

"He'll never go for that. I think he's already done all of that."

Carson sat back into the couch motioning towards Uncle Bob. "Then, don't worry about those things. That's how he copes."

I looked back into the kitchen noticing someone made enchiladas. My stomach growled. "You're right. I just worry about him."

Carson looked over at Uncle Bob. "You know, he doesn't bother me. Actually he's been a big help with the combat data."

I set my things down and watched Tommy go into the kitchen. Tommy had a gentle way with Uncle Bob too. Uncle Bob really responded well to him.

"So, enchiladas! Who cooked?" I didn't think anyone here knew how to cook.

"Pam. She went back out again."

"Yum."

Unlucky and Pam were also our new house guests. She still liked to take long walks during the day with her dog. She just took them in a different park now. The duplex had two rooms off the kitchen that Pam and Uncle Bob slept in. However, Pam stayed in there during the day if she wasn't taking her walks. She liked being alone. I was looking over at the open door to her room that revealed an empty space within. I got worried.

"But, Pam's not here."

Carson kept his eyes on the machine. "Uh, no. She took her walk late today. The dog is already back, though. But you know, he usually out runs her home?"

I looked through the kitchen window after Tommy and Uncle Bob sat down for a snack and saw Unlucky chasing his tail outside.

"Good."

"So what's on the agenda for this weekend?" Carson hollered from the living room.

I sighed. "Prom."

"Eww … prom? Have fun," Carson told me and got up to bring his device upstairs to his unit. It must have been ready to test.

CHAPTER 36

The Serpent

The dreaded prom took place at Brenning's Country Club the next night. Kiki was so excited that I was back at school and work, but more so because I was going to prom with her. To be ultra-rebellious to her mom, as usual, Kiki turned down offers from guys and asked me instead. Well, she asked me several times to the point of begging. She knew how much I hated being around people, especially crowds of people. When she told me I owed her because she covered my shifts at work, I had to give in.

We arrived in Carson's Mustang and both went in together. Kiki was wearing a pale blue sequined gown and had her hair pulled up in a bun. After a bribe, she convinced me to wear her burgundy gown from last year's Mardi Gras Debutante Ball. I agreed until the night of the prom when I put it on. It was cut low in a *V* at the top and hugged my curves from top to bottom. I had trouble walking in it because of its long mermaid skirt. My legs felt like they were taped together.

In fact, when I was leaving the house, Carson made fun of me in it. Thankfully, Tommy kept his mouth shut. Tommy looked like a deer in the headlights when he first saw me in it. The boys were making me extremely uncomfortable before I had ever even left. Tommy hugged me and reminded me to dance all night for him. He was staying active tonight with Carson. Since lots of schools were holding their proms this weekend, it was a good idea to monitor police scanners just in case.

"Tickets please," Ms. Jolly said.

She was the greeter at the door of the country club, and she appeared to be lavishing in it. Every time a boy went in, she gave him a short talking to about what he better not try to do later. All the boys knew her already. They just walked by saying things like, "Yes, Ms. Jolly", "Got it Ms. Jolly", and "Thanks, Ms. Jolly."

"Here you go." I handed her mine and her eyes lit up.

"Téa, you look beautiful. One thing missing."

She stood up and moved over to me with bobby pins in one hand. Then, she took my wavy hair and pulled it all over to one shoulder. Next, she pinned it in place on that one side. With a big smile, she took a pic with her phone to show me how I looked.

"See, even more lovely?"

Lovely was not an adjective that ever described me. I wasn't comfortable going to prom in the first place and now I really didn't feel comfortable in my own skin. I thanked her and turned to Kiki.

"Thirty minutes, and I'm out of here."

Kiki smiled. "I know. Let's get our formal picture, dance one, and taunt the boys for a few minutes. Then, we go home."

I rolled my eyes as I followed her in. The dancing area was lit up with LED Christmas style lights everywhere and strobes that were blinding me. The music was playing too loud and the crowd was insufferable. I didn't think I'd make it thirty minutes.

After taking our picture with the photographer, we went out to dance to an up-tempo song. I didn't dance. I had never danced. I had no business dancing. I kind of just swayed with my trapped legs until the wannabe belle of the ball, Lexi Sampson, came around with her new beau, Kyle.

"Kiki, Téa, don't y'all look nice. No dates?" The Sampson toad grinned with pleasure.

I had a new found confidence, because of what I had been through, that I jumped at the opportunity.

"Oh, Lexi, I thought you wanted to come with Tommy?" She frowned.

"Oh, that's right, he turned you down. Good thing Kyle was still available."

Lexi shook her head and grabbed Kyle's arm to walk off.

"Love it. I loved every minute of that," laughed Kiki. "So how did Tommy convince you to let him be your roommate for college?"

I didn't answer. I just looked at my phone.

"Hey, do you think he'd go out with me?"

My jaw dropped. "Tommy?"

"Yeah, if you're not interested in him."

I smiled. "He is a little too much of a gentleman for you."

She slapped my arm. "Hey! I'm starting to warm up to nice guys. I've been talking to Ralph."

I thought of Tommy's smile. I'd hate for him to lose it. But Kiki's a good girl when she wants to be.

"I'll ask him."

"Yes!" she exclaimed and moved her hips with the music. "Hey! Time for a drink?"

Margaretville started playing on my phone telling me Carson was calling. "Hang on," I told Kiki and stepped away.

I answered, "Yes, sir."

"I'm hearing on police scanners that someone was speeding down highway 59 carrying two young women. The officer pulled him over and when the perp got out, he snapped the officer's neck."

"That's *not* normal. But I didn't sense anything. Are you sure this is what you think it is?"

And I would have sensed it. My abilities to hear threats started when I got out of the hospital. They came on like echoes. It was really weird. Sometimes they were crystal clear and sometimes they were mumbled. However, I hadn't heard anything in weeks.

"I don't know but still, this is not normal. I'm sending you license info and directions. The police are engaged in pursuit."

"I'm on it."

I rushed over to my selfie-addicted friend, Kiki. She was taking another pic with Ralph.

"Kiki, I've got to go. Do you want to stay and I come back for you?"

Ralph blurted, "I'll take her home."

"Is that okay?" I asked her when her smiled disappeared.

She looked back and forth between us. "What the heck, goodnight Téa, love you."

With that, I was wiggling out the door. Lots of eyes were on me, but I didn't care. I was above the social scene. I heard Ms. Jolly in the background too but kept going. I got to the car and realized that I did not have a change of clothes. I guess I thought that since it had been quiet lately that surely nothing would happen tonight. Surely Tommy and Carson were being too paranoid. Well it was happening. I swore and then ripped the entire bottom of my skirt off from my thighs down.

"Man, I hope this dress wasn't too expensive."

I grabbed my weapons out of the trunk and turned on the scanner when I got in. Sure enough, it was big news and surprisingly the chase was coming in my direction. I skidded out of the parking lot as a couple of teens yelled at me to slow down. I did what I'd always wanted to do and never could, I flipped the rod at them.

A few turns, and I was on the highway. I could see the police cars in the distance, so I knew the killer was not far from being on me. When I saw the black Kia, I swerved at him pushing him onto a feeder road. He slammed into me and almost made me lose control of the car. I got back on the road and put the Mustang to use like it was meant to be used. I gassed it and caught up to the assailant in no time. This time, I slammed into him harder causing him to lose control and go off the road. My heart dropped. The girls.

I pulled up next to the flipped over vehicle and the police cars started coming down the feeder. I didn't have much time. I rushed to the driver's side hoping it was just some druggie until I saw the serpent's mark. Should I keep him and question him, or finish him now? I looked at the unconscious girls in the car with brutal marks all over their bodies and my decision was obvious. I stabbed the alien just as he was coming to.

I pulled my daggers back out of his chest, pulled him out of the car, and lit him up on fire. Then, I ran back to my car and gunned it right before the police rounded the last curve.

"Carson!"

"Téa?"

"I killed him. Geez, that was definitely an alien and he had the serpent mark."

"I figured. How are the girls?"

"Good. But Carson … "

"Yes."

"You know what that means?"

CHAPTER 37

Surfacing

"Téa, you're not going to believe this. Another one!"

Carson had greeted me at the door as soon as I got back. I followed him to the monitoring room where Tommy was.

"No way. I didn't feel anything again."

Tommy countered, "There is a lot of buzz on the police scanners about something going on in West Chase."

"What kind of things?" I eyed the twenty-four-inch monitor.

"Two girls missing, ages thirteen and fifteen."

My heart sank, "That young?"

"Yes."

"So, two in one night?"

"Something must be going down," Carson said behind me.

"Are you thinking what I'm thinking?"

"Yea, they're no longer being patient."

I took in a deep breath. "I'm on it."

I ran up to my room to change into my black combat gear and then to the equipment room to grab my weapons. If it *was* an Epex, I wouldn't have much time before he finished them both off. Tommy stayed behind as Carson and I took off in Carson's Mustang. I thought he'd flat a tire the way he was skidding out of the driveway.

"Slow down, you'll hurt Baby!"

Baby was what he named his car. He loved that thing. I'm so glad he hadn't noticed the smashed passenger side yet. Or maybe he did. We sped around to the area in question and saw the police lights immediately. Hiding my weapons under my jacket, I approached the scene. The first cop I came to had a badge that said, Pearson. I got my lie ready.

"Mr. Pearson, that is my cousin's house. I can't get ahold of them by cell."

He answered back, "I'm sorry, but this area is closed right now."

"Was there a fire?"

"I can't disclose that, ma'am."

Then, he looked up at the tall business building down the road and turned away from me to listen and speak to dispatch. For any normal human, talking low would have worked. However, for me, I heard every last word the police officer tried to hide from me. From the look he gave that building and after hearing him tell the dispatcher, "I've got eyes on it", that was all I needed.

I took a few steps back and then ran down the road to the back side of the building the police officer had drawn attention to. Policemen were already starting to rush over to the building now. I whispered into my com, "Carson, I'm at the Nestle building. The police are already here. I'm climbing."

Carson came back over. "Roger that. Tommy is pulling up the building plans now."

Behind the bushes up close to the building yet out of sight, I closed my eyes and began to feel movement under my feet. When I opened my eyes, I was already two stories up. Flawless. However, that was still only how far I could get without help. I grabbed the side of the building and began to climb.

Carson came back, "What floor, Téa?"

"I don't know yet; I haven't felt anything. It's odd."

"Be careful."

I kept climbing as my hand slipped twice from my sweaty palms. I was able to catch myself on the ledge and keep going. I still felt or heard nothing. By the time I got to the sixth floor, I was spent. I pulled a dagger out and broke the window.

The alarm didn't go off. I was home free. I jumped through the broken window and immediately felt something. It was like an electrical surge had run all through my body. I took off running towards the direction of the source. When I got to the elevator, I heard, "Floor ten."

I pushed for floor ten and started going up. Pulling off my coat, I grabbed both daggers and had them at the ready. As soon as the elevator dinged and the door opened, I was confronted by not one but three Epex. They didn't bother hiding their true from. They came at me like vicious animals. I wasted no time getting the first one down.

In two movements, I pushed the daggers in and then back out ready for the second. However, he kicked me to the ground. I paused. It actually afforded me time to take in my surroundings. Both came at me quickly. I got up and jumped on top of a set of filing cabinets and ran across them knocking the cabinets on the assailants like dominoes. At the end of the row, I hopped down and came on top of the first alien. His kill spots were easily visible. I took him out and turned for the other. But, that was when I heard a voice from behind that I didn't want or expect to hear.

Borax.

"Téa. So nice to see you—"

Before he could finish his sentence, I attacked.

He blocked me once, twice, and then a third time before he managed to get a kick in on me. I fell to the ground again but this time dropping my daggers. Then, it got worse. There were sounds everywhere that were deafening. All of them came out of the woodwork, alien after alien. I took off running for the staircase, broke through the door, and rushed down the stairs.

"Carson, come in, Carson."

"Téa? You okay?"

"There is a whole dang army up here. Why didn't I sense that?"

"Where are you?"

"I'm heading down the stairwell. I dropped my daggers. I need another set."

"No ma'am. You're not going back in there. How the hell did he still have that many? I'm calling Des."

I was already short of breath and took the next steps two at a time. "That may be a good idea." Then, below me I heard movement coming up the stairs my way. "Someone is coming up."

"Duck into the offices on that floor."

"Right, I'll get out through the window," I reasoned.

"What floor are you on? I can give you cover."

"Fourth."

I busted through the door into the new set of offices and saw that there were no windows. "Carson, there are no windows," I whispered into my com.

He came back, "Crap, Tommy says that's an old Bell building."

"What does that mean?"

"The first few floors were the original building for the phone company. They are made to be bomb proof. No windows on purpose."

"What the hell?" I asked and heard the stairwell door open. Borax knew I was there. I ran down passed a few desks and hid behind a tall cabinet.

"Any ideas, Carson?"

"We're working on it."

Borax's voice echoed through the offices. "Téa. You underestimated me and overestimated yourself again."

I wiped the sweat off my lip and leaned against the wall catching my breath.

His grating voice came across again, "I guess a Watcher would have come in handy right now. Too bad yours was, how I should I say it, worthless."

I paid no mind to his words until he said, "You want to know what really happened to your parents?"

I slowed my breathing and poked my head around the cabinet. I couldn't see anything. "You're lying."

He continued, "Oh, and your brother. See, it's all their fault."

"Enlighten me," I wiped my lip again. I knew if I kept him talking it would buy me time.

His voice seemed closer now. "Aepi. Aepi and their thieving. They—"

Boom! Boom!

Something loud blew ahead of me pounding out my ear drums. Debris was falling from everywhere. The smoke made it hard to see and my ears were ringing. A bomb? Maybe two?

Carson came over my com, "Téa, what's happening up there?"

My head was spinning from the force of the explosion not ten feet from me.

"I don't know. Bombs just went off on this floor." I started coughing.

Then, I saw him.

Between the flames and shattering glass was Ben stabbing aliens one by one. Each one was injured from the detonation and couldn't heal in time to react. I stood to go help and my head felt like it was cracking open. Ben ran over towards me.

"Téa, are you alright?"

I had to squint my eyes to make sure it was *really* him. "Yes. I thought you died or that you left me."

"No time to talk now. I'm here. Borax got away. He went back up to the tenth floor."

"I'm on it!" I stood ready to go. To finish this.

Ben grabbed my arm. "Listen. Whatever you do, don't charge him when you get off the staircase. Stay up against the wall until he comes to you."

I eyed Ben strangely.

"You got it?"

"Yes!"

"Then, go. I've got these."

I took off running for the stairwell and made my way up to the tenth floor. Ready to bust down the door to kill myself an Epex, but I stopped. Ben said not to charge in. I opened the door and moved flat against the wall when I heard him.

"Good, Téa. I was planning on killing this young thing if you tried to attack me."

Borax was standing farther into the room with what looked like the missing thirteen year old girl braced in front of him with his mouth at the ready on her neck.

I looked to the young brunette and put my hand up. "It is going to be okay."

Borax was clearly enjoying that. "Don't lie to her. You can't help her. If you come after me, I'll kill her and then you." Then Borax's eyes turned beady red like last time, and he spoke in an even more menacing voice causing the poor girl to shiver, "I will enjoy it."

"Stop! Take me instead. Look, I'm removing my weapons."

I pulled them off and tossed them to the side. The young girl was extremely frightened and started screaming.

Borax yelled at her, "Shut up!"

"Now, I'm going to slowly come your way defenseless. Let her go and I will be yours."

Borax smiled. "Yeah, I don't know about that. I thought we already tried this."

"I give you my word."

"The word of an angry little human."

"But you want me."

He sneered. "Yes, I do. That's what all this was for tonight. To get you."

I thought my knees gave out on me. "What do you mean? Was this some kind of a trap?"

"Why do you think you couldn't sense me? There are too many of us. It clouded your senses."

"What do you mean? What's going on?"

He grinned and the girl kicked.

I swallowed my fear and steadied my legs. "Just let her go."

He smelled the young girl's neck. "Your life for hers? Someone you don't even know. Someone that I picked up outside a mall shopping for expensive clothes to wear at her expensive mansion. These are the people you cannot stand!"

"Do you want me or not!?"

He laughed. "Deal." And he shoved the poor girl down towards my feet.

I leaned over to her. "Take the staircase all the way down to the first floor. There are police out there. Go!"

She took off through the door, and I could hear her little feet running down several floors. I returned my focus to Borax. I put my hands in the air and walked towards him.

When I got within arms length of him, he grabbed me and twisted me around for easy entry to my neck.

His mouth hovered right above my skin as he said, "An Aepi Protector killed my best soldier. But that same worthless Protector couldn't even save your father."

Borax squeezed my arm with nails tearing through my skin. "But he made off with your brother. Too bad you'll never see your brother again."

I was confused.

"Now, I will finish what I did not complete the last time, and this will open the door to the Epex taking the whole galaxy."

I cringed as I remembered the way his teeth felt in that same exact spot weeks ago. The skin was still tender to the touch. My vision blurred as I thought of that young girl running down the stairs to safety. If this was the end, I was actually glad I was at least able to save one. This, I realized, would be a death that was worth it. I closed my eyes and let myself go.

Then, I felt it.

Something altogether different among the tranquil. I was suddenly freezing. Was I in the morgue now dead? Was I locked in a drawer after being turned into ashes? I opened my eyes, but surprisingly did not see anything but *fire* everywhere. It was swirling around me like a tornado. I lifted my arms to watch it dance off my skin. That was when I noticed that my arms could move freely.

I looked around and saw a few desks in the distance catching on fire. Was I still in the office building? I turned and saw Borax on fire behind me.

"You witch!" he yelled at me.

He was moving sporadically trying to come back at me. I dropped to the ground and crawled back to my daggers. As soon as I grabbed them, he was on top of me. The fire slowed him down, but it wasn't burning quick enough to stop him. I kicked him off and jumped up heading towards him. He was trying to get up, I stopped right above him.

"We're not in any rush. This time I will make sure I correctly hit my targets, a-hole!"

Just as I saw them, I aimed precisely into the kill spots and this time, hit them dead on. He fell back and continued to burn.

CHAPTER 38

Unconditional Love

" … the heroic efforts of a young lady that has not yet been identified. Mrs. Hensley is offering a $10,000 reward for the identity of the person who saved Kylie. Kylie is set to return to school next week to finish the last few weeks of school. Kylie, can you tell me what you are most looking forward to?" the news anchor, Gloria, asked.

The small teen's hair was brushed back into a headband showing off her struggling bubbly smile. She was having a hard time recovering from what she saw. I almost didn't recognize her. She had on a white blouse and floral pants that screamed girlie.

"The summertime! This summer, I will be going to horse camp to ride my first horse ever."

"Are you glad to be able to finish seventh grade with your classmates?"

"Of course. I never thought I'd see my friends again."

"Is there something you would like to tell the unknown girl that saved you?"

Kylie dropped her smile and looked up. With those solemn eyes, I recognized her instantly as the child I saved a few weeks ago.

"Téa, if you are out there watching, I wanted you to know that I owe you everything. Not just because you saved my life. But more so because you showed me that there really are unselfish people out there that will help others. Even people that they do not know. With the divorce of my own parents, I was really questioning people these days. You showed me that the stuff talked about in church is true. We *can* love each other unconditionally. Thank you."

Carson walked in. "Oh, turn that mushy stuff off."

Tommy glared at Carson. "That's the girl y'all saved."

"Not me. That was Téa and her new firestarter ability. We don't need thanks. It's our job."

I chimed in, "You're right, Carson."

Uncle Bob sat up in the recliner. "Téa?"

I cut my eyes over. "Yes?"

"Carson has been hogging the remote lately."

Off to the side of the room, I saw Carson break out into a silent belly laugh.

Uncle Bob knew it. "I'm just looking for permission to snap his neck."

I looked back and forth between the two. After just a little while of living close to them, I figured out how it worked with military men. Uncle Bob was in the army and Carson from the navy. Those two types didn't mix. If they weren't fighting over tedious crap like a television remote, then they were making fun of each other's division. I decided to pay them no mind.

Tommy on the other hand was always thinking we needed peace. Peace, perfection, blah, blah, blah. He didn't quite get it yet.

"How about we just get another television?" he asked me.

I turned to Tommy. "It won't matter. They will always find something to argue about. They feed off of it. It keeps them going."

Uncle Bob drew his black brows together. "Téa, you taking the side of the youngin over there?"

Carson pushed off the wall, put on his colorful cap, and went to head out the front door. "Well, she knows not to side with a crayon eater."

"Ha, Ha, pretty boy," Uncle Bob retorted because that was what the Navy called people who served in the Army. "Now go get us some chicken. I'm firing up the grill tonight. Oh and some premade sweet tea incase Ms. Pam isn't back in time to make some."

Carson saluted sarcastically, "Yes, sir," and headed out.

I stood up and made my way to the kitchen with my empty coffee cup in hand. When I got to the kitchen sink, I saw them. Blue bonnets. Ben must have placed them in a vase on my windowsill. I smiled and looked out the window. There was nothing out there but Unlucky barking at the neighbors.

Tommy came up beside me. "You want to train at the park today?"

I looked outside again. "Yes, it's a pretty day."

Tommy and I were set to graduate high school in two weeks. He was going to attend Sam Houston, and I was going to Rice on an anonymous scholarship. Usually I wouldn't take a handout, but I've changed a lot in these last few months. I didn't win at the State Science Fair after all, so no internship. However, Leroy gave me a raise at work. So, it was all good.

I was still planning on studying astrophysics, though. Funny, my whole life I thought I would one day meet aliens from another world. Here I was, fighting them.

"It is a pretty day." Tommy said to me. Tommy was just going to college to play football. His major was undisclosed. However, he got a full-ride scholarship because of football, so there was that.

I hadn't seen Ben again since that night he set those detonations off in that office building giving me the chance to chase after Borax. Not only was it good that the explosives were on a floor that was stable enough to handle them, but also because he saved my rear again. How did he know to set those and when? I got the feeling that his special abilities were more than just being able to track me down. Either way, it felt good to know that he was alive and watching over me.

It hurt to be apart from Ben, but I knew it was for the best for now. At least until more intel could come in on what all we were still dealing with. Borax had hinted at something I couldn't quite put my finger on.

I picked up a flower from the vase. "So you never told me how it was possible that Ben helped me in the building. Y'all told me he was taken from the reservation by Borax's men and presumed dead."

Tommy eyed the flower spinning between my fingers and smiled like he knew something.

"I don't know." He turned abruptly and walked out. Bad liar.

I poured out the rest of my coffee and grabbed my combat boots to meet up with Tommy. Uncle Bob waved at me on my way out as I waved back still thinking of Ben. Yes, it was a nice day to train and hope that Ben was watching me do my thing. Either way, I was realizing that I had loved these days with my friends. I also realized really quickly, that I couldn't do this job without my team or my Watcher.

It takes a village.

❈ ❈ ❈ ❈

For the next two months, there was radio silence. No abductions and no NORAD transmissions that stood out as extraterrestrial either. I began to think Borax's group were the only Epex and that maybe we were going to be safe. I also paid Cheyenne a visit in July after stewing on Borax's other lie. The one about my brother, Bryce, being taken by a Protector. Cheyenne denied it, and I believed her.

My little family and I started celebrating our birthdays together at Tacky Tacos with the other staff. It became a tradition. The only one missing was Ben. It has now been three months since I last saw him. I dreamed of him. Felt him close sometimes. I even tried to catch him once after I found the latest blue bonnets left for me after work. I couldn't see past the crowd. Just a figure with dark hair weaving through it and then he was gone.

For Uncle Bob's birthday in August, we opted to stay home and have a hurricane party instead. I made Uncle Bob a butter yellow sheet cake with Bavarian cream filling and simply wrote, 'Bob the Vet's B-day' on top. He got a kick

288

out of that. We were poised around the table, our misfit family, singing the birthday song and enjoying each other's company.

We were also watching the Weather Channel closely monitoring, Greg, a category four hurricane that skirted the lower Texas coast and was beginning to make landfall south of Victoria. That put Houston on the east side of the storm, the wet side. As the wind and harsh rain blew in, Unlucky scattered to Pam's room. The storm door on the back of the house slammed violently and our pendant lights blinked off and on. Carson took a bite of the rich cake and set his paper plate down.

"I'll go get the flashlights."

Uncle Bob touched my hand. "Thank you for this, Téa."

I patted his hand and heard another gush of wind. "No thanks needed, old man. Do you like the cake?"

He nodded and the lights flickered again. His dark chocolate face turned ashen. Both of us sat there flinching at the external noises. A few days ago the governor issued a mandatory evacuation and just roughly half of Houstonians heeded the request. But we did not want to go neither no matter how much we feared a repeat of last year's storm. Not when Borax's threat was still a possibility here. If Borax contacted other Epex, they would land somewhere around here. We were the first line of defense, and the only ones that could get a message out to the other Protector teams if an invasion occurred. Tommy walked back in with Carson and handed me a flashlight just as the lights went out permanently.

The howling of the wind outside had us huddled together under the dim light of the flashlights. Then, a huge sound boomed across the backyard followed by something slamming down to the ground. Tommy and I were up instantly and looking out the back door. Our eyes followed the moonlight around the yard. Something the size of a tractor with rounded edges and a red glow encompassing it was now where our tomato garden once grew. Tommy opened the door.

"Téa, wait right here. If a tornado could throw something that big, it could certainly throw you into Louisiana."

"No, sir. I got this."

I shoved passed him and was slammed with slapping rain that drenched me in seconds. The rain was coming down so hard, I couldn't see but a few feet in front of me. Just the outline of the object in question. When the wind blew again at probably fifty miles per hour, I lost my balance and landed flat in the mud. Tommy pulled me up, and I heard Carson yelling from the back door.

"You two, get back in here. I don't like it."

I stood back up with Tommy's help and we forced our legs to take the next few steps against the powerful wind. With Tommy supporting my right arm, I took my left and touched the material of the large structure that landed in my backyard. I froze.

"Tommy, this isn't metal. This isn't a tractor or a car."

Tommy pulled me back. "Not good."

Just as we were about to dash back to the house something yanked us up and smacked me in the head.

"Téa!" Tommy's yelling was the last thing I heard.

CHAPTER 39

Mistaken

Voices were speaking at low levels all around me. I opened my eyes. The room was not my room at the duplex. It had metal walls and no windows. Tommy was standing over me with a two inch long gash on his forehead. I sat up.

"Where are we? Are you okay?"

"What?"

"The big cut on your head."

He acted like he didn't know what I was referring to.

"That looks painful. It doesn't hurt? It's huge!"

Tommy frowned. "You don't remember, do you?"

"No." My own head was screaming.

Tommy's mouth opened slightly like he was about to say something. Then, there was a knock on the door next to me. In came an Epex. He didn't bother hiding his skin or purple eyes.

"Good morning, human."

"What's going on?"

The monster looked at my stomach. "What's going on? What's going on is you have something I want."

I hugged my middle. "I won't give it up that easily."

My breathing started coming faster. This meant that Borax's crew wasn't the only ones to find us. How am I going to stop them or even get a message out? I had to focus. My only concern now was taking out as many as I could.

I continued, "Either way, that seed you want has long been digested and the remains flushed down the sewer."

"It doesn't work that way. It's still racing through your veins," he said and his baritone voice shook the room. "And after we extract it, then we'll begin the annihilation."

I stood up unsteadily. "Good luck with that."

He smiled with vicious teeth. "Borax was weak. A worthless soldier because he was a greedy soldier. He wanted to have the glory of bringing the seed's powers home himself. Something about you had him a little worried, though. When the high council got his final transmission with Earth's coordinates, we couldn't believe it. Of all the habitable planets, Earth? The same measly planet that one of our ancestor's ships went down on a long, long time ago."

The Epex alien before me scratched at his prickly chin. He wasn't as huge as Borax had been, and he also had an almost human expression that crossed too easily over an otherwise terrifying face.

"Earth. If we only knew back then the opportunities it held, we would have had less losses against the last planet we conquered." He shook his head. "But now we'll have the seed's powers and a huge stock of female eggs. We'll take this galaxy and move on to the next."

He lowered his chin at me. "It will be an honor to tear all the traces of that seed from your worthless human body."

"Come and get it." I fisted my hands by my side. Then, more Epex came into the room. I couldn't deny, I felt nervous when I saw them all. I started weighing my odds.

He stepped forward. "I heard you can levitate and set fires with just your thoughts. This last seed you carry is a powerful one indeed. But there's no way to levitate in a room and we're prepared for your fire abilities, too. This is your last stand."

I closed my eyes, felt all the heart beats of the room's occupants. How many could I take out? A strange fragrance passed under my nose leading me to open my eyes again. There was smoke everywhere. It was blackening the entire room. I started coughing and watched as each Epex before me fell to the floor passing out.

A mask was shoved onto my head and over my face before I was rushed out of the room into a hall. I looked up. It was Ben who had pulled me out. I ran with him and we followed Tommy farther down. The three of us jumped onto a staircase and went down another hall until we found an open room to hide.

Ben yelled, "Exits are all blocked."

Both men barricaded the door as soon as we walked through to give us time.

"Epex are everywhere and are coming in fast," Tommy said and his eyes met mine. "Téa, it's time you knew something."

"Knew what?" I asked while taking off the mask and breathing a sigh of relief to see Ben.

Ben slammed the back of his head into the door. "Dammit, they came in too quickly. We're trapped. There are too many of them."

Tommy continued, "Téa, you always wondered what happened to your brother. Borax told you a little of the truth."

Ben shoved off the wall and checked my arms and face. "Are you okay?"

"Yes," I told Ben and looked back at Tommy standing in front of me with a blank expression.

"What is it Tommy? What could you possibly know?"

Ben challenged Tommy, "No, Tommy, don't!"

Tommy ignored him. "Ben, you know it is the only way. And in this case, a little anger is a good thing."

"Anger? What are you talking about?" I asked looking at both of them.

"The truth," Tommy said and stepped closer. "I'm your adoptive brother. Téa, I'm Bryce. Or at least I was."

"What?!? Am I supposed to believe that?" I asked now smiling.

"You used to call me your sidekick Patrick."

"Whoa … how did you …"

"Shhh … let me finish. There is not much time. This part will be the hardest to swallow. I am not human. I am also not Epex or Aepi. I am from another galaxy. We are called the Nebuli in human language. We shapeshift. I shapeshifted into a little boy, so our parents would adopt me a few years after you were born. I needed to be close to you. You are more than just my sister. You are my other half."

"Wh … what are you saying?"

"You were originally a Nebuli like me. Our job was to come to this galaxy and restore balance after the interplanetary war began between the Aepi and Epex. When it made its way to Earth, you started watching the Earthlings. You were fascinated by them but more so by their God. You don't remember, but you were always more of the rebel among our kind. Before you were to pass judgment, you wanted to try to do what the Earth's God did."

"Which is what?" I asked, noticing Ben's downturned face.

"Become human. Walk among them like them. Upon your visits you saw something that interested you. A couple that was infertile but still worshipped this Earth's God. That was when you decided what you wanted to do. Without my approval, you shapeshifted into the woman's womb and fertilized her egg. The only problem was that you didn't know that the chemical reaction upon implantation rendered you unable to ever change back. You lost your memories and were forever stuck in that state. You are now a product of human *and* Nebuli."

"Hold on, hypothetically, let's say that I believe you. How do you know I can't change back? And Michael Lane is not my father?"

I heard a stampede running through the halls on the other side of the door. We were running out of time.

"He is your father. Just not your biological father. He couldn't be anyway."

"No, no, this is all wrong. If this is true, then why was my father killed? Is this all related to his death?"

Tommy deliberated long enough for Ben to speak up, "Michael Lane was killed by an Epex alien before a Protector could stop it."

I turned to Tommy. "What? Is this true?"

I loved my father so much. Did a Protector let him down?

Tommy frowned at Ben. "That part is *not* true."

"Tommy don't," I heard Ben say but ignored him.

Tommy pushed through, "The Protector was the one that killed your father. That is the truth. Michael Lane was an Epex. That was why he was infertile. That was why your parents couldn't conceive."

Ben said nothing to dispute it.

"An Epex? It can't be. Tommy, why are you telling me this?"

My anger was brewing up under my skin.

"Téa, I want us to go home. You have your own people back on Nebuli. I've waited for so long to have you back. I'm tired of these humanoid wars. Let's finish what we started. Restore balance and go home. I know when you first got your wild idea to do this, become part human, that you made me promise you that I would wait to tell you the truth when you reached human maturity age. But we can't wait any longer."

"No. I am home, Tommy. And so are you!"

His pleading disposition turned to a grave expression. "This *home*? These horrid beings that value conquest and power? The same things you once detested? This is not your home!"

He put his hands on his hips. "Let's end this and then you can come back with me to the Black Eye galaxy."

"The Black Eye galaxy? You're kidding right? I did a report over that galaxy in the fifth grade. Black Eye my ass …"

I shook my head looking around at the floor.

"Not kidding. And half human or not, they will still take you back if they see you have restored balance to the Milky Way galaxy. This part of the universe has been growing in hostility for years. They sent us to this galaxy because we were the honored, the reliable ones. You most of all. You were royalty among our kind. I wish you could remember."

Tommy put his hand on my shoulder, and when I looked up he was glowing with a gold energy all around him. I had never seen anything like it. It wound on his forehead was gone and his entire body grew several inches. It was true. He was not of this world or anything I had ever seen. Could I really be like him? All this time, I had been trying to fit in. Could it be that I was never meant to?

He spoke again but in a different voice. One that was more whimsical with an echo.

"I'm sorry you yearned to find me for years. That you mourned for your brother who was with you all along. But I knew the humans would separate us once we were placed in foster care. So, that's when I just changed into your friend, Tommy."

I looked between him and Ben.

Tommy persisted. "Come with me. It's time. *All* the Epex have arrived now. The full power and weight of the

Epex will now devour Earth. They will slaughter every human and remaining Aepi."

"But we have Protectors and we are a strong people, the humans. We will not have the same fate as the Aepi, right Ben?"

This being that I once thought of as just Tommy turned to Ben and said, "Tell her."

Ben's grim face gave it away. "It does explain the record numbers of Epex. But we can't just give up."

Tommy spoke again, "Humans and Aepi are dead already."

Tommy grabbed my hand and energy surged up to my elbow. "This your chance to destroy the Epex too. Join with me and let's end what we came here to do. End them all, Téa and go home."

"No, there has got to be another way. The humans and Aepi are good beings. Epex have the potential too. Look at my father, Tommy. He was a great man. He loved me. He loved us."

"Good beings?"

Ben jumped in, "Tommy, no!"

Tommy ignored Ben and proceeded, "Tell her about the necklace, Ben."

I swung around. "What necklace?"

Tommy raised up his hand and a chain was hanging from it. It had that same fish medallion that my cottage key from the res had on it. However, it also had my mom's initials on it. Tommy asked, "Ben, did you or did you not have this in your possession? Or at least the Aepi had it?"

"Ben?" I asked now shaking.

Ben nodded his head yes. "It *was* your mother's. But I can explain."

Tommy's now unnatural huge size grew to tower over Ben. "Your cousin's father killed Michael Lane. He wouldn't listen to Michael saying that he was a deserter from the Epex. Michael told him over and over that he loved his family. The Protector was too scared. It was his first Epex face off."

Ben looked at me.

Tommy turned back to me. "See what Ben kept from you? After the ordeal, your mother then figured out the truth about aliens. About her husband. About the Aepi. She went into shock. When she came around, the loss of her husband, no matter who he had been, was all she talked about."

I was shaking. "And you, Tommy. She loved you too. I know you were adopted, but they loved you the same. If what you say is true, why didn't you help her, help our father?"

"You told me not to interfere with your life here. You wanted to experience it without protection so it would be authentic. So you could judge correctly. Now judge!"

I took a breath. "Tommy, I remember when she became ill. She would have nightmares and say she saw things. She would stand by my bed saying someone was in my room. I remember it all now. After they took her away, I went into one horrible foster home after another. I hated her! I hated her for lying. I thought she was lying!"

I frowned at Ben. "Did you know about all this?"

He nodded. "Des' father, Simian, gave her the necklace as a way to apologize, I guess. We didn't realize it then, but she tried to send it back to him before she died. For some reason, my father had it. But yes, it was in our possession."

I stared off into nothing away from everyone in the room. "When I visited her one day, she appeared to be well. Very lucid. I … I … thought things would go back to normal. That I could have a normal mom again and a normal life."

I squinted trying to recollect more. "I remember seeing the necklace now."

Tommy raised his hands out to me. "Téa, what happened after? Tell Ben. After your mother committed suicide, what happened to you that I couldn't stop?"

I stared at the ground. "I slit my wrists."

Ben walked over and tried to grab my hand. "I'm sorry. I'm so sorry, Téa."

I shoved him away keeping my eyes diverted. "I fell into darkness that night and was awakened by a doctor. I cried because I was trapped in hell. No matter what I did, I couldn't get away from the pain. I tried two more times, both on the same scar tissue. Still on all attempts, I was unsuccessful."

"Until Ms. Adele?" Ben asked but in more of a placating way.

I didn't answer him.

Ben continued, "Téa, I'm so sorry. I didn't know."

Tommy swung his hand up at Ben. "Don't do that now. If your cousin's father would have admitted to the doctors and her mom that the person he killed *was* in fact an alien, our mother would still be alive!"

Ben swore. "You know we couldn't do that."

Tommy spoke, "Téa, your mother begged the Protector, Simian, to admit what he did and to admit to the authorities that Michael was an alien too. She loved Michael, but she saw with her own eyes what he became when he was stabbed. Simian denied her over and over again. Isn't that true Ben? Téa, the Aepi wanted to protect themselves. To stay hidden. They are a selfish, horrible race. Just like the humans. Our mother didn't deserve that."

My mom. The woman I hated for so long for giving up so easily was actually a victim of their foolish games. In that moment, I hated myself for doubting her. I hated the Aepi for forsaking her. I hated the Epex and all humans. Something suddenly snapped inside me.

Tommy was by my ear instantly, "Ever wonder why you have more superhuman abilities than the other Protectors?"

I did wonder that.

"You *are* Nebuli. And your mother was indirectly killed by Des' father, an Aepi," Tommy said.

My mouth went dry. No wonder Des never liked me. Of course … he knew.

Tommy touched my shoulder. "Come with me. Let's go home."

I shook my head and felt the panic attack building. I was shaking so hard. Tommy and Ben disappeared from my mind. The loud noises outside the room disappeared. I started moving around violently.

I grabbed my mom's chain and stood up solidly on both legs. The anger had now built into a whirlwind of power all around my body. I couldn't think straight. It was like I was slitting my wrists all over again, but this time my attempts would be successful. I was tired. I was so tired of everything. I started fighting for breath as fire exploded from every pore of my skin consuming everything around me.

The walls of the whole compound fell down around us. Outside, people were running. Swarms and swarms of them mixed in with the Epex. I saw them all, Epex and humans running for their lives in the deadly bands of the hurricane that I was conjuring. I could comprehend that much for sure. Tornadoes were coming down from the sky formed by me. I tried to steady myself, so I wouldn't lose it completely. I didn't really want to hurt anyone or did I? I couldn't think straight. My oldest best friend, *rage*, had all the control now.

Just before I was to finish it all, I saw Ben and yelled, "Run Ben!"

My voice sounded deep and raspy. I didn't feel like I was me anymore. Was I becoming a Nebuli? A shock wave of energy left my body and slammed into the city buildings collapsing them all around us.

"GO NOW!"

No matter how mad I was, I still couldn't hurt him. I couldn't blame him for wanting to protect me from all of this.

This truth.

This truth that was now tearing me apart.

I couldn't see Tommy anymore, but I saw Ben. He stood there with his hands out, palms up, and approached me slowly.

"I won't leave you!"

I yelled back, "A Protector killed my father. A Protector forsaked my mother! Humans stood idly by and didn't help her or me. They only persecuted her more! I'm done with this crap! Tommy is right. I will fix it. I will restore balance. End the abuse. The cruelty."

Ben took another step and with every ounce of sanity I had left, I tried to keep the fire laced tornado from engulfing him. He still approached.

"If you want revenge, you will have to start with me, Téa."

By that point, the hate was all consuming. I no longer cared. "So be it!"

I lifted my hands to send the rest of my strength into my powers with the intent of destroying the whole damn world.

"Grace," I thought I heard him say.

"What Ben?"

I asked and saw several feet of ocean begin to cover our bodies. In the vision, we were hundreds of feet below the ocean. The fire was gone. The ocean waters were beautiful with sparkling coral and shiny fish drifting by. Ben's face was smiling and admiring me. He said something else that I couldn't make out.

"What?"

Then, he spoke again. "Grace. The human's God decided to give them *grace*. He saw all the same flaws you're seeing, but he also saw the good. Think of Ms. Adele ... think of Cheyenne ... Uncle Bob."

"No! There is *no* good!"

The water cooled my body as if there were no flames to begin with. Ben moved his hands and what looked like a current appeared moving in a circular motion in front of me.

"If there is no good in this world, then why did the Native Americans take my ancestors in? Us, aliens? Why did they make us one of their own? If there is no good, why did Adele take you in? Cheyenne loves you as her own. If there is no good, then why is there love at all still? If any love exists in this world, even the smallest, then it is a good world. Protect that, Téa. If you are meant to protect anything, please protect that at least. And I know there is love left, Téa! I know there is love left because I love you."

All I remembered next was Ben rushing towards me. We were back on the dry ground in the stormy city. The water was gone and the fire tore through my hands making me feel the amazing power it gave me. Ben grabbed my face and kissed me so urgently, sweetly causing everything in me to shift. As I thought of his words, my memories began to turn from blurry red thoughts to cool blue images of Uncle Bob, Adele, and Cheyenne smiling at me. Kiki too.

And then ... my mother.

My mother who forgave me and loved me, even though I hated her for leaving me on my own. I berated her the times I visited her at the hospital. She still would reach for me and say she loved me. A Protector's fault or not for her death, I had always resented her for everything. I blamed her. I couldn't believe I actually blamed her all this time. But there she was now smiling at me with an unconditional love that was so incredibly hard to comprehend.

"Mom?" I asked and felt tears seer my cheeks.

As the rest of the buildings started to fall down on top of us, I pushed Ben back out of the way just before I purposely let the biggest and final piece of a ten story building fall on top of me.

Stopping me.

Only darkness was left.

CHAPTER 40

Redemption

Were those wind chimes? I could hear like a crystallized clicking sound. My eyes fought to open. I couldn't decide whether or not I wanted to open them, but it seemed so natural to do so. When I did, the light was so bright that I regretted it. Had I been taken back to Black Eye galaxy? Was I dead?

Figures of white and pale grey moved around me. No faces were discernible. It was like peering through the window of dreams. It was so peaceful. A hand touched my shoulder, and I could barely make out a smile on the being's face. My only thought was *loss*. I hurt people.

"I'm sorry," I said with tears running down my cheeks. "I'm so sorry."

The figure nodded and smiled again. "I know," it said slowly just above a whisper. "I know." The voice was so kind and comforting. And then without another word, there was blackness again. The warmth was all gone. I was shivering now.

"Téa!"

I opened my eyes again to see. "Ben?"

His reddish disoriented eyes peered down at me. "Thank God. You've been in a coma for months."

Another coma!? What is my deal with comas?

"So, I'm alive?"

"It was close. But yes, you're alive. It took several surgeries, Téa. The doctor said you will heal fully, but it will take months. They took the tube out the other night when you started showing signs of awakening and breathing on your own. You don't know how much shock the doctors were in when they saw that you were coming out of it. Téa, they're calling it a miracle. But I guess you are more powerful than we all thought."

I twisted in the cold bed towards him remembering what I did. "Oh no ... did I hurt anyone?"

"No. Everyone was able to get away."

"Am I going to prison?"

He leaned forward laughing and took my hands. "I don't think your kind can go to prison. But you really don't know what all happened, do you?"

"I threatened people's lives, spewed hateful accusations, and destroyed everything around me. I guess that about sums it up, huh?"

He stood above me and his sincere smile took my breath away. I had missed him so much and to think I was going to hurt him, too. He traced my forehead with his forefinger.

"I knew I had to help you. I knew what was going to happen. At first, I could only see a few hours ahead into your life. As I got stronger and closer to you, I began to see twenty-four hours into your future. Now, my Watcher abilities show me a few days into your future."

"That's how you knew Borax got out a message and more Epex were coming?"

"Yes, but it only works when you are in danger. The Epex aliens that came, trapped you and it signaled my visions. I can't see everyday things, just images that show you in trouble. So, I knew they were coming just like I knew Borax was setting a trap for you in that old building."

I squeezed my blanket. "Thanks, Ben."

"Don't thank me. It's my job."

"So seriously, what happens to me now? Am I banned from Earth?"

I wondered, do I fly back to this unknown world I'm actually from? Would they even want me now that I didn't follow through with destroying everyone here in this galaxy? I looked around at the white walled hospital room and thought of Carson, Uncle Bob, and Pam. Will I ever see them again?

"And what happened to Tommy?"

"I don't know about Tommy. He just disappeared. But that's what I was getting at. You see, Téa, a miracle happened."

I laughed. "Yeah, I unleashed my true nature."

He leaned over and kissed my forehead. His soft lips and intoxicating smell rolled all over my senses. Then, he looked deep into my eyes. I was more interested in drowning in those silver hued eyes in that moment than what he was keeping from me.

He continued, "The tree chose you to be a Protector for a reason. A reason I couldn't figure out til all this happened. It knew that you were the only one that could protect the last seed because of who you *really* were. Your special abilities did not come from the seed. They were in you all along."

"Because I'm Nebuli. But I could have killed others."

"You wouldn't of. You were of sound mind, even though you thought you weren't. You allowed everyone time to get away."

I noticed the sunlight coming through the hospital blinds appearing all angelic and peaceful. I still hurt for my parents and knew I had a long way to go to forgive Simian, Des, and the human doctors for their callousness. But more so to forgive myself for hating my mother and bringing out so much wrath on the poor city of Houston. However, deep down, I felt that since I had been forgiven for what I could have done, I surely should be able to forgive myself. And everyone else.

Then, I thought of Tommy. Would I ever see him again? Is he okay? I should have tried to convince him to let it all go. Did he head back to our home world? The what ifs and questions were swirling all through my mind.

Ben just stood there watching me with a faint grin on his face.

"What?" I asked.

"Téa, it's over. It's all over. The Epex retreated back to where they came from when they saw what you were capable of. You were what the legend referred to that I was raised my whole life hearing about. The being that would restore balance. But now … " he paused, "... will you stay here on Earth ... stay with me?"

I smiled. "If I do stay, will you stay with me, too? I know I'm a mix of … well who really knows. Let's just say I'm a mutt. But …"

"Stop. We're all messed up. But, I know one thing for sure, you are Téa Lane and I love you. There is no way I'm leaving you again."

He raised up one finger up in front of that sexy grin of his. "But I *do* have one condition."

I dropped all my worrying right then and thankfully my heart could sing. "What?"

He was on the cusp of laughing when he said, "You majorly need some anger management classes."

THE END*

*But will the other Nebuli aliens from Téa's home back in the Black Eye galaxy all agree with her decision?

References

Elon Musk, "The future we're building--and boring", Filmed April 2017. To watch the full talk, visit TED.com

Acknowledgements

There are so many people that I want to acknowledge for their support while I've been writing like a crazy woman these last few years. However, my biggest supporter is my husband, that continues to be believe in me and pump me up, even on the days that I let that ugly thing called *doubt* creep in. I also want to thank my daughter, Claire, who helped me find Téa's voice. My daughter and my sons are my world, and I write these young adult stories with them in mind. I thank my publisher and editor, Amanda, for believing in this story and for all the rest of my friends and family who keep questioning when the next book will come out. You guys keep me going!

About the Author

Jacqueline Anders has been an obsessed reader and lover of all fiction her entire life. As a young adult growing up in Louisiana, she never missed an episode of *The X-Files* or *Stargate*, or the release of any of the *Terminator* movies. Jackie holds a Bachelor's degree in Business Management and a Master's degree in Educational Leadership from W.TX A&M.

She currently teaches at a public school in the Houston, Texas area. She hopes to inspire her students to use their imagination and to think 'outside the box' to uncover their creative side.

Anders is a mom of two teenagers, one elementary kiddo, and a part husky dog named India. She is also married to a proud Texan (he reminds her how great the state is ALL THE TIME!), and enjoys cheering on the Houston Astros!

Follow Jackie on:
Twitter: @jandersbooks
IG: @jandersbooks
Facebook: Jackie Anders - Author
YouTube: Author Jackie Anders

www.ingramcontent.com/pod-product-compliance
Lightning Source LLC
Chambersburg PA
CBHW061551100726
47898CB00002B/324